Praise for Pe

COGHEART ADVENTURES

"Vivid and gripping."
Kiran Millwood Hargrave

"A gem of a book."
Katherine Woodfine

"A stormer of a plot."
Abi Elphinstone

"A glittering clockwork treasure."
Piers Torday

"A blend of Philip Pullman,
Joan Aiken and Katherine Rundell."
Amanda Craig

"A thrilling Victorian adventure."
The Bookseller

"Marvellous fun."
New Statesman

"Prepare yourself for the adventure of a lifetime."
Jo Clarke, *Book Lover Jo*

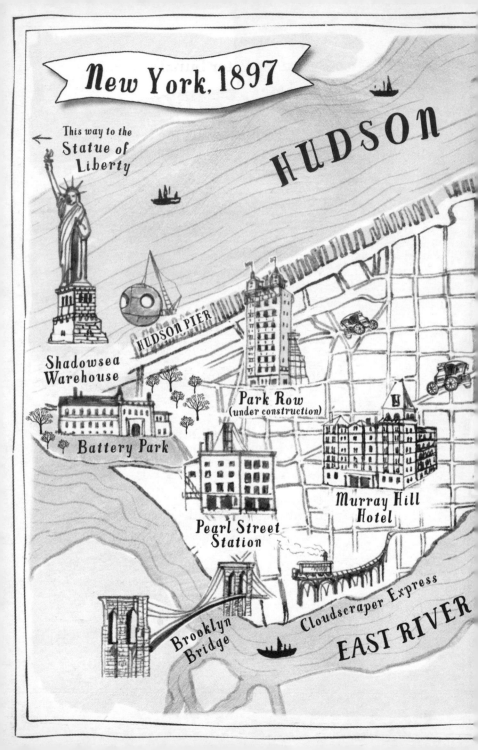

RIVER

BROADWAY

Opera House

CENTRAL PARK

Croton Reservoir

FIFTH AVENUE

Metropolitan Museum of Art

Grand Central Depot

BLACKWELL'S ISLAND

For Lyra and Avery

First published in the UK in 2020 by Usborne Publishing Ltd., Usborne House,
83-85 Saffron Hill, London EC1N 8RT, England., usborne.com

Text © Peter Bunzl, 2020

Photo of Peter Bunzl © Thomas Butler

Cover and inside illustrations, including map by Becca Stadtlander ©
Usborne Publishing, 2020

Clockwork Key © Thinkstock / jgroup; Border © Shutterstock / Lena Pan; Crumpled paper
texture © Thinkstock / muangsatun; Plaque © Thinkstock /Andrey_Kuzmin; Newspaper
© Thinkstock / kraphix; Old paper texture © Thinkstock / StudioM1; Brick Wall ©
Thinkstock; Brick Wall © Istock / forrest9

A CIP catalogue record for this book is available from the British Library.

ISBN 9781474964388   05325/1   JFMAMJJASO D/19

Printed and bound in Great Britain by CPI Group (UK) Ltd, Croydon, CR0 4YY

PETER BUNZL

USBORNE

PROLOGUE

First there was darkness.

Then patches of watery green light.

Then fish, whole schools of them.

With luminous fins bright as knives, glowing scales that shimmered like armour.

They swam past the shadow of a submarine base that clung to a cliff edge beside a fathomless trench, which stretched like a scar across the ocean floor.

The base was the shape of a giant rusted wheel, with spokes that ran from the exterior to its centre. Parts of it were unfinished – the ties that bound it to the seabed still under construction. Fixed with rope and cable in place of iron trusses, the base bobbed slightly in the current. Rising from the hub was a tower with a turbine at the top, turning slowly.

Through the tower's only porthole, a blond boy of thirteen with bright, inquisitive eyes could be seen sitting on the cabin floor. The boy was humming a tune to himself – a tune that matched the buzzing in the walls – as he worked on a miniature wagon. Jam-jar lids made up the wagon's wheels, flattened cans its carriage. It had pencils for axles and wire for its yoke.

When he was done, the boy plucked a white mouse from his pocket and tied it to the wagon. He placed the mouse on the floor and geed it along like a long-whiskered, pink-snouted pony. The mouse tottered forward on tiny red paws, pulling the wagon behind it.

After a moment it broke into a run, skittering beneath a table, where two adults, a man and a woman with the same blond hair and inquisitive eyes as the boy, sat working.

The boy chased the mouse under the table and followed it out the door.

Hot on its heels, he ran down the passageway.

The mouse crossed grates and vents and wove beneath pipes, sticking close to the walls. It clattered its cart past damp bulbous diving suits that stank of the sea, tumbled across galleys and mess halls where crew members sat eating.

Still the boy chased it.

Finally it ran through a crack where a door stood slightly ajar.

In the room beyond, row upon row of mice scrabbled about in cages.

The white mouse stopped in the centre of the spotless floor.

The boy crouched, mouth half-open, stretching out a hand to pick it up.

A *swish* of a skirt.

A shiny leather shoe stepped across his path.

The boy glanced up. "Hey, Aunt Matilda!"

A gaunt-faced woman with short slicked-back hair, wearing a white lab coat and goggles pushed back on her head, was putting on a pair of rubber gloves. "That's Professor Milksop to you."

Professor Milksop scooped up the mouse and dropped the cart unceremoniously on the floor. "This rodent's valuable. You should never have taken it from the lab."

"He looked sad," the boy said. "I named him Spook, on account of his colouring. He looks like a Spook, don't ya think?"

The boy glanced at the mouse, scrabbling in the professor's hand.

It squeaked softly.

"Don't be naming them," the professor said. "Name a thing and you start to have feelings for it." She turned away and made a sharp, jerking motion with her hands.

The squeaking stopped.

"Go back to your quarters now, Dane. You shouldn't be here. Could be bad for your health."

The professor kicked aside the cart and headed for a second, lead-lined door at the far end of the room. A door marked:

REANIMATION LAB

DANGER! KEEP OUT!

Above these words was a picture of a snake curled in a circle, eating its own tail.

Dane rubbed away a stinging tear as he watched his aunt go.

Then he narrowed his eyes and stared at the door.

"No," he said softly. "I won't."

He stepped forward and gently pushed against the sign, peering round the door's edge.

In the room beyond, a large white laboratory, a mechanical nurse with a red cross on her chest was adjusting a square metal machine on a table. A phonograph on a wheeled stand in the corner played ghostly opera music from a wax cylinder.

"Ready to wake the dead, Miss Buckle?" Professor Milksop joined the mechanical at the table and examined the four glass lenses arranged on the front of the square machine.

Miss Buckle frowned as she checked a tangle of copper wires that emerged from the rear of the machine. They stretched out to a control box and socket inside a lead-lined observation booth on the far side of the room. "Is that one of your jokes, Professor?" she asked. "I can never quite tell. My clockwork doesn't easily compute humour..."

"Forget about it." Professor Milksop laid Spook in a tray on the table in front of the machine and adjusted a blue glinting shard of diamond inside its workings. Then, when she was satisfied all was ready, she pulled down her goggles and stepped away from the machine into the lead-lined booth. Miss Buckle followed her.

Dane peeked further round the door, watching Professor Milksop through the observation booth's porthole window as she shut herself and Miss Buckle in.

Then the professor pressed a series of buttons on a control box.

Soon, the machine on the table hummed to life as a tidal wave of electricity buzzed through it.

Miss Buckle peered out through the porthole and saw Dane sneaking into the lab.

"STOP!" she shouted, half at him, half at her mistress.

But it was too late…

Crackling strands of blue lightning were already shooting from the four lenses of the machine. They waved around the lab like a tangled ball of angry, energetic snakes. Their lightning strands latched onto Spook's body, engulfing it.

The little mouse writhed and jerked in rhythm, then opened its eyes, wiggled its whiskers and crawled back onto its feet like a newborn.

Soon the lightning found Dane…

Winding round him like a nest of vipers…

Biting electrically into his skin.

His body spasmed.

His feet danced a random rhythm.

Silver scales burned his eyes.

His limbs scissored and jiggled.

He fell to his knees…

Keeled over on the floor…

And was still.

The arms of lightning crackled onwards, through the open door, arcing along the passageways of the base... slipping serpent-like around each crew member in turn and dancing them to the same jerky death.

Soon there was only darkness once more. And two last shadows: Professor Milksop and Miss Buckle, who ran from the open doorway of the observation booth and kneeled down beside Dane.

Sparks flew off Miss Buckle's metal body as she shook Dane by his shoulders. "Master Milksop!" she called, her mechanical voice wavering. "Wake up!"

Professor Milksop kept her distance. She didn't want to get an electric shock.

"Dane," she asked. "Are you still in there? You still alive?"

CHAPTER 1

Lily woke on Christmas morning to find herself not at home, as she had been dreaming, but on a top bunk in the cabin of a sleeper zep that was crossing the Atlantic Ocean.

She blinked her green eyes and rubbed her freckled face until she felt entirely awake. Then, with her fingers, she began combing out the worst of the knots in her tangled fire-red hair.

Under the thrum of the airship's purring engines she could hear the beat of her Cogheart: a mechanical heart of cogs and springs that her papa had given her. It sat ticking in her chest like an overwound carriage clock. Because it was a perpetual motion machine, the Cogheart might go on for ever. Lily didn't quite understand what that meant, but she knew one thing: without it she would not be alive today. Nor would she be taking this trip.

Papa, whose name was Professor John Hartman, was lying in the middle bunk beneath her. He wore a nightgown and nightcap and snored softly in his sleep. His feet stuck out the end of the bed, for he was quite tall, even lying down.

Robert Townsend, Lily's best friend in the whole wide world, comrade in arms, first-class clockmaker and her co-conspirator in all things adventuresome, was asleep on the bottom bunk wearing blue-striped pyjamas. A coal-black cowlick of hair curved over his forehead like an upside-down question mark.

Malkin, Lily's pet mechanimal fox, most trusted confidant and a red furry-faced know-it-all, lay next to Robert, curled up beside his pillow. Lily was only relieved he wasn't sleeping on Robert's head, which he sometimes did.

Malkin, of course, was frozen still. That was how mechanicals looked at night, when they were run down, before you took their winding key and wound them up again in the morning.

Christmas Eve had been most diverting. The three friends and Papa had set out from Liverpool Airstation on the *Firefly* airship, for what promised to be a once-in-a-lifetime adventure: a four-day flight to New York.

The *Firefly* was the grandest ship in her class and had all the modern conveniences of the most up-to-date sleeper zep in the Royal Dirigible Company's Transatlantic Fleet. There was a control room where the captain and navigation crew worked. A radio room where they sent and received telegrams. An officers' mess where the crew relaxed. A galley kitchen that serviced a dining room where two mechanical waiters in white silk jackets served breakfast, lunch, dinner and afternoon tea, with two different types of cake and sandwiches with the crusts cut off. A port and aft side promenade for exercising. A writing room. A thirty-four-foot passenger lounge, which had extra-light tubular-metal cushioned chairs and a duralumin grand piano.

And nestled on top of the zep was a magnificent viewing platform called the Crow's Nest, which was accessed via a spiral staircase that wound through the centre of the balloon.

It was rather like travelling in a floating hotel. And Lily loved it.

In New York they would be staying in a real hotel, which she hoped would be just as good. They were due to arrive on the twenty-eighth of December. Robert's mother and sister, Selena and Caddy Townsend, would join them at the airstation.

Since June, when Selena and Caddy had last seen Robert, the pair had been travelling across the states with their vaudeville act. Selena had written to her son and then to Lily's papa to invite Robert and the Hartmans to meet them in New York for New Year's Eve.

Luckily, Papa had been planning a trip to America himself. He'd been invited to speak at the Annual American Conference of Mechanists and Electricians in January at Hardwood University, near Boston. Or was that Aardvark University...? Something like that, anyway. To be honest, Lily hadn't been listening to that part. Papa took his speech with him everywhere he went. Every few hours, in between his holiday reading, which was a hefty book on Shakespeare, he'd been practising snippets of his speech on Lily and Robert and Malkin. Just the thought of it was enough to make Lily feel like falling back to sleep.

She finished combing her hair and crawled down to the end of her bed. There was a stuffed stocking that she hadn't noticed before, beneath her thrown-aside blanket. It must've mysteriously arrived in the night.

She eagerly examined the stocking, then climbed down the cabin's wooden ladder to shake Robert awake.

"What is it?" he asked her, sleepily rubbing his eyes and crawling out of bed.

"Santa Claus has been!" Lily whispered. "We have stockings!"

She took Malkin's key from round his neck and began winding him with it. The fox's gears and cogs clicked into action and he shook himself awake.

They glanced up to find that Papa was yawning and wide awake too. "It's rather early for gifts, isn't it?" he asked.

"We're in the middle of the ocean," Lily said. "We are neither on British Time nor American. So it is neither early nor late. In my opinion, that is *exactly* the right time for presents!"

"All right then," Papa said, getting up and putting on his dressing gown. "I suppose you can open them."

Gleefully, Robert and Lily fell upon their stockings to see what Santa had stuffed them with.

There was an orange and three whole walnuts in each. Plus a brightly-striped twist of paper that contained a handful of lemon drops, barley sugars, chocolate drops, caramel creams and humbugs. Lily hated eating humbugs, especially on airships, but she would be able to swap them with Robert later.

"There's more." Papa reached up into the luggage rack

and, from inside his suitcase, produced three finely-wrapped presents – one for each of them.

Lily opened hers first. It was a real magnifying glass, like the kind used by her favourite detective: Sherlock Holmes.

"To help you solve mysteries," Papa explained.

She tried out the lens by examining the patterns of the carpet. Every minute detail blew up magnificently, even the worn-away threadbare parts.

"It's perfect. Thank you." She put the magnifying glass away in her pocket.

Robert opened his present next. Papa had got him a beautiful compass in a gold case. "So you always know where you are," Papa explained as Robert examined it. "I found it in a second-hand shop in the village. I think it was made by your father."

"It was. Thank you." Robert ran his thumb over the maker's mark on the side of the device: *T.T.* for Thaddeus Townsend.

Tears pricked at his eyes. This was only the second Christmas without his da, but it was the time of year when he missed him most of all.

Last but not least was Malkin. He tore the wrapping from his present with his teeth to reveal a bright green jacket, knitted by Mrs Rust, their clockwork cook and housekeeper back home. Mrs Rust was a legendarily awful knitter, but she didn't look to have made such a bad job of this. Lily wrestled the jacket onto Malkin, with relatively little complaining and gnashing of teeth on his part.

"There," she said when she was done, imagining the look of pride on Mrs Rust's face. This was the first Christmas they'd spent apart since Papa made Rusty. Lily missed her so much, and the three other mechanicals Papa had built and created to look after her – Captain Springer, Mr Wingnut and Miss Tock. The four clockwork servants were like family and Christmas didn't feel the same without them.

At least she had Malkin and Robert and Papa.

The fox grizzled at the jacket, pulling it this way and that until it sat comfortably across his back. "How do I look?" he asked.

"Rather smart," Robert replied.

The scruffy tail part that sat over Malkin's backside was a bit of a mess – it tangled with his wagging brush. But on the whole, the jacket gave him a raffish air.

"Unfortunately, I don't have gifts for any of you," the fox announced. "But I shall give you each a lick on the cheek and hopefully that shall suffice."

This he promptly did and they laughed at him warmly.

They spent the rest of the morning playing charades in the cabin, before dressing excitedly for the lavish Christmas feast, which was to be served to all the guests in the airship's dining room.

"Lead on, Macduff!" Papa said when they were ready.

"I think you'll find it's 'Lay on, Macduff'." Malkin hopped into a little picnic-style basket with handles, which Lily rushed to pick up.

"What are you doing?" Papa asked.

"Joining you for dinner," the fox said.

"Mechanimals aren't allowed on deck, you know that."

This was true, unfortunately. It was a rule on public airships that all mechanimals were to be stowed away in travel trunks in the hold for the whole duration of the journey. But Malkin couldn't abide such treatment, and neither could Lily.

The fox fidgeted in the basket, getting comfortable. "It's Christmas Day. A time of goodwill to all creatures great and small. You can at least allow me this little indiscretion."

"Fine," Papa relented. "So long as you stay hidden."

They closed the cabin door and followed Papa along the passage. Lily couldn't wait to eat Christmas dinner with her two best friends, and the thought of doing so on an airship made a bubble of joy rise inside her, higher than the zep's balloon itself.

In the dining room, the two mechanical waiters were busily showing the other passengers to their seats. A clockwork concert pianist sat at the duralumin grand piano, playing Christmas carols to welcome everyone to dinner.

Each table was set with bone china and silver cutlery, starched white napkins and red-and-gold crackers. There were even specially designed seasonal menus with sprigs of holly printed around their edges.

Lily put the basket down by her feet and checked to see how Malkin was doing. He'd dozed off already. Mechanical foxes, she found, did not take Christmas half as seriously as humans.

She fidgeted about in her seat to get comfortable. She intended to enjoy the festivities, yet she couldn't help notice that everyone else was staring at her. Lily bit her lip and held the menu in front of her face, pretending to study it.

"What's wrong?" Robert asked.

"Every time I come in here, people gawk at me as if I'm some kind of medical anomaly!"

"Nonsense!" Papa said.

"Cream of artichoke!" One of the mechanical waiters placed a gold-rimmed soup dish in front of each of them.

"I don't see anyone staring." Papa adjusted his napkin on his lap, while Robert tried to work out which of the diverse denizens of the dining room was gawking the most at Lily.

"That's because you don't pay attention, Papa," Lily admonished. "You're so lost in your own head, reading your patents and papers, practising your important speeches or inventing things, that you barely see what's in front of your nose."

"I don't know what to say…" Papa stopped eating and reached up to clutch his nose comically, as if that was the culprit.

"You don't have to say anything." Lily dipped some bread in her soup. "But know that since we've been on this airship – in fact, even before that, at Liverpool Airstation – people were pointing me out to each other and whispering about me behind their hands."

"Is this true?" Papa asked Robert.

Robert nodded. He had been having trouble deciding on which of the many different-shaped silver spoons to use, but had finally settled on the biggest one, which, it turned out, barely fitted in his mouth.

"Lily's famous now," he gargled through a sloppy spoonful of soup.

"Infamous, more like," Malkin said, poking his head from under the table. "Thanks to that clanking article Anna wrote."

"I knew no good would come of that," Papa cried exasperatedly as the waiters swapped the barely-finished soups for a main course of roast turkey with the full trimmings. "Curse Anna and all her pals on Fleet Street."

Anna was one of Lily and Robert's closest friends – a journalist. She'd written an article about Lily two months ago in which she'd revealed the secret of Lily's clockwork heart and, since then, people had become interested in Lily, often seeking her out.

Life at Brackenbridge Manor – the country house where she lived with Papa, Robert, Malkin, Mrs Rust, Captain Springer, Mr Wingnut and Miss Tock – had changed in many small ways. When journalists and other interested parties would knock on the front door in hope of an interview, Mr Wingnut, the mechanical butler, or Miss Tock, the mechanical maid, would send them packing. And if they sneaked round the back, then the indomitable Mrs Rust would threaten them with her meat-cleaver arm-attachment and shout, "COGS AND CHRONOMETERS! BE OFF, BEFORE I CALL THE

CONSTABULARY!" Even Captain Springer, who was normally so calm and collected, had taken to chasing off any visiting reprobates with his rake.

All of which was lucky, as, oftentimes, Lily had no idea what to say to these people. She felt like she was an imposter and unworthy of their attention. But still, every week, dozens of letters arrived asking if Anna's article was true, whether she really did have a clockwork heart, and how it felt to be the only one in the world with such a thing.

Of course, these were questions Lily didn't know how to answer.

Anyway, they weren't really about her. They were about Papa's machine.

No one ever asked how she'd rescued Papa when he was kidnapped, or how she'd survived being almost drowned in the Thames by notorious criminal Jack Door. Nor what it felt like to meet Queen Victoria and ride on the back of her mechanical elephant. They never asked Lily about being held prisoner in the Skycircus, or enquired about how, along with the other acts, she'd fought for hybrid rights.

Things would be different, Lily thought, when she wrote her own story. Then she would explain what it was like to live through such adventures. She'd made a start already in her journal. It was slow going because writing was hard, but the important thing to stress was that being a hybrid was not dissimilar to being anyone else. It was how you lived your life that mattered; that made you who you were. Not whether you possessed a flesh-and-blood heart or a mechanical one.

"TELEGRAM FOR TOWNSEND! IMPORTANT TELEGRAM FOR MASTER TOWNSEND!" a voice called out, interrupting her thoughts and everyone else's Christmas dinner.

Lily's Cogheart tick-tocked wildly. That was Robert's name. She looked up to see a mechanical porter in the blue uniform of the Royal Dirigible Fleet trundling across the floor on his wheeled feet, carrying a silver tray.

"Quick, hide!" Lily told Malkin.

Grumbling to himself, the mech fox clambered back into his basket beneath the table. Lily tucked him away and studied Robert's nervous face. Who could possibly be sending him a telegram at Christmas dinner?

CHAPTER 2

"That's me!" Robert called out, a knot forming in his stomach. "I'm Townsend!" Anxiously he pushed aside his Christmas meal.

The mechanical porter approached their table. His wheels squeaked loudly, cutting through the chatter of the other diners.

"Here you are, Sir," he said, holding out the telegram to Robert on its silver platter.

Gingerly, Robert took it.

"Thank-you-Seasons-Greetings-and-good-day," the mechanical snapped quickly, before snatching away his tray and trundling off towards the exit on the far side of the dining room.

Robert ripped open the telegram and scanned it; the knot in his stomach loosened and his heartbeat slowed. It was from his ma. He read it aloud to everyone.

WESTERN UNION
TELEGRAM

The filing time shown in the date line on domestic telegrams is STANDARD TIME at point of origin. Time of reciept is STANDARD TIME at point destination.

ROBERT. MERRY CHRISTMAS! I HOPE YOU ARE TUCKING INTO A PLATEFUL

OF TURKEY! OUR STEAM SHIP IS A DAY BEHIND. WE WILL NOW ARRIVE

IN NEW YORK ON 29TH DEC. WE WILL MEET YOU AT HOTEL AT 2 P.M. I AM

OVERJOYED TO BE SPENDING NEW YEAR WITH YOU AND THE HARTMANS.

CADDY CAN'T WAIT TO SEE EVERYONE. I HAVE SURPRISES UP MY SLEEVE ALSO.

LOVE, YOUR MA. SELENA XX

Lily felt relieved the telegram wasn't bad news. "It's a shame your mama and Caddy are going to be a day late," she said. "But you still have plenty of time to see them," she added soothingly.

"What do you think she means by surprises?" Robert asked her.

"I don't know." Lily took a mouthful of buttery turkey. "Perhaps she just means she's brought you a nice Christmas present?"

"A snotty hanky, perhaps?" Malkin suggested, poking his head up between Robert's legs in a most alarming fashion. "Isn't that what most humans keep up their sleeves in winter?"

John Hartman looked up from his food. "I don't see the point of trying to read these various meanings into such a short message, Robert."

"Papa's right," Lily said, eating a Brussels sprout. "You've done that every time your ma's sent you something."

"Yes," said Malkin, nudging Robert's leg with his nose. "You need to calm down about seeing them again."

They were right, Robert observed to himself. He clasped his ma's Moonlocket that he wore around his neck, stroking its ivory inlay as he always did when he was worried about her. Since he'd been getting closer to the reunion with his ma and sister, his nerves had become more and more frayed. This would only be his second time seeing them, and yet, despite their differences, he'd missed their presence in his life. He wanted everything on this holiday to be perfect. "I suppose I *am* concerned about how it will be," he said. "I want to prepare myself for every eventuality. Including..." He broke off, and finished quietly to himself, "The fact that we might not get along..."

The journey across the Atlantic took three more days, during which time Robert and Lily ate far too much Christmas cake, watched various ships passing in the night, and played a clank of a lot of hands of whist and cribbage. Malkin would've joined them in their games, only he found he couldn't hold the playing cards in his teeth.

Every evening, before bed, they took it in turns to read aloud from Papa's guidebook, which was called *Appleton's General Guide to the United States and Canada* and had an illustrated section full of tips and advice on New York.

Finally, on the afternoon of the twenty-eighth of December, when they were due to arrive, the three of them pressed their noses against the cabin's porthole window and peered out, expecting to see the city beneath them. Instead, they saw nothing but the bulbous shadow of *Firefly*, sweeping over the ocean.

"There's nothing to see but sea!" Lily moaned. "We needn't have bothered getting dressed up!"

In honour of their imminent arrival in New York, she'd put on her emerald-ribboned bonnet and a smart velvet blouson. Malkin wore his new green knitted jacket, which he'd barely taken off since receiving it. Robert had on his flat cap, which he always wore, and a woollen winter coat that had once belonged to his father. It was rather old now, but it was one of the last gifts that Thaddeus had given him before he'd died and it was Robert's favourite item of clothing.

"Four-fifteen," Lily said, checking the time on her pocket watch, which she'd reset to United States Eastern time.

"We must be getting close," Robert said. "I imagine the coast will come into view quite soon."

"Not likely." Malkin hooked his forepaws over the edge of the porthole window and pressed his leather nose to the glass. "This clanking zep travels so slowly that the Christmas holidays will be over by the time we get there."

Lily gave a disheartened sigh and hiked up the ends of her yellow-and-black striped scarf, tucking them into her coat pockets. The scarf was one of Mrs Rust's early knitting experiments. Malkin said it made her look like a swaddled giraffe, but Lily felt more like a tiger when she wore it. The perfect beast to face New York.

Just then, Papa burst into the cabin. He was dressed for the outdoors too, in a dark grey overcoat with a silk cravat tucked into the heavy collar. "Lily, Robert," he cried as soon as he saw them. "You must come at once to the viewing platform. The captain tells me we'll begin our descent to New York in the next five minutes. As we cross the harbour, we'll float straight past the Statue of Liberty and see the whole of the city."

Lily peered out of the window and noted, with delight, that he was right. In the time they had been talking, a dark strip of coastline had appeared.

"What about me?" Malkin asked.

"You'll have to watch from the window," Papa said. "Mechanicals aren't allowed on deck."

"Ridiculous rules," Malkin muttered, waving his brush angrily at Papa.

Suddenly, Lily had second thoughts too. "I don't think I shall come either," she announced. "I'm sure I'll see well enough from here." As thrilled as she was to see that statue from the very best vantage point, she didn't want anyone goggling at her to mar her first view of the city.

Papa must've known that was what she was fretting about, for he put his arm around her and gave her a squeeze. "I promise no one will be staring at you on the viewing platform, Lily. They'll be too busy looking at the sights."

"Come on, Lil." Robert flashed his friend a smile. "It'll be no fun without you."

"I suppose," Lily said, feeling a bit better.

"Jolly good!" Papa was already on the move, marshalling them towards the exit. "And so, to the Crow's Nest!"

Lily picked up her wicker basket and glanced down at Malkin.

"I wish you could come too," she whispered.

"He can," Robert said and, while Papa wasn't looking, Malkin jumped into the basket. Robert threw a blanket over him so he was hidden beneath it. Then the three of them set off together after Papa to go see the view.

They traipsed along a corridor filled with numbered passenger compartments and took the winding spiral stairs at the far end that led right up through the centre of the zep's balloon. It was a long climb past giant geometric frames that kept the silks in place, depleted oil tanks and gas envelopes and empty leather water bags that hung from various straps and girders. Through it all, Lily's excitement rose at the thought of seeing New York.

They reached the top of the spiral stairs and clambered through a hatch onto the zeppelin's roof. Lily felt her belly drop and heart tick-tock nervously in her chest. It was harder to breathe out here. The chill wind blew through her woollen winter stockings. The airship was crossing New York harbour and, far off, beneath the heavy clouds, the sun had started to set.

Lily squeezed into a gap at the viewing rail beside Robert and Papa and sensed a faint rustle against her leg. Malkin was poking his head from the wicker basket. He stuck his tongue out to taste the sea air and rested his snout over the foot rail, his ears flapping wildly in the wind as his bulging black eyes took in the view.

The rest of the passengers were leaning against the railing, staring at the miniature islands that crowded the bay and holding onto their hats to stop them blowing off. Papa and Robert had been right, Lily realized, everyone was too busy sightseeing to notice her arrival.

Then Lily spotted Liberty. And, in an instant, the sense of dread she'd felt at her own predicaments burned away. Papa was already staring at the giant metal lady, shading his eyes with a hand. Lily shook Robert by the shoulder and tapped Malkin's head, pointing out the details on the statue.

Alone on her island, beset by the raging waves of the harbour, Liberty looked small and slight beneath the burgeoning grey clouds, holding her torch aloft. But, as the airship swooped closer, accompanied by the loud *oohs* and *aahs* of the passengers, she seemed to grow in stature.

Soon Lily could see every fold in her dress, every rivet on her bronze skin. Then they were passing right by her, beneath her raised arm – so close that Lily felt as if she might lean over the rail and touch Liberty's hand.

The statue had her back to the troubled ocean and was staring with concern at the island city. Lily followed her gaze and saw a hundred thousand windows twinkling like fallen stars embedded in the surface of the earth.

It had started to snow. A flurry of flakes pinched harshly at Lily's cheeks. She stuck her tongue out and swallowed her first New York snowflake. It tasted of ice and excitement.

As the *Firefly* dipped towards the southern tip of Manhattan, Lily, Robert and Malkin traded exhilarated glances, readying themselves for the start of this new adventure…

CHAPTER 3

Lily took a deep breath and stepped down the gangplank of the airship, letting her lungs burn with the smoky sharpness of the city.

Following behind her, Robert pulled his cap low and wrapped his collar tight around him. Clapping his gloved hands together, he huffed out clouds of steam into the cold winter twilight. Sharp noise and chatter echoed off the warehouse buildings on the wharf, assaulting his ears.

Mechanical porters in red pillbox hats swarmed about inside the *Firefly*'s open hold, unloading everyone's trunks and transporting them through the white slush to a warehouse filled with officious-looking customs officers in smart blue suits with starched white collars.

The sheer number of people in this airstation made Robert's head spin, but it would be hard to lose Lily amongst them, thanks to her brightly-striped tiger scarf and the basket with Malkin's brush sticking out.

As Lily and Robert walked with John through the crowds, not a single person stopped and stared, and Lily's spirits were buoyed by the sudden and complete realization that no one here knew who she was, or the first thing about her.

Here, in New York, she was free.

"Malkin," she said, stuffing his swishing tail back into the rear of the basket, "you'd best stay hidden. If you cause an international incident, they might send us back home before we've even properly arrived."

"As if I would!" Malkin stuck his leathery nose out from the basket's other end, sniffing around at everything that was coming his way. "You know me. I'll be discretion itself."

In the customs warehouse, the serious officials in the smart blue suits inspected each trunk in turn, overwhelming their owners with questions. Robert hoped he wouldn't have to speak to any of them. He tended to get tongue-tied in those sorts of situations.

They found their luggage – three large travelling trunks that were as tall as he was – and waited by them, while one of the customs men came over to check their passports and papers.

"It says here you have a mechanimal with you?" the customs man said to John, consulting the manifest on his clipboard.

"That's right," John said. "He's a mech-fox."

Malkin tried to pop his head out of the basket then, but Lily pushed him down. The customs man glared at her. "He should really be packed away in a travel trunk. I hope you've filled in all the necessary paperwork for him."

"We have," John said.

"Good." The customs man ticked a few boxes on a form. "Because it's illegal to bring a mechanimal into this country unless it's been properly registered." He lowered his clipboard and gave them an uninterested smile. "All right, I'm done. You've cleared customs. You may leave."

When he'd gone, John engaged a mechanical porter in one of the red hats to take their trunks on to the hotel. The porter gave him a brass tag for their luggage and agreed to receive payment when he met them at the other end.

"Look!" Robert said, tugging Lily's sleeve and pointing out some of the other steerage passengers, who were being corralled off to a ferry boat at the edge of the quay by uniformed officials. "Where do you think they're being taken?"

"I don't know," Lily said, "but it seems a bit ominous."

"They're going to Ellis Island for further processing," John explained. "They've come to the US to stay for ever, unlike us, and so they need to be inspected properly before they're allowed to enter the country."

"But they're wearing threadbare clothes," Lily whispered to Robert.

Robert had noticed that too. The folk being waved through, like the Hartmans, were richer-looking. "Seems there's one law for the better-off and another for the rest," he told Lily quietly, and she nodded in agreement.

The Arrivals Hall was filled with people of all ages and races in outfits from every different kind of place. The air sang with their joyful babble, a mix of various accents, languages and dialects. Robert recognized snatches – French and what he guessed was Italian. Plus Polish, German and…Irish? Families and friends were meeting for the first time in a long time and their faces glowed happily in the warm electric light.

Lily fidgeted excitedly with her basket. Malkin was still hidden inside it and would occasionally stick his head out to glance around, or poke out his swishing brush. And Robert, who was walking behind Lily, would have to sneak over and stuff it back in.

They crossed the lobby and stepped through a row of swinging glass doors that led onto the sidewalk and the bustling streets of the city, where clouds the colour of roof shingles sprinkled snow on a cobbled road, busy with traffic.

"Come on," John said, flagging down an electric taxi carriage and winking mischievously at the three of them. "Let's go see New York."

No one talked much as they set off in the brand-new electrical-wagon. They were too busy taking in the view. Robert had never seen the like of it before and neither, it seemed, had Lily. She swayed in her seat and lifted Malkin to the window so that he could see too. It wasn't long before the fox had his snout pressed against the glass.

"Look!" he called out excitably, staring through the falling flakes of snow.

Robert wiped away the condensation and peered through the soot-and-dust-stained window as they chugged under an iron bridge that spanned the street.

A train sped across above them. Robert realized this was New York's famous elevated railway, raised on heavy columns and stanchions above the road.

The train's chimney puffed smoke that showered hot, hissing flecks of ash onto the roofs of the low tenements that edged up to the tracks. Behind those, taller buildings spread out in a forest of bricks, concrete, glass and electric light, which streamed from every window, making the cobbles and slush piles radiate a brilliance that twinkled like the joy in Robert's heart.

The city appeared to be set out on a grid, for every crossroads had four junctions. They passed alleys crisscrossed with bare frozen washing lines and a humungous, half-finished tower on the edge of a park, whose top floors, concealed in scaffolding, almost touched the clouds.

"That's Park Row," Robert said, pointing it out eagerly to Malkin and Lily.

"How do you know that?" Lily asked, her eyes shining in the light from the tower.

"We read about it," Robert replied, "in John's *Appleton's Guide*, remember?"

"That's right," John said. "When it's finished, it's set to be the tallest building in New York. A skyscraper, they're calling it."

"Impressive," Lily said. And she meant it. It was a far cry from the short and dumpy houses she was used to seeing in Brackenbridge. Then, in the gap between Malkin's ears, she glimpsed the Brooklyn Bridge.

With its imposing metal cobwebs of suspended steel cables, it was even more breathtaking than the skyscraper.

After ten more minutes, the cab turned off at a junction and pulled up before an eight-storey brownstone. Trees in white fluffy overcoats lined the avenue out front and the tall pyramid-roofed towers on each corner of the building's roof looked like they were sprinkled with icing sugar. Three red words glinted on an electric sign at the front of the building:

"We're staying here?" Lily asked breathlessly.

Papa nodded. "That's right. I booked us a suite."

"Blimey," Robert muttered, gaping wide-eyed at the

place. It looked like a palace. "I've not even stayed in a regular hotel before, let alone one that's so…"

"Swanky?" Malkin suggested, finishing off his sentence.

The three of them stared at the building and then at each other in amazement, as Papa rapped on the roof of the cab to signal the driver to stop.

"To the hotel!" Papa called as the electric taxi juddered to a standstill. Then he opened the carriage door and jumped down from his seat.

His mouth still hanging open, Robert bounded after him.

Lily gathered a bouncing Malkin up quickly in his basket, and with a chest full of twitching excitement followed the pair out into the street.

CHAPTER 4

MURRAY HILL HOTEL
ALL GUESTS WELCOME

NO MECHANIMALS ALLOWED

"It's not really *all* guests welcome, if mechanimals aren't allowed," Malkin said, peeking out of the top of Lily's basket to read the sign in the entrance lobby. "In fact, I would go so far as to say that's discrimination."

"Hush, Malkin," Lily said. "We can't make a scene." She pushed the mech-fox back down beneath his blanket and hoped the staff hadn't noticed.

"At least, not until we're checked in!" Robert said, taking off his cap and stuffing it in his pocket.

John strode purposefully across the marble floor to meet the airstation porter, who was waiting with their trunks beneath a giant gleaming crystal-studded electric chandelier. While he returned their tag to the porter, Robert and Lily looked about.

To their left were two elevator grates. A curved row of numbers and an arrow above each indicated what floor the elevators were on. Beside these stood a pair of telephone booths with glass-panelled doors. Each booth contained a mounted transmitter to speak into and a receiver on a cord to hold to your ear. Robert and Lily had heard of telephones, of course, but had never actually seen one.

To the right of the telephone booths was a fine Christmas tree taller than any of the pines in Brackenbridge Woods. It was festooned in glass baubles and striped candy canes and long red candles, whose flames flickered every time the entrance door swung open.

Robert ran a hand across one of the branches and sniffed his fingers. Pine. The scent of Christmas. The best smell in the whole wide world.

"This is quite the place!" he whispered to Lily.

"I don't imagine Queen Victoria stays anywhere better when she comes to visit New York," she replied.

"She most certainly does not!" John said with a wry smile. He'd finished paying the airstation porter and dismissed him, and now he put a hand on each of their shoulders. "But I have it on the highest authority that there's much more to see than this! So come along, you whippersnappers, let us go and procure our key!"

As they approached the long marble reception desk, they saw that someone was already waiting in front of them: a gaunt-faced woman with short slicked-back hair and a heavy wooden case handcuffed to her gloved wrist. On the side of her case, stamped in black ink, was a snake curled in a perfect circle, eating its own tail. The sight of it sent a shiver slithering down Robert's spine.

DING!...DING!...DING!

The woman dinged the bell on the marble desktop three times. "Hello! Anyone here? Service, please. We wanna check in!" She had a loud New York accent. Beneath her coat, a silver lightning sigil was pinned to the collar of her dress. It reminded Lily of the golden cog Papa wore on the lapel of his suit to indicate his membership of the Mechanists' Guild.

Stood to one side of the woman was a mechanical nursemaid – a square-jawed, iron lady with a red cross painted on her chest. The nursemaid held the handles of two very large leather suitcases within one enormous fist and the thin wrist of a forlorn-looking boy tightly within the other. "I'd advise you don't make a scene, Professor," the nursemaid said. "Humans rarely get what they want from us that way."

"You're wrong, Buckle," the woman at the desk said. "Service mechs ain't like you. They need some geeing up to get 'em going."

The boy said nothing, merely blinked sleepily as if he was half-awake.

Lily studied the boy closely. He seemed around her and Robert's age, maybe a year younger. He held a cage draped with a velvet cloth. His face was pale as a peeled potato, his expression melancholy as a rain cloud and his eyes were like tiny black holes into an infinite nothing. Nevertheless, something about him made Lily hold her breath. He seemed older than his years, as if he'd seen many disturbing things.

As Lily watched, a little white mouse poked its head out of the breast pocket of the boy's suit; it blinked at her, peeked around and sniffled its whiskers. Lily wondered if the mouse was a mechanimal. It seemed very docile for a real pet.

The mouse ducked back down inside the pocket, but

Robert had seen it too. He and Lily both gave the boy warm smiles and Malkin popped his head out of the basket and gave the boy a foxy grin to show he too was friendly.

The boy's eyes lit up when he saw the mech-fox, but then the dark rain cloud of sadness that he seemed to carry with him descended once again.

Lily wondered what was troubling him and whether he had any friends he could tell his worries to. He certainly had a lonely aura about him.

"Can I be of assistance, Ma'am?" A mechanical receptionist with a countenance like a feature doorknocker had appeared in the doorway behind the desk and was addressing the woman.

"Yeah," said the woman. "We just arrived. We wanna check in. Booked a quiet suite. Don't want regular maid service." She nodded at the nursemaid and the boy. "My nephew's sick. Needs peace and quiet. No disturbances. No one's to speak to him. Tell your staff. It'd be much appreciated."

The mechanical receptionist smiled sympathetically at the boy and gave his aunt a darker look. "Of course," he replied. "What did you say your name was?"

"I didn't," the woman replied. "But it's Milksop. Professor Matilda Milksop."

Papa, who'd been studying his *Appleton's Guide* while they waited, looked up with a cry. "Professor Milksop, can it really be you? What a wonderful surprise!"

The woman took a moment to realize she was being addressed by someone else. She wheeled around and stared at Papa as if she couldn't quite place him.

"Have we met, Sir?"

"Professor John Hartman," Papa said cordially, taking her hand and shaking it. "We were introduced at a conference in Sweden some years ago. You were working on the prototype of an oceanic turbine to generate electricity."

"That's right," Professor Milksop said. "Delighted to see you again, Hartman. A real joy." She smiled coldly and pulled her hand away from his. Half-hidden beneath her coat-sleeve was a circular tattoo: a black ring on the inside of her wrist. With alarm, Lily recognized the same snake symbol that was stamped on the wooden case.

"What are you doing in New York?" Professor Milksop asked.

"I'm here to give a speech in January," Papa replied. "For the Annual American Conference of Mechanists and Electricians at Harvard. Meanwhile, I'm taking a holiday with my family. This is Robert Townsend, and this is my daughter Lily—"

Professor Milksop's eyes widened. "Oh yeah! I read about her. And her Cogheart. In the *New York Daily Cog*, of all places. The article said that you made the heart, Hartman. And that Lily and her friend escaped a freak-circus that kidnapped them. Interesting stuff."

Lily felt a flood of disappointment. She had thought she'd be safely cloaked in anonymity in New York, yet here was someone else who knew her story.

"And this is your nephew?" Papa asked, staring at the boy and then at his mechanical nursemaid.

"Yeah. His name's Dane. He's not well, I'm afraid. He don't speak with strangers. It's part of his condition."

"Oh dear! I'm sorry to hear that," Papa said. "What condition is that?"

"Oh it ain't contagious," Professor Milksop reassured him. "It's a form of mutism. He'll be fine…eventually." She glanced at Dane, who seemed dazed and barely taking in the conversation. "Right now he just needs plenty of rest. Miss Buckle here looks after him. Does a real good job."

The mechanical nursemaid gave them a friendly but firm nod.

"Well, at least that's something," Papa said. Then, after a brief pause, he added, "Perhaps the pair of you would like to join us for dinner? We'll be eating right after we've unpacked. Even if he doesn't speak much, your nephew might enjoy some company his own age."

"Unfortunately not," Professor Milksop said. "Dane has a rather delicate constitution. Can't stomach dinner chit-chat." She put her fingers in her coat pockets and rocked back and forth nervously on her feet. She seemed hardly comfortable with small talk herself.

But then, to her obvious relief, the receptionist returned with her key. "Here you go, Ma'am. Room one hundred, on the third floor. You can take the elevator. Our concierge will show you the way."

"No need for that," Professor Milksop said, snatching the key. "We can make our own way. Well," she added to Papa, "we've lots to do. Should be getting on. Pleasure to meet you again, Hartman."

"Likewise," Papa said.

"See you around." Matilda Milksop put the key in her pocket. "Buckle!" she called out. "Our bags, if you please!"

She didn't wait for her mechanical's response, just set out for the elevators, clutching her wooden case tightly in her gloved hand. Miss Buckle followed dutifully, dragging Dane and the suitcases along behind her.

As he went, Dane threw a brief glance over his shoulder and mouthed something at Lily. Two small, silent words. It took her a moment to work out what they were…

Help. Me.

"What strange people," Robert said when the three of them were finally gone.

"And rather rude," Malkin added.

"Funny," Papa said. "I don't recall Professor Milksop being that way. I wonder what she's doing in New York? The last I heard of her, she was researching the properties of diamonds for a sort of electrical machine she was building, but she got sidelined onto a submarine project at the behest of one of those banking barons – a fellow named Nathaniel Shadowsea, I think."

Robert thought that Matilda Milksop had seemed like a rat caught rather unexpectedly in a trap. And Dane's expression had been even worse. There was something odd about him. Like he was not quite…all there. Just as he was thinking this, the mechanical receptionist addressed them.

"Can I assist you, Sir?" he asked John.

"Yes," John said. "I'm Professor Hartman. We're here to check in too."

"Of course." The receptionist studied a book behind

the desk, then fetched their key from the room next door. There was a wooden plaque attached to it, painted with a number. "Room ninety-nine. A triple suite on the third floor."

With a start, Lily realized it was right next to the Milksops.

"Our concierge'll take you up. And one more thing…" The receptionist stared hard at the basket over Lily's arm. "No pets are allowed in the hotel, either real or mechanimal. I hope that won't be a problem?"

"Not at all," Lily said brazenly.

"Good. If you need anything else, don't hesitate to ask. You can call in at reception at any time and one of us will be here to help. Have a pleasant stay."

The receptionist waved at a mechanical concierge in green-and-gold livery, who gave a curt nod and made his way over to them.

When they stepped into the elevator, the elevator boy tipped his peaked cap to them, revealing a head full of brown fuzzy hair, and gave them a grin. He was the first human Lily had seen working here.

"Floor?" he asked.

"Third," the mechanical concierge said.

The boy slammed the grate and pushed the control lever.

As the elevator rose, Lily's thoughts turned to Dane – the mournful-looking nephew of Professor Milksop who kept a mouse hidden in his pocket. Had he really mouthed *Help me*? Or had she imagined that? Papa always said she had an overactive imagination from reading too many penny dreadfuls. She pondered the conundrum for a moment, remembering the shape of Dane's thin downturned mouth making the words...

No, she was sure he'd said *Help me*.

But did that mean he was *actually* in trouble? Or was it a sarcastic and long-suffering aside, because his aunt was so awful?

Lily couldn't quite tell yet. Nevertheless, she'd felt such an odd affinity with Dane. It wasn't just that they were both smuggling pets into the hotel, it was something more that she couldn't quite put her finger on. She had the feeling that Dane's short life had been a somewhat troubled one. And that probably, in his time, he'd seen as many strange and disturbing things as she had.

She peeped past Papa's shoulder, over at Robert, who was standing on the far side of the elevator. If anyone would know how to assist Dane and resolve his predicament, it would be Robert. After all, he'd helped her uncover the Cogheart, saved her from the circus and unravelled the riddle of his own past. With his aid, and Malkin's, Lily felt certain she could remedy whatever was troubling Dane. As soon as she had a moment alone with her two friends, Lily vowed to tell them the two words Dane had silently said.

CHAPTER 5

"Here we are." The concierge unlocked the door. "Room ninety-nine. One of our *premium* suites." Robert stepped in first, followed by Lily and John.

It was a beautiful space. Elegantly furnished, with finely woven Persian rugs thrown across the floor and heavy brocade curtains that hung over the windows to block out the street sounds.

As Papa spoke with the concierge, Lily and Robert hung their coats and scarves on a hatstand in the corner and walked about the lounge room, examining things.

A comfortable-looking sofa and a pair of matching armchairs, upholstered with roses, framed a roaring fire in a grand fireplace. A sideboard, bookshelf and a table with four high-backed chairs filled the rest of the space.

They opened each door in turn and poked their heads around them, finding first a bathroom with wall-to-wall marble that looked good enough for the gods of Mount Olympus, then two bedrooms, each containing a king-sized bed and a polished rosewood wardrobe the size of a mausoleum.

Finally, there was an even larger bedroom that was decorated with the bright, flowery wallpaper of a nursery, which contained three child-sized beds.

Instead of a window, behind its curtains, the room had French doors that led onto a snowy balcony. Beyond the high balustrade, Robert could make out the snow-strafed buildings on the far side of the street.

"This room shares a wall with suite one hundred next door," the concierge explained. "So there might be some noise. But that's a nursery room too, so your neighbour will most likely be that kid you saw. He seems the silent type, if you ask me!" He laughed.

Robert wondered if the concierge ought to be gossiping about guests.

"Well," said John. "One of you will have to take this room. What do you think, Lily? It *is* the biggest, and Robert will probably have to move in here as well when Selena and Caddy arrive tomorrow..."

"I—" Lily clutched her basket close to her chest. She seemed about to argue – it was what she'd normally do. And who could blame her? Robert knew Lily didn't like it when John did anything to suggest she was still his little girl.

But, after some consideration, Lily said, "All right. I'll take it."

"Splendid!" John replied. "Then Robert and I can each take one of the other two."

Robert wondered if the balcony was the reason Lily had agreed so readily to taking the nursery room. Then he remembered that special and particular scheming look she had got in her eyes when the concierge mentioned it abutting the Milksops' room – it had to be something to do with that.

But what?

The mechanical porter arrived and deposited their trunks in each of their rooms. "You folks have a nice vacation," he said. And when he and the concierge had finally disappeared, and Papa had gone to take off his own coat and inspect his room, Robert was finally able to ask Lily what was going on.

"I need to tell you and Malkin together," Lily said, tipping the fox out of the basket.

Somehow Malkin managed to right himself quickly

so that he fell with four legs outwards, like a cat, and ended up standing on the floor.

"About time!" he complained. "My joints were getting stiff in there. I thought I would be stuck scrunched up for ever with your old sweet wrappers and handkerchiefs."

"No time for grousing, Malkin," Lily admonished. "I need to tell you and Robert something about the boy in the lobby."

"Dane Milksop?" Robert asked, taking off his cap and running a hand through his mop of unruly black hair. "He looked rather unhappy."

"Probably didn't want to be on holiday with that awful aunt of his," Malkin said, shaking out his brush.

"It was more than that," Lily said. "Dane mouthed something at me as he was leaving. I think it might have been *I lelp me.*"

"Are you sure?" Malkin asked. "That seems a tad odd."

"I'm not making it up," Lily snapped.

"I never said you were," the fox yapped back.

"That mechanical, Miss Buckle, was holding onto Dane rather tightly," Robert said. "A bit too tightly, if you ask me... And what about Professor Milksop's wooden case?" he added. "The one she had handcuffed to her wrist, with that drawing of a snake on its side, eating its own tail. Have you ever seen anything so creepy? What do you think's in there?"

"Snakes?" Malkin suggested. "Lots of them. Sliming about over one another and eating their own tails." He scrunched up his snout in disgust.

"She had that same symbol tattooed on her wrist," Lily told them. "I saw it when she shook Papa's hand."

Robert gave a shudder. "So I assume we're going to investigate?" he asked. "Try to speak to Dane on his own?"

Lily nodded. "But don't tell Papa. He won't believe any of it."

"Won't believe what?" John asked, stepping back through from the lounge with a folder of papers under his arm that contained his speech.

"Nothing," Lily said.

"We were just saying how unbelievably hungry we are," Robert said.

"Hungry enough to eat our own tails," Malkin added, though the truth was he didn't eat at all, being a mechanical.

"Then let's adjourn to the dining room," John suggested. "I think they're still serving."

"That sounds a grand idea," Malkin barked, his tongue lolling out excitedly. He jumped down from the bed, slipped through Papa's legs, headed across the lounge and bounced up at the main door of the suite, scratching at it with his claws and making awful pining sounds.

"STAY! MALKIN! STAY!" Papa admonished, chasing after him, papers flying everywhere. "Foxes and fine dining don't mix." He yanked the fox back by the scruff of his neck and deposited him by the fire. "You wait here," he said, tapping the mechanimal brusquely on the snout.

"Oh, what joy!" the fox snapped snottily, looking down his nose at John. He licked a few stray pages of the speech that had fallen at his feet.

"We'll take you for walkies tomorrow, I promise." John rushed around picking up his papers as quickly as possible before the angry fox had a chance to start chewing them.

"It's all right, Malkin," Lily whispered, picking up her basket as Papa wedged his folder back under his arm and opened the suite's front door. "I'll sneak you in. You can help us keep an eye out for Dane."

"Good-o!" Malkin jumped into the basket, while Robert stood in the way so that John wouldn't see what was going on – but it wasn't necessary, for he had already stepped into the corridor. Lily hid the basket behind her back, then she and Robert walked a few steps behind Papa, so he wouldn't realize what they were up to and send Malkin back before they arrived at dinner.

"Good evening," the maître d' greeted them as they stepped into the dining room. He was only the second human they'd seen working in the hotel and had a friendly, lived-in face with a broad freckle-spattered nose and tight white curls that were plastered to his head with pomade. "You must be Professor Hartman, Miss Hartman and Master Townsend."

"Yes," said Lily. "How did you know?"

The maître d' smiled. "Apart from Master Milksop, you're the only other children currently staying in the hotel. Would you like me to put your papers in the cloakroom, Sir?" he asked Papa.

"No, thank you," Papa said. "They're rather vital. I have to work on them at dinner."

"And your handbag, Miss Hartman?" the maître d' asked, reaching for the basket hidden behind Lily's back.

Papa gave a sigh of angry frustration. "You haven't brought him with you as well, have you?" He stared down pointedly at the lumpy shape beneath the blanket in Lily's basket. "Well, you tell him to stay hidden and quiet!"

"I will." Lily tucked the basket tighter under her arm and gave the rather confused maître d' her most innocent look. "I'd rather keep hold of this, thanks. It contains… important stuff too."

"Very good." The maître d' was still at rather a loss as to what was going on, but he turned smoothly like he was a mechanical on oiled castors, and led them through a dining room packed with smartly dressed, chattering guests. "I have a table for you in the family section. That should be quieter and more amenable than the main dining lounge."

Robert had never been anywhere quite so imposing. It was grander than the dining rooms at Brackenbridge Manor, the London Mechanists' Guild and the *Firefly* airship all put together. The walls were hung with boughs of holly and ivy and red Christmas ribbons, and the ceiling was ablaze with crystal chandeliers that illuminated plates and plates of exotic-looking dishes.

"This hotel was one of the first in New York to get direct current electricity," the maître d' explained as he showed them to their table.

"That's right!" said Papa, suddenly interested. "Didn't it come from Edison's power station on Pearl Street, near the Brooklyn Bridge?"

"Correct, Sir." The maître d' pulled out an elegantly-carved oak chair for him, and another each for Robert and Lily. "Though that station burned down. Now we're powered by General Electric, and Mr Tesla's technology." He flicked their napkins out and dropped them on their laps. Then, with a modest bow, he returned to the front of house.

"I wish we had electricity at home," Lily said, tucking Malkin's basket away beneath her chair. "It seems almost like a magic power. Eventually it could run *everything*... even mechanicals." She gave the basket under her seat a kick to warn Malkin not to comment on that.

"Too right," Robert replied. "I suppose, in the end, it'll take over completely from gaslight, steam and clockwork."

"What?" Papa stared up at them from his reading matter. "Oh no, I don't think so. Not for a long while."

"Why not?" Lily asked.

"Right now, electricity is far too unpredictable," Papa said. "Far too dangerous... We've barely scratched the surface in discovering what it can do."

A mechanical waiter brought a carafe of freshly-made lemonade and poured it into three glasses, one for each of them. Then, with a flourish, he presented everyone with a menu.

Robert opened his to find row upon row of dishes

he'd never heard of. Thanks to an incomprehensible mishmash of French and English words, he had trouble understanding what anything was. He stared down in consternation at the pile of gold-rimmed plates in front of him and the rows of knives and forks. At least, by now, he was getting used to the armoury of cutlery these places tended to provide.

Finally, Papa read through the choices and ordered for each of them. Bouillon to start with, then baked halibut with potatoes Parisienne for him, and beef à la mode with green peas and mashed potato for Robert and Lily.

While they slurped their bouillon soup, Lily and Robert scanned opposite ends of the dining room for any sign of Dane Milksop.

Lily could not see him at first, and was about to give up looking around her half, when her eyes were drawn to a glamorous black lady in a blue silk gown, who was dining alone at the next table and seemed awfully familiar.

The lady had brightly painted eyes and long lashes, but it was her sparkling, ostentatious gold necklace that had attracted Lily's attention.

The necklace was in the shape of a snake, which curled around the woman's neck in a circle, its head and tail meeting just above her breast. In its mouth, between its pointed fangs, the snake held a bright blue diamond. Its golden tail wound around the other side of the diamond, clasping it securely.

Lily perceived with shock that the necklace was the very same symbol that was tattooed on Professor Milksop's wrist, and stamped on the side of her wooden case!

Subtly, she pointed out the necklace to Robert.

"Who is that lady?" she asked, tugging at Papa's sleeve. "I recognize her."

Papa glanced up from his papers. "That's Miss Aleilia Child," he said, squinting at the lady. "The famous soprano singer from the new New York Metropolitan Opera. I have some recordings of her in my music collection."

"I've heard those cylinders," Robert said. "She has a beautiful singing voice."

"We should all go and see her at the opera sometime," Malkin whispered from under the table.

"A mechanical fox at the opera," Lily said. "Whatever next?"

Robert giggled.

"I'll have you know I'm quite cultured," Malkin huffed.

"What now?" Papa angrily abandoned his papers. "Malkin, didn't I tell you to stay hidden and quiet?" He gave an immense and agitated sigh. "Oh, never mind! I give up! On all of you! Just don't let him be discovered, please."

"What kind of necklace is it?" Lily asked, changing the subject back to Miss Child.

"It's an Ouroboros Diamond necklace," Papa said. "The stone is very expensive. Very rare."

"As rare as Queen Victoria's Blood Moon Diamond?" Robert asked, tucking into his beef, which had just arrived.

"Almost." Papa took a mouthful of fish. "Like Blood Moon Diamonds, Ouroboros Diamonds supposedly have life- and death-giving properties."

"I wonder where Miss Child got it from?" Lily said. "It looks almost exactly like the symbol on Professor Milksop's case."

"Case? What case?" Papa asked.

"Clanking chronometers!" Lily exclaimed. "You really don't notice anything, do you?"

As she said that, she finally spotted the professor. She was dining with Dane at a table off to their right, partly hidden by wooden screens painted with bright fishes and seaweed. Miss Buckle, the boy's mechanical nursemaid, stood beside the professor, not eating or talking, just watching Dane and making sure he was behaving himself.

The Milksops had the only screened table, Lily observed. She wondered if Professor Milksop had asked for it to protect her nephew Dane from prying eyes. Or was it actually the other way round – to stop *him* from seeing anyone or anything.

She nudged Robert and pointed the pair out to him.

Through a gap in the screens, they could just make out Professor Milksop's wooden case at her feet. The professor kept gently kicking it to check it was still there.

Dane, on the other hand, she was practically ignoring. The boy sat silently opposite her, searching the dining room with an expression of deep unease.

Suddenly, his eyes locked onto Lily's.

Her heart skipped a tick as he smiled sadly at her.

Help me, he mouthed.

Lily frowned and pinched Robert's knee under the table, nodding in Dane's direction.

He watched with Lily as Dane once more mouthed the same words through the gap in the screen:

Help me.

Lily was sure now that the message was meant for the pair of them. After all, they were the only other children in the hotel and the only people paying attention to Dane, while Papa read his papers and everyone else in the dining room sat eating and talking ebulliently.

No. Dane wanted *their* help specifically. Hers and Robert's... But why?

Before Lily could observe anything more or speak directly to Robert about what they'd seen, the waiter brought tea and dessert – chocolate meringue puffs – blocking her view of the Milksops' table. By the time he moved away, Dane was staring fixedly down at his plate.

Lily tucked into her dessert as she thought about the matter. The cocoa was so good it made her taste buds itch, and the nutty spun sugar melted in her mouth like fragments of fluffy cloud. Robert and Papa ate their desserts almost as fast as she did, Robert licking his lips with each bite.

"Delicious!" Papa said when he was finished, and then he stood up and put his napkin on the table. "Now, if you will excuse me, I intend to retire to the smoking room and work a little more on my speech. It's probably the last chance I'll get before your mother arrives tomorrow, Robert. Lily, you may stay here with him while the pair of you finish your tea. Malkin, since you're here, you might as well make yourself useful. Be sure they go straight up to bed after tea. And you're to go with them."

"Must I?" the fox complained.

"Of course you must!" Papa said. "We can't have our feral fox wandering the corridors of a top-drawer hotel. What will people say?"

When Papa was finally gone, Robert, Lily and Malkin huddled together to talk.

Dane hadn't looked at them again since dessert.

"His aunt and Miss Buckle have been watching him," Robert said. "But I don't think Dane's finished with what he's trying to tell us."

"In which case we'd better stay here and wait," Lily replied. She licked her finger and dabbed it in the remaining cocoa on her plate.

Robert poured himself more tea from the pot.

And Malkin, aware that no one was looking, chewed the table leg to sharpen his teeth.

A moment later, as Lily and Robert watched the screened table, Dane did something quite extraordinary – especially for a boy who seemed so quiet and withdrawn. With a sweep of his arm, he sent his knife tumbling to the floor.

His aunt said something angrily to him and Miss Buckle tutted and folded her arms. Dane apologized and crouched down to pick up the offending piece of fallen cutlery.

The legs of the screen hid his hands, as Lily tried to see what he was doing.

Suddenly, Dane's little white mouse scampered across the carpet stopping in the shadows of a far-off table.

As they watched it, it dodged between the feet of various hotel guests, slunk past a waiter with a silver tray and zoomed towards them.

It was a miracle it wasn't seen, but it was fast.

Lily and Robert waited with bated breath, until eventually the mouse arrived at their feet. It was carrying a teeny piece of paper in its jaws.

Malkin sniffed at the creature from his basket. "It's not a mechanical," he informed them with a snort. "But – the strangest thing – it doesn't smell alive."

"How can that be?" Robert asked.

"I don't know," the fox replied.

"Hello, little one," Lily whispered to the mouse.

She picked the creature up, cupping it in her lap to avoid anyone else seeing it. It felt strangely ice-cold to the touch. The mouse nuzzled at her fingers with his soft snout. Lily took the twist of paper from his mouth, picking at its edges, trying to unroll it.

The mouse hopped down from her lap, skipped across the hem of her skirts, zigzagged quickly around Malkin's basket and scarpered back across the room to Dane.

Lily unfurled the paper beneath the table. Dane's minute handwriting filled the interior page, the words crammed so close that Lily and Robert could barely read them.

Lily got out her magnifying glass and tried that. Immediately the message jumped out clear as day. She and Robert put their heads together and peered through the lens reading what Dane had to say.

Lily, Robert,
  you're the only ones I can trust.
  I need your help. I can't leave my room without being watched.
I can't recall anything before last week. I need to remember
what happened to my parents. Please, find out what you can.
When my aunt goes out, come to room 100 and knock three times.
Let no one know I contacted you, least of all my aunt.
          Kind regards, Dane Milksop

"He's lost his memory," Robert whispered. "He *does* need our help."

"That's why he sent a rodent," Malkin added. "He doesn't remember what a real postman looks like."

"See?" Lily said. "I was right. I knew there was something wrong with him. I wonder what has happened to his parents? And why he's with his aunt?" She glanced up to see Dane dropping his napkin over the mouse and bending down to carefully hide it back in his pocket.

Lily pondered how she, Robert and Malkin were going to discover more about Dane's parents. And how they were going to contact him in his room tomorrow without his formidable aunt finding out. Especially if his nursemaid, Miss Buckle was guarding him – she looked somewhat of an intimidating foe herself.

It was a difficult task, and Lily couldn't figure out why Dane had chosen to entrust it to her, Robert and Malkin, rather than an adult. Then she remembered the weird connection she'd felt with Dane in the lobby. Had he sensed that too? Perhaps that's why he'd chosen the three of them...

Either way, now that he had, Lily realized they had a new mystery to solve and they couldn't let him down.

CHAPTER 6

Robert, Lily and Malkin watched as Matilda Milksop got up and handcuffed the wooden case back to her wrist, then she and Miss Buckle each took one of Dane's hands and guided him from the dinner table.

As she passed Miss Child, the professor's eyes flicked to the Ouroboros Diamond around her neck. Lily wondered once again what the link was between the symbol on the professor's wooden case and the singer's ostentatious piece of jewellery. Her brain fizzed with ideas. There were so many questions to answer, so much to find out – but where to start?

"They must be going up to bed," Robert whispered, as the pair of Milksops and Miss Buckle stepped through the dining room's archway, past the maître d' and on towards the elevators. "I don't think we'll get to speak to Dane again tonight."

"Maybe Papa knows more about the Milksop family?" Lily suggested.

"Seems unlikely," Malkin yipped. "Given that he's only met Professor Milksop briefly once before at a conference."

"Malkin's right," Robert said. "My hunch is he's told us all he knows about the Milksops already, and even if he hasn't, we can't really ask him about Dane's message."

"Why not?" Lily asked, touching the twist of paper in her pocket.

"Because it specifically says not to tell anyone," Robert reminded her.

"Oh." Lily had forgotten that part of the message. She felt a flood of disappointment. With Dane's stipulations, this mystery was going to be even more difficult to solve than she'd first thought.

"Maybe we could look around the hotel instead?" Malkin suggested. "We might find out something else that way?"

"Good idea!" Lily brightened up. "Perhaps his aunt stays here all the time? Or his parents used to, and the staff know them?"

"Or perhaps they're strangers here, like us?" Malkin suggested.

"Both are equally possible," Robert said. "We won't know until we do some digging."

They finished their tea and set off, determined to investigate the other public rooms of the hotel to see what they might find out.

First, they peeped in on the Ladies' Sitting Room, where ladies in various feathered hats that made them look like plumed blue jays sat drinking their evening cups of coffee and glasses of *digestifs* before bed.

Then they found the Grand Ballroom, which was empty except for one mechanical polishing the gold fixtures and fittings.

This was followed by the Tea Lounge, which was vacant too, since high tea was only served in the afternoon.

Then came a Gentlemen's Smoking Room, which was filled with smoking gentlemen – the worst kind. They were careful to peer only briefly round the door of that one, because they didn't want Papa to know they'd disobeyed his decree at dinner about going straight up to bed.

Then there was a Games Room, full of card tables, and finally, at the end of a long ill-lit corridor, they found a Reading Room. A sign on its door proclaimed it was for the use of all guests and that it was open all hours.

"Maybe we can find some information about Professor Milksop and the Milksop family in here?" Lily tried the door handle, but it was locked. The reading room, it seemed, was open all hours except this one.

Still, that had never stopped her before.

She knocked once to make sure the room was empty. Then, while Robert peered up and down the corridor to check no one was coming, Lily felt around in the bottom of her basket for her lock picks.

"Watch it!" Malkin snapped as her fingers scrabbled about beneath his undercarriage.

Eventually Lily found what she was looking for – a dinky leather wallet, hidden beneath Malkin's brush. She pulled it out.

The lock-picking kit had been a present from her friends Anna and Tolly, back in England. Even before she'd got it, Lily had been a pretty dab hand at picking a lock with a hairpin. Now, with the kit, she considered herself an expert.

She unfolded the wallet's flaps to reveal the two neat rows of lock picks, each held in its own special pouch, and selected one to open the door.

"Are we really going to start breaking into hotel rooms

now?" Malkin asked, climbing out of the basket as she crouched beside the room's keyhole.

"It's not a hotel room," Lily said. "It's a *reading* room. And besides, it's not like we're going to steal anything."

"Except knowledge," Robert said.

"And you can't steal that," Lily added. "It's free."

"The end doesn't always justify the means, you know," Malkin grumbled.

But in the time they had been talking, Lily felt the lock shift. It let out a quiet *click*.

She pulled out the picks and replaced them in the wallet, before sneaking into the room. Malkin followed her as Robert picked up the basket and shut the door softly behind them.

The reading room was filled with plush carpet and floor-to-ceiling oak shelves packed with books. In the centre of the room was a long table and many upright chairs. Off to one side, two red leather armchairs stood beside a marble fireplace with a fire crackling in the grate. A magazine rack sat beside the hearth, where there was a dented coal scuttle and basket of old newspapers for burning.

"This is quite the library," Robert whispered, running his hand along the polished tabletop.

"Isn't it?" Malkin agreed. "A relaxed place, for anyone

so minded to sit and study, or enjoy forty winks by the fire." He peered longingly at the pair of easy chairs.

"No time for that now," Lily told him. "Why don't you and Robert check the recent magazines for any mention of Matilda Milksop? Professors are always in the news. Especially female ones – they're as rare as hen's teeth." She was thinking of her mama and Dr Droz, the only other two female professors that she knew of.

"What are you going to do?" Robert asked, but Lily was already scanning through the far shelves.

"I am going to find an encyclopedia and look up the word *ouroboros*," she announced.

"Good plan." Malkin prowled over to the fire and threw himself down before it. "But someone needs to keep an eye on the door. The lion's share of the work."

Robert made himself comfortable in one of the armchairs and began searching through the magazine rack for anything about the Milksops.

Lily stalked the shelves and found a twelve-volume encyclopedia. Each volume was thicker than the breadth of her palm. She pulled down *O–P* and brought it over to the seat opposite Robert. Then she licked her finger and flicked through the pages.

"Obey, obfuscate, oboe, orang-utang…ouroboros. Here it is!" she said triumphantly, turning the book around.

And there it was. At least, a drawing of it. It looked *exactly* like Miss Child's necklace, and the picture stamped on Matilda Milksop's wrist and the side of her wooden case: a circular snake eating its own tail.

Robert gave a shudder. "That symbol doesn't get any less gruesome the more I see it."

"Let's have a look at what more there is to learn." Lily frowned and read out the definition. "'Ouroboros comes from the Greek *oura*, which means *tail*, and *boros*, which means *eating*. The ouroboros symbolizes infinity and wholeness. The cycle of life and death and the duality of creation and destruction.' It's just like Papa said!"

"What does duality mean?" Robert asked, shuffling through the piles of magazines in his lap.

"It means something that's two things at the same time," Lily explained, reading from the encyclopedia.

"I see." Robert gave up and stuffed the magazines he had been examining back in the rack of newspapers.

"No good?" Lily asked.

"No." He shook his head. "There's nothing in any of them about Professor Milksop, or her orba…her ora-bora…" He gave up trying to pronounce the word. "Her snake suitcase. Nor anything about the work John said she was doing for the fellow Nathaniel Shadowsea on his submarine project."

"That's probably old news," Malkin yapped.

"Unless…" Lily glanced over at the basket of newspapers beside the fire. She put the encyclopedia aside, walked over to the fireplace and began pulling the papers out of the basket.

When Robert grasped what she was doing, he got up and joined her.

They flicked through each newspaper in turn. Robert enjoyed reading various headlines out to Malkin and Lily in an important-sounding voice. Headlines like: *Reporter Nellie Bly Solves the Mechanical Mysteries* or *Survivor of the Lost Arctic Airship Found* or *Secrets of the Stolen Steam-Engines Revealed*.

But after a while he stopped. "None of this is any use for our case," he said sadly.

"No," Lily agreed, scanning the articles with her magnifying glass.

"It does clean one's canines most agreeably though." Malkin grizzled at the papers, shredding them to ribbons.

"Malkin! Wait!" Robert called. He had glimpsed a headline that seemed promising, but it was about to get ground to a pulp by the fox's yellow teeth.

Luckily, he managed to tear the page from Malkin's snapping jaws in time.

"Give that back," Malkin barked, snorting and scratching at Robert's leg. "I haven't finished chewing it yet!"

"No!" Robert snapped. "I need to read this!"

He squinted at the article in the firelight. Lily joined him, peering over his shoulder.

NEW YORK DAILY COG

FIRST MODULES READY
TO BE SUBMERGED FOR BUILDING
OF SHADOWSEA SUBMARINE BASE

NYC Late Edition , March 1, 1896   All today's news!

Mr Nathaniel Shadowsea, Professor Matilda Milksop and guests met President McKinley on the dockside of the Shadowsea Warehouse near Battery Park yesterday. They were there to celebrate the delivery of the first module of their newly designed Shadowsea Submarine Base. Also present were Professor Milksop's brother Daniel and his wife Lucille, who will be living and working on the base along with their young son, Dane. Other employees destined to play a role on the base include one Miss Buckle, a mechanical nursemaid, who will be primarily programmed to look after Dane as his protector, but who will also be able to help Professor Milksop with some of her undersea experiments. Miss Aleilia Child, the famous opera singer, seen here wearing a rare Ouroboros Diamond necklace, was also invited to sing at the celebration. The Shadowsea Submarine Base will be built on the edge of the Darkwater Oceanic Trench. A submersible named the *Diving Belle* will be used to take down supplies needed for the work. When finished, the structure will harness undersea currents using a gigantic turbine and will create enough electricity to power the entire Eastern Seaboard. It is scheduled to start operating on December 1, 1897.

Beneath the text was a photograph of a group of people lined up on the dockside.

Professor Milksop and Miss Buckle were standing next to a smart-suited man, who must've been Mr Shadowsea, the project's financier.

Miss Child, wearing the same golden snake-shaped necklace she had on at dinner, stood beside President McKinley. Robert recognized the president by his square head and slick side-parted hair. He'd seen his face before on John's dollar bills. Behind the president, a crane was lowering a metal sphere the size of a small house, with portholes in the side, onto the deck of a ship.

As Robert pored over the picture, he saw a younger-looking Dane with his parents, blurry in the background among the crowds. He pointed them out to Lily, who took out her magnifying glass and stared at their teeny faces. They and Dane did look alike. But no matter how hard, or how carefully Lily and Robert stared at the minuscule figures, their expressions told them nothing new, and the closer they got the more indistinct the image became, until eventually the three Milksops just disappeared into the crowds, melting away into itty-bitty blobs of black-and-white newsprint.

"Well, we know the names of Dane's mama and papa now at least," Lily said, ripping the article with its picture out of the paper and putting the page in her pocket. "Lucille and Daniel."

"But we don't know who or where they are," Robert said. "Apart from that they were on this Shadowsea base with everyone. And we don't know why Dane's aunt is hiding out with him and Miss Buckle at this hotel for New Year's Eve."

"Nor anything about that ouroboros case his aunt constantly has handcuffed to her wrist," Malkin added. "It's very suspicious!"

Lily shook her head. "We may not have the answer to any of those questions yet," she said, "but I intend to find them out. They're all mixed up with Dane's situation somehow, I just know it."

"We could speak to some of the hotel staff?" Robert suggested.

"Good idea," Lily replied. "They might overhear something over the next few days from Professor Milksop or Miss Buckle. Something we might miss."

She was about to say more when Papa suddenly appeared at the door on the far side of the room. "There you are!" he cried. "I've been looking for you everywhere. Malkin, you were meant to take them straight up to bed. Come on, all of you, it's late now. You need your sleep... perchance to dream!" he laughed.

After shooing them off to bed, Papa had quickly become distracted by the many interesting books in the reading room; including a thick two-volume biography of Shakespeare, which looked even more in-depth and boring than his own, and so they ended up walking back to their room alone.

"Tomorrow we're going to have to relay everything we've learned to Dane to see if any of it helps him remember," Lily told Malkin and Robert. "And we'll need to do it without arousing suspicion from his aunt or Miss Buckle."

"It's not exactly Sherlock-Holmes-level sleuthing," Malkin said, jumping up and burrowing himself into Lily's basket before they reached the more public part of the hotel.

"Maybe not," Robert replied, "but we've only just started looking. Perhaps," he suggested, "the article alone will be enough to jog Dane's memory?"

"Hopefully," Lily said. "My hunch is, whatever it is Dane's forgotten about his parents and everything else, it has to do with the project in the news story – his aunt and her work on that submarine base, and probably her wooden case as well. Maybe tomorrow we'll find out."

They were approaching their door when suddenly Malkin poked his head out of the basket and pricked up his ears. "Hush!" he said urgently. "No more talking."

"Why?" Lily whispered.

The mechanical fox's expression had taken on a wild air.

"Because," he hissed, "there's a stranger in our suite."

CHAPTER 7

Lily pressed her ear to the wooden door of room ninety-nine, just above the lock.

There was indeed a noise coming from inside – the noise of someone shifting things about.

She tried the door handle. It was unlocked.

She motioned to Robert and, brandishing the magnifying glass, she stepped through the door.

Malkin sprang from the basket, teeth bared, and crept down the short entrance passage to peer around the corner into the living room.

Immediately his tail went up and his hackles dropped. "It's only room service," he barked back at them.

There, by the hearth, was a maid dressed in grey with

a white pinny and a starched white cap that stood out against her brown skin. She had a patch over one eye, which made her look a mite piratical and endeared her to Robert straight away.

"Excuse me," she said, looking up from where she was busily setting the fire. "I didn't mean to cause any trouble..."

"That's all right," Robert replied, slightly embarrassed. "We thought there was an intruder."

"An intruder?" The girl looked aghast. "Why'd you think that? You in some kinda trouble?"

"Not yet," Lily said, "but we soon might be."

"Intriguing," the girl said. "S'pose I'd better not ask why?"

Malkin crept up to her and butted his head under her hand.

He purred softly as the girl obligingly stroked his ears.

"Never seen a mech-fox before," she said. "What's his name?"

Mechanimals weren't allowed in the hotel. Robert felt queasy. He hoped she wouldn't tell management, but she seemed friendly enough.

"It's Malkin," the fox said.

"He *can* talk!" the girl said. "I thought I'd imagined it."

"Oh yes," Robert said. "He barely shuts up."

"How dare you!" Malkin snapped.

The girl opened her mouth wide and guffawed in delight. Malkin seemed to like that. He gave her his foxiest grin. "You may scratch behind my ears, Miss, if you so desire," he said, giving playful yelping noises when she complied.

"Oh." The girl put a hand over her mouth. "I clean forgot. I need to finish the fire." She let go of Malkin and turned back to the grate. "You won't rat me out, will ya? It'll only get me in deep with the head housekeeper."

"What rat?" Lily asked. The girl's words had confused her.

"You won't tell 'em I started a conversation with you?" the girl explained. "Or that I was tardy lighting the fire. It's against regulation. They'd dock my pay."

"As long as you don't tell them we smuggled a mechanimal into our room," Lily said. "Then I think we have an agreement."

"Deal," the girl said. "I won't breathe a word. Besides, your Malkin is quite the character." She beamed at him.

Robert felt relieved. He liked this girl. "My name's Robert Townsend," he said. "This is my friend, Lily Hartman."

"Pleased to meet ya," the girl said.

"And you," Lily replied.

A flicker of recognition appeared on the girl's face. "Hey! Weren't you the kid in the paper?" she asked Lily. "The girl with the clockwork heart? You're practically famous!"

"Practically," Lily said. "I wish I wasn't."

"I'm sure it ain't so bad," the girl said. "'Specially if you get to lord it up in these sorta places. Name's Ida Winkler, by the way. But my pals call me Kid Wink, on account of my missing eye."

"How did you lose it?" Lily asked.

It felt a bit blunt, but Kid Wink didn't seem to mind. "It was pecked out by a crazy crow that belonged to a witch," she said.

"Really?" Robert asked.

"No." Kid Wink chuckled. "Gullible, ain't ya? Truth is, I lost it in a fight. The other kid was no good. Shot me with a catapult. Now I wear an eyepatch because I ain't got the dough to buy a mechanical eye, nor even a glass one." Kid Wink tapped her eyepatch with a finger. "Before I worked in this classy joint, I was always getting into brawls like that. Now I have to watch my back. If the super or the head housekeeper sees me, they'd chew me out for sure, and I'd lose my job. It was hard enough getting this gig in the first place, looking the way I do."

She kneeled back down by the fireplace and began

filling the grate with folded circles of paper. On top of this, she tipped out a handful of coal from her bucket.

Then she took something from her pocket – a tiny silver box that fitted in her palm. She flipped its lid open on a hinge. Inside was a miniature wheel of flint and a wick in a small steel basket.

"What is that?" Lily asked, intrigued. She had never seen such a thing before.

"You like it?" Kid Wink brightened. "I named it the Wonderlite. One day it's gonna be bigger than Lucifer matches. The whole city'll have one."

"You invented it?" Robert asked, slightly flabbergasted.

"You got that right."

"But how…?"

"Trial and error. Me and my buddies are rogue inventors. We collect junk from the street – stuff no one wants, from places no one goes – then work with it to make things."

Kid Wink spun the wheel of the Wonderlite until sparks flew from it, igniting the wick into a glowing flame. She held the flame to a twist of paper in the fireplace and waited while the fire spread along its length, licking at the coal.

"Folks call us the railway children, but we call ourselves the Cloudscrapers," she explained. "'Cause we live in an abandoned carriage on the IRT."

"What's the IRT?" Lily asked.

"The elevated railway – the Interborough Rapid Transit." Kid Wink flipped the lid of her Wonderlite shut, extinguishing the flame, then put the silver box back in her pocket.

Robert thought of his father and the fire that had ravaged their house, as he did sometimes when he saw flames, and felt a sudden flood of sadness.

"Do you fix the fires in every room in this hotel?" Lily asked Kid Wink. She was thinking of what Robert had said earlier, about asking the hotel staff to help them learn more about Matilda Milksop and Dane.

"Only the rooms on this floor," the girl replied.

"But that's perfect," Lily said. "We were wondering if you knew anything about a boy named Dane, or his aunt and her mechanical? They're in room one hundred – next door. They arrived earlier today."

"Ah," Kid Wink said. "They're strange ones." She leaned in closer. "I tried to set their fire earlier, but they wouldn't let me. Woman said her nephew was ill and no one was allowed in the room. I overheard her talking to the mechanical too, later in the hall. Something about a plan she had to fix an engine that she keeps in her wooden case."

"The one with the ouroboros stamped on it?" Lily asked.

"The what?" Kid Wink said.

"The one with the circular snake stamped on the side."

Kid Wink nodded. "Yeah, that's the one. She kept looking at it while she was speaking."

"So there's an engine in it!" Lily felt delighted. At last she was learning more about the mystery. "I wonder what it does?"

"Wrangles snakes?" Malkin suggested.

Lily shook her head. "Seems unlikely."

"It'll be something more abstract represented by the symbol," Robert said.

"Like what?" Lily asked.

"Something to do with creation and destruction. Life and death," he suggested.

"So, an engine that creates and destroys?" she asked. "Brings things to life or kills them...?"

Robert nodded. "One of those, or all of them," he said.

Lily frowned. Could a machine create life like that? Surely not? "No engine has that much power," she said. "It would require too much energy."

"Like the energy generated by a brand-new underwater base?" Malkin suggested.

"Whatever it is, this engine sounds dangerous." Kid

Wink picked up her coal scuttle. "I'd best be off. Been shooting my mouth off too long. I still got a ton of fires to light on this floor."

"Thanks for your help," Lily said. "If you find out anything else about Dane and his aunt, or her engine…"

"I know," Kid Wink said. "I'll be in touch. Catch you later." She bobbed them a brief curtsey. Robert could see there was a studied casualness to it. "So long and good night. See you on the flip side!" And, with that, she stepped out the door.

When she was gone, Robert and Lily brushed their teeth together at the bathroom sink. Then Malkin went with Lily to her room, and Robert bade them both goodnight and retired to his bed as well.

It had been a long day, what with arriving on the airship and travelling across New York, before stumbling upon this new mystery right next-door in the hotel. Suddenly, Robert felt more weary than he had in a long time.

He climbed beneath the covers, sank his head onto his pillow and shut his eyes. The mattress felt extraordinarily comfortable, but he could not sleep. Not yet. He kept thinking about Dane's missing parents and the thought made him circle round to his own da, who had died last Christmas. Oh, how he missed him!

Still, his ma and Caddy would be here tomorrow afternoon. He fiddled with the Moonlocket around his neck as he thought of them.

Perhaps Caddy could speak with the spirits about Dane and find out what was going on with him and his aunt and the engine? It was worth a try at least. She knew about those kinds of things, after all. And so did his ma. That was what they had been doing, travelling around the States – seances and the like.

Robert knew his relationship with his ma and sister was new. Sometimes he felt like he was the moon to their sun, and at other times he was the sun to their moon. Either way, they were forever orbiting around each other, forever travelling in opposite directions. Barely fated to meet.

Would they have anything to say to each other now, after another six months apart? Or would the thread between them have broken, like last time?

So many things to worry on. But, thought Robert, as he snuggled deep beneath the warm covers, the thing about worry was that entertaining too much of it got you nowhere. What would happen would happen. And most of your worst fears never came to pass. This past year,

Robert had learned that it was the mammoth random things that crashed across your life like tidal waves that made a difference and those were torments no amount of worry could predict.

As he was fond of saying to Lily: all you could do was enjoy life and, when needs must, try to be brave in those treacherous moments.

Gradually, with that last comforting thought in his head, Robert drifted off to sleep.

CHAPTER 8

Even with all there was to do in New York the next morning, Robert found the wait for his ma and Caddy to arrive interminable.

After an early breakfast in the dining room, where the Milksops were not present, he, John and Lily put on their hats, scarves, gloves and coats and left the hotel, along with Malkin in his green jacket (who was relieved to be let out of Lily's basket once they were outside), and took a brisk promenade through Murray Hill.

It was a smart neighbourhood of grand houses and sidewalks still heavy with snow. Up above, a cold winter sun was shining.

While they walked, Robert, Lily and Malkin tried to

catch a moment to discuss what they'd learned yesterday about Dane's family and the engine in his aunt's wooden suitcase. But this turned out to be impossible, for John was always close by, keenly interrupting their conversation to point out landmarks, like a tour guide, or shepherding them across a busy road. And though they needed to talk urgently, they couldn't risk him overhearing what they had to say.

Two blocks west of the hotel, they took Sixth Avenue, arriving eventually at Central Park, an immense white eiderdown of a space that was dotted with snow-capped trees.

They skirted an enormous frozen pond, where local people were ice skating, and walked back along Fifth Avenue, stopping for a lunch of breaded mutton and peas at a local diner, before returning to the hotel at two to meet Selena and Caddy.

Robert took a seat on a red leather settee in the lobby that was partly hidden by the Christmas tree, beside a grand stone fireplace with a roaring fire.

Lily and John joined him. Lily was holding her basket on her lap with Malkin once again hidden in it.

Then they waited.

Robert removed his cap and clutched it in his lap, turning it round and round and fiddling with its brim.

He was so nervous he would jump to his feet whenever someone came through the door.

Malkin was overexcited too. He was constantly popping his head out of the basket to tell them how much he was looking forward to seeing Caddy again. Lily had to push him back down on multiple occasions so he wouldn't be discovered.

Two-thirty rolled around and his ma and sister still hadn't shown up.

Robert stood up and paced the floor, disturbed. Perhaps some disaster had happened to their ship? Or perhaps they simply weren't coming?

So many possibilities churned around in his mind.

Then, all of a sudden, he caught a glimpse of his ma and Caddy stepping through the swing doors at the far end of the hotel lobby, and his heart soared.

They had yet to see him and they glanced anxiously about, walking towards the reception desk.

Lily and John hung back beside the fire to give Robert time alone to greet them.

Robert took a few small steps forward, but for some reason didn't wave just yet. Instead, he stood and took them both in, trying to fix them in his mind like a photograph. It was a habit he had when he thought a moment might not ever happen again.

His ma had on a long blue velvet coat dotted with glass beads that twinkled in the light. It was reminiscent of the starry stage costume she'd worn when she and Robert had first met at the Theatre of Curiosities in London. A waist-length black woollen winter cape was thrown over her shoulders, and atop her head was a large felt hat trimmed with feathers. A few locks of her black hair trailed down beneath the hat brim, framing her face. They reminded Robert of a trail of ink.

Caddy sported a stylish black velvet jacket with green glass buttons, matching green walking gloves, a scarf and a bonnet trimmed with red Christmas ribbons. She looked a lot smarter than the last time he'd seen her. But she hadn't changed completely, for her hair, which always used to have a tendency to tangle, hung down beneath the bonnet like a bundle of twigs.

The pair finally saw Robert. His ma's hazel eyes shone and she broke into a bright smile, waving her gloves and rushing at him.

Caddy waved too. Her grin was so big it made dimples appear in her apple cheeks. "Robert!" she called out across the lobby.

"Hiya, Ma! Hi, Caddy!" Robert cried as the pair of them hurried over. "Merry Christmas! Can we still say that now that it's passed?" He was gabbling. The nervous twinge in his belly fluttered like a hothouse full of butterflies.

"Of course we can." His ma pulled him into a huge hug, kissing him on the cheek. "Merry Christmas, darling. I'm looking forward to seeing in the New Year with you! Sorry we're late. I hope you got our telegram? We would've been with you last night, only our arrival was put back a day. Then I had to look up the hotel's address because we didn't know where it was..." She stared around nervously. "We've never stayed in such a smart place before!"

She was babbling too. Perhaps Robert wasn't the only one nervous about their meeting?

"Hello, Selena, Caddy," Lily said, stepping in quietly beside Robert.

"Hello, Lily!" they both said in unison.

Selena shook Lily's hand while Caddy gave her a kiss on the cheek.

Malkin poked his head out from Lily's basket and licked both their hands.

"Feel free to ignore me," he chirruped. "I'm disguised as the contents of a picnic basket."

"So you are!" Caddy ruffled his ears.

"Mrs Townsend. Miss Townsend. I'm delighted you made it finally." John lifted his hat to both Selena and

Caddy as he joined the group.

"Pleased to meet you again, Professor Hartman," Selena said, with a slight bow. "Call me Selena. I think you did before."

"And you may call me John." Papa beamed at them. "How are you both?" he asked, while Lily tucked Malkin away again, peering at the lobby staff and guests to check none of them had seen him.

"Better now we've finally arrived," Selena said. Then she turned properly to her son. "Now, Robert, let's get a good look at you…" she said, grasping him by the shoulders. "I swear, you look more and more like your father each time I see you! Doesn't he, John?"

"Thanks." Robert shrugged her away. He didn't like it when she brought up Da. It was so long since the pair of them had been together. She hadn't even been there at the end, when Thaddeus had died.

He turned to Caddy instead and looked her up and down. "All right, sprout?" he said. "I think you've sprouted too!"

"That's because I'm nearly ten," Caddy said, beaming. "Practically grown. My birthday's in fifty-nine days!"

"How long exactly have you and Caddy been in America?" John asked Selena.

"Almost six months," Selena said breezily. "Virtually

from the moment we left Brackenbridge. We were in Manchester and I saw an advertisement for cheap fares to America, so I thought why not try our luck in the theatres over here? We've done almost fifty spiritualist shows since we arrived – all the way down the East Coast – including some personal seances."

John gave a grumble of disapproval. "Perhaps it's time you thought of a more sensible career? One less onerous to a young girl."

Selena ignored this remark, or at least pretended to. Lily thought she had become rather frosty all of a sudden.

"Ma can't do that," Caddy said in reply. "Not now we've got new cards printed up. Look, she put my name on them, see?" She took a calling card from her pocket and showed it around to everyone.

With the compliments of

* *Miss* **Cadence Townsend** *
&
* *Mrs* **Selena Townsend** *

Mediums, Spiritualists & Fortunetellers etc.

We bring messages from loved ones who've passed.

"Very nice," said Robert after he'd read it.

"You can keep that," Caddy said proudly. "We've got loads of them. Ma hands them out in whatever boarding house we're staying at. We've been right around the States with them."

"Thank you." Robert kissed his sister's forehead. Then in a sudden fit of elation, he picked her up and twirled her around the lobby.

When he stopped he felt dizzy with happiness. His family were all together again!

"Well," said Selena, when they arrived at the suite. "I think I might just freshen up. It's been rather a long journey."

"And I shall catch up on some reading," John said, settling himself in one of the living-room chairs, with his big book on Shakespeare.

Lily and Malkin started moving Robert's things into their room so that Selena and Caddy could have the third bedroom to themselves. Robert tried to pack his clothes into his case for the move, but Malkin grizzled half of them away from him and insisted on carrying them in his mouth instead.

Caddy immediately set to helping as well. All the way

up the stairs she had barely left Robert's side – she seemed to want to spend as much time with him as possible and that made his heart sing.

As soon as the four of them finished moving Robert's things, Robert shut the door of the nursery, so they wouldn't be overheard by John or Selena. "Lily," he said, "are we going to tell Caddy about Dane now?"

"Who's that?" Caddy asked.

"The boy next door," Lily said, flopping down on one bed. "He sent us a secret note at dinner last night, asking for our help."

"How did he do that?" Caddy furrowed her brow.

"By post-mouse," Malkin explained.

Lily got out the note and showed it to her.

"It does sound like he's in trouble," Caddy said when she'd finished reading it. "Do you know anything more about him?"

They produced the newspaper article, which she studied as well.

"Dane's aunt is a professor of electricity," Lily said. "She has a wooden case that she keeps with her the whole time, handcuffed to her wrist. Very odd. It has a snake drawn on the side."

"An ouroboros snake," Robert added.

"Which means life and death," Malkin said, settling

himself on the bed beside Lily.

"But where are his parents and why can't he remember anything?" Caddy asked.

"That," said Lily, brandishing her magnifying glass, "is what we intend to uncover with our detective work."

"We're going to see him today," Robert said, "and tell him what we've discovered so far. Perhaps it will jog his memory, and he'll remember more of his past and how it connects to all this."

"When?" Caddy asked.

"As soon as possible," Lily said. "We just need to wait until his aunt and that mechanical nursemaid Miss Buckle are out. Then we need to find an excuse to get away from Papa and your ma, and knock on his door, like he asked."

"It's a simple plan," Malkin said, sarcastically. "What could possibly go wrong?"

"So, do you want to help us?" Robert asked.

"It sounds the most exciting mystery! Just like my penny dreadfuls, and I love those. So, yes, I would love to help!" Caddy handed the note and article back to Lily. "Perhaps we can use my second sight to see into Dane's past and recover his forgotten memories?" she suggested. "Or maybe even read his future – that might help too."

"That's what I was thinking," Robert said.

"There's something else." Lily leaned forward on her bed. "It would be better if you stayed in this room with us. That way we could make our plans together."

"Good idea," Caddy said, plonking herself down on the spare mattress. "I can take this third bed."

There was a knock at the suite's door. Malkin hid under the bed.

It was a porter from the lobby, arriving with Selena and Caddy's baggage.

Before he could even put down their trunks, Caddy burst from the nursery,."Why don't you let me stay here with Robert and Lily, Ma?" she said.

"Are you sure?" Selena asked. "Wouldn't you rather share with me?"

"We have plenty of space," Lily reassured her. "There's even a spare bed."

Selena studied her daughter doubtfully. "As long as the rest of the Hartmans are fine with it?"

"I am," John said, looking up from his papers.

"I am too," Robert said quickly. Then he noticed he had lumped himself in with the Hartmans. He was more of a Hartman now than he was a Townsend, despite how much he cared for his ma and sister, and that thought made him feel quite odd.

The porter left Caddy's trunk in the nursery with Robert's and Lily's, and set Selena's trunk in the other bedroom, before tipping his hat to everyone and bidding them good day.

Lily thought then that there might be an opportunity to slip out and speak with Dane, but before she could suggest it to the other three, Selena called them back to the lounge.

"I have some presents," she announced, taking various brightly wrapped boxes out of her hand luggage. "This is for you, Robert," she said, handing the largest package to him. "From me and Caddy. Sorry it's so late!"

"That's all right," Robert said. "Our gifts are late too." He put the package down and nipped back to their bedroom, bringing out the presents he had purchased for his ma and Caddy in England. With the help of Lily and John, he had neatly wrapped both gifts in shiny red paper and green ribbons.

They sat and unwrapped their gifts together. Selena's was a bottle of perfume in a glass jar that was shaped like a crescent moon. "Thank you for this, darling," she told Robert, dabbing her neck with the perfume stopper.

Caddy's was a book about spy craft from the Brackenbridge Bookshop, called: *The Secrets and Techniques of World-Class Spies*. "How marvellous!" she said as she flicked through the pages. "Now I've something to read for the rest of our stay."

"It does have a happy ending, doesn't it?" Selena asked.

"It's not a fiction book, Ma!" Caddy said.

Robert's present was a set of binoculars in their own case, with a strap so you could hang them round your neck. "Thank you," he said, trying them on.

"I thought they might help with your zep-watching," Selena said.

"They are fantastic." He kissed her on the cheek.

Lily and John both got chocolates and Malkin an old-looking bone wrapped in ribbon.

"So," John said, when everyone had finished opening their gifts, "how do you Townsends want to spend the rest of the afternoon? I thought perhaps a spot of sightseeing? I've earmarked the Metropolitan Museum in my *Appleton's*, I hear it has the most startling collection. Or how about the Croton Reservoir? The walkway at the top is rumoured to provide marvellous views of the city. But perhaps we should save that one for New Year's Eve, eh? It would be a great place to see the fireworks. Apparently the display this year is going to be extra-extravagant to celebrate the unification of the five boroughs of New York!"

"Oh, good idea," Lily said. "That sounds like a great place for New Year's Eve."

"Yes!" Caddy said. "Let's save that one. Then you can try out your new binoculars on the fireworks, Robert! Can't he, Ma?"

"Hmmm?" Selena seemed suddenly distracted. "What time *is* it?" she said, searching for her pocket watch. "My goodness," she cried when she found it. "Four o'clock already! I'm afraid I can't go sightseeing today, John. I have an errand to run. I have to visit the British Embassy before it shuts at five. Caddy and I need to renew our tourist permit before everything closes for New Year's Eve."

"But why the hurry?" John asked.

"Yes," Robert said, wringing his fingers with a flash of despondency. "You only just got here."

Selena bit her lip. "I'm afraid it's rather delicate – we only have a few days left on our current permit. On top of that, we weren't exactly supposed to be working while we were here." She stared sheepishly at John. "But you could probably help me, actually, Professor. There're a lot of forms and I really am quite hopeless at that sort of thing!"

"What kind of forms?" John asked.

"Oh, you know..." Selena counted them off on her fingers. "There's the permit renewal, the travel declaration, oh, and there's also the residency forms – and references – which need to be filled out in triplicate."

"Residency forms?" Robert asked.

"That's right." Selena nodded. "You see, I was thinking Caddy and I might stay in the States...on a more *permanent* basis, and I wanted to get a start on the paperwork needed to seek permission for that. At least while there was someone of sound legal mind to help me." She patted John's arm.

Robert felt a tad queasy. Did that mean his ma and Caddy would not be returning to England and Brackenbridge ever again?

Selena smiled at him, as if she knew exactly what he was feeling. "Of course, the residency part's not certain," she explained. "And either way, we'd still come and see you as often as we could, back in England."

"Well," said John, "it sounds like you have a lot to sort out, and relatively limited time to do it. We'd best get going right away."

"Thank you," Selena said. And to Robert, Lily and Malkin, she added, "Perhaps you three could look after Caddy for me, while John and I are gone? You could show her around the rest of the hotel. That might be fun?"

Robert sighed with disappointment. His ma had barely arrived and already she was flitting off on this new errand. More than that, he worried that this might be the last chance he'd have to see Caddy and his ma for an unthinkably long time. But at least they were here right now. That made up for it.

Then Robert remembered they had a mystery to solve. And that Lily had said if they could get away from the grown-ups, they could try and contact Dane.

"Of course we'll look after Caddy," he told his ma, secretly pleased that his sister would be part of their adventure. "I'm sure we can find something to do with her for the rest of the afternoon."

CHAPTER 9

When Selena and Papa finally departed for the British Embassy, Lily and Robert stuffed Malkin in Lily's basket and took Caddy down to the lobby to check whether Professor Milksop and Miss Buckle had gone out.

The mechanical receptionist had seen Professor Milksop leave that morning among the crowds of guests. He wasn't positive that Miss Buckle had been with her, but since the key was not in the return box, he had to assume that the mechanical was still in the room – either that or the professor had taken their key with her.

Robert asked the receptionist if the professor had been with her nephew, Dane. The receptionist shook his head.

"That I'm certain of," he said. "I'd remember if I saw that strange boy again. He hasn't been down to the lobby or left the building since they arrived."

"So he must still be in the room," Robert said to Lily and Caddy as they stepped away from the front desk.

"It seems likely," Lily said. "Which means now would be a great time to try and speak with him. If we can get past Miss Buckle."

In the elevator up to the third floor, they tried to make a plan, huddling in the corner and whispering so the elevator boy wouldn't hear. He seemed nice enough, but they couldn't take any risks.

"How are we going to lure Miss Buckle away from the room?" Caddy asked.

"Knock Down Ginger?" Robert suggested.

"Good idea," Lily said.

"What's that?" Caddy asked.

"It's a game," Robert explained, "where you bang on someone's door as many times as possible and as loudly as you can. And then, when they come to answer, you run away to make them chase you."

"Except in this case," Lily added, "only one of us will do the running. The rest of us will be hiding in our room and sneak in when Miss Buckle runs off."

Malkin sighed, poking his snout from the basket.

"Obviously I should do the running, since I have the fastest paws."

"THIRD FLOOR!" the elevator boy shouted, pulling the stop lever and beaming at them, as if he'd been listening to everything they'd just said.

They hurried down the passage to the Milksops' suite. Then, while Caddy and Robert stood in the open doorway of room ninety-nine with the empty basket and kept a lookout, Lily knocked on the door of room one hundred. Malkin waited at her feet to goad Miss Buckle away when she answered the door.

But no one came.

Lily knocked again, banging out the loudest and most annoying racket she could, so that if Miss Buckle was inside she would be forced to answer.

Yet still no one came.

"I don't think she's in," Malkin said.

"I think you're right." Lily tried the handle. The door was locked.

She took out her lock-picking kit and quickly and quietly picked the lock. Carefully, she pushed the door inwards a crack and Malkin slipped past. She pushed it wider and wedged it open so he'd be able to get back out. Then, with Robert and Caddy, she hid in the doorway of their room and waited for Malkin to flush Miss Buckle out.

"It's fine!" the fox called after a minute. "You can come in. She's run down."

Robert and Caddy shut the door to their own room and followed Lily into the Milksops' suite. They found Malkin sniffing around the feet of Miss Buckle, who stood frozen by the fireplace with her arms outstretched.

Stilled mechanicals were always odd-looking, especially when they'd stopped halfway through an action. Miss Buckle's eyes were open, but she could not see them, for she had run out of ticks.

"Well, that was easier than I anticipated." Lily let out a deep breath and shut the door to the passageway before someone could come past and see them, then she and the others examined the suite.

"I wonder which one is Dane's room," she said. "We'll have to check behind each door in turn."

Apart from the exit, there were three doors that led off the sitting room. The one in the middle was ajar, and Lily could see the same marble bathroom as theirs behind it.

Dane had to be in one of the other two.

"He's in here," Caddy whispered. She'd wandered over to the far door and the colour had drained from her face. She clutched the handle. "I can feel it."

Lily and Robert joined her.

Lily pressed her ear to the door's wooden panelling but heard nothing.

Caddy tried the handle, but it didn't give. "They really do lock him in!" she whispered.

Lily took out her lock-picking kit again.

"Wait! Here, try these." Robert handed Lily a set of keys he'd just spotted, hidden behind the lamp on the sideboard.

"Hello!" a scared voice from inside the room called suddenly.

It had to be Dane. He sounded American, with the same New York accent as his aunt.

"Hello," Lily said through the wood. "It's Lily Hartman, from the room next door. I'm the one your mouse brought the message to, at dinner. I'm here with my friends, Robert, Caddy and Malkin. We picked the lock and sneaked in so that we could help you, like you asked."

"Where's Miss Buckle?" Dane asked.

"She's run down," Robert said.

For a moment there was no answer. Then the relieved voice from behind the door asked, "Will you pick this lock too?"

"We don't need to," Lily said. "We've got the keys from the sideboard."

Lily nodded to Robert, who searched through the

117

keyring until he found the right key, then turned it in the lock.

"Keep quiet and let me do the talking," she told him and Caddy confidentially, before they opened the door. "We don't want to overwhelm Dane with too much information from too many new people."

"All right," they agreed.

"Malkin," Lily said to the fox. "You're to stay here in the lounge and listen out, in case Professor Milksop comes back."

"Aye aye, Captain!" The fox flicked his ears and slunk off to a shadowy corner from where he could see everything.

Lily grasped the handle and pushed Dane's bedroom door open.

Robert peered around her shoulder.

The room beyond had the same three beds and flowery wallpaper as theirs, but it was ill-lit, which gave it a dark and unfriendly air.

Dane sat on the edge of the nearest bed, his thin fingers clutching the little white mouse. He wore green polka-dot pyjamas, a checked woollen dressing gown and plaid slippers. There was a cold stillness to his posture that made him seem out of place in the room, as if he was barely there.

"Thanks for coming," he said faintly. "I'm glad you got my message."

"Sorry we couldn't come sooner," Lily said.

Caddy and Robert stepped in behind her.

On top of the chest of drawers was a wire mouse cage lined with old newspaper. Robert examined it. Everything within had been created from scavenged pieces of wood and metal. Each piece had been fashioned into amazing runs or slopes. There was even a home-made running wheel and a mouse-sized ladder made of string and sticks and broken cutlery.

"Did you make these?" Robert asked Dane, forgetting at once what Lily had said about doing all the talking. "These mouse-runs?"

"They're for Spook, my mouse," Dane said. "So he has something to do when he's locked up. I wanna be an inventor when I'm grown, like my aunt."

"How long have we got until she gets back?" Lily interrupted.

"About an hour," Dane said. "I overheard her talking to Miss Buckle before she left. She must've forgotten to wind her."

"Have you discovered any more about what your aunt's up to since your message?" Robert said. "Why she's brought you here?"

"She invited that Miss Child over to the suite this morning to try and buy her diamond necklace," Dane said. "I heard them through the wall. Miss Child refused to sell. Now my aunt's gone to the jewellery district to see if she can find a shard of the same stone. I don't even know what she wants it for. She don't seem the jewellery kind. I mean, I don't remember her with jewellery, and since we've been here, I ain't seen her wearing nothing like that." He stood up from the bed. "What've you found out about my mom and pop and what happened to them since me and Spook sent you that note?"

"We found this." Robert's hand shook as he handed the newspaper clipping to Dane. He wasn't sure what the other boy would think of it.

"Here." Lily gave Dane her magnifying glass so he could take a closer look.

Dane ran his finger across the caption before holding the lens over the picture to stare at himself and his parents.

"*These* are my folks," he whispered in surprise.

"Do you recall anything about them?" Lily asked.

Dane shook his head. "I don't think so." He furrowed his brow and peered closer at their faces. "They look kinda happy," he said. "Oh…wait, I just remembered… Mom and Pop were excited for their new jobs on the

Shadowsea. I was glad for them." He stared closer at his parents in the picture. They each had a hand on his shoulder. "After this, they must've worked on the submarine base, like the article says. We all must've, me too, plus the rest of the crew, and my aunt."

He paused, screwing up his eyes. His body was taut, as if it strained his every muscle trying to recall these few things. "I know I was down there a long time. Under the sea. From the very start, I think. We were supposed to be finished by the first of December this year. My folks and I were gonna be leaving for the surface that day, to get back home for Christmas."

"Where's home?" Robert asked.

"I don't recall," Dane replied, a faraway look in his eyes. "But it ain't here. Not with my aunt. Not...*without* my mom and pop." He blinked away a tear and gave a long, fidgety sigh. He seemed to be finding it uncomfortable to dredge up these memories, as if they were coming from somewhere deep and dark inside him.

"So you don't remember your parents being with you when you left the Shadowsea Base?" Lily asked.

"No." Dane shook his head. "Me and my aunt and Miss Buckle came up early for some reason. Alone. Maybe my folks stayed down there on the Shadowsea to work some more? I dunno..." He scratched his head and looked pained. "I'm sorry, I'm not being much use, am I? But that's why I wanted…*needed* you to find things out for me… It's like my memory's blocked out what happened down there. And that's made me forget about my folks too."

"Maybe I can help?" Caddy said quietly. She looked paler than she had outside the door. "I'm a medium."

"What's that mean?" Dane asked.

"It means I have second sight. I can see things others can't," she explained. "Spirits seek me out and speak to me. They can go anywhere, see anything. Track people both living and dead. They tell me memories and stories from people's pasts. They can even give me a glimpse of someone's future."

"Ain't that an awful burden?" Dane said. "A thing like that… Spirits talking to ya. Seeing the future and past of every kinda person you meet?"

Caddy shook her head. "It doesn't work that way. The person I'm giving a reading to has to *want* my help; they have to believe and let me in. Only then will the reading succeed and the spirits show me things." She held out her hands to him. "So if you want those things, Dane, and you truly trust me, then I might be able to see where your parents are."

Dane bit his lip and frowned, thinking about it.

Robert could see he wasn't quite sure what to make of Caddy's offer.

"What if you see something bad?" Dane asked at last.

"Then we're here for you," Lily said soothingly.

"All right," Dane agreed. "What do I need to do?"

"Give me your hands," Caddy said, sitting down beside him on the bed.

Dane let go of Spook, placing the tiny white mouse carefully on the eiderdown. It curled up into a ball and watched warily as he held out his long, pale fingers to Caddy.

Caddy took them and gave a shiver as she clasped his hands tightly in her own. "You've such a cold grip!" she exclaimed. "Ice-cold!"

"I have?" he asked, slightly taken aback.

"Yes." Caddy shut her eyes and began to hum softly. Then she commenced muttering strange incantations. Robert remembered some of the words and phrases from her seance at the Theatre of Curiosities last summer.

Gradually, as she said the weird words, Caddy's breathing began to slow. Her eyes moved behind their closed lids, and she went into a trance.

She was silent for a long time before, finally, she spoke afresh...

"The spirits are here," she said. "Close by. Offering to show me things…"

"What do you see?" Dane asked, his voice cracking.

"Darkness. Ripples of green water. And fish… Lots of fish."

Caddy paused. Her brows furrowed as she peered deep into the past.

"I see the Shadowsea Submarine Base…and your parents, Dane. They're working in a cabin and you're with them, sat on the floor playing with Spook beneath the table. You've made a cart for him, from old things. You chase him out the door, through winding passageways, past people and pipes and diving suits, until you come to a room full of caged mice."

"What happens then?" Dane asked. He was clasping her fingers so tightly that his hands were practically fists. Robert could see the veins around his knuckles, blue beneath the skin.

"Your aunt steps across your path," Caddy said. "She's wearing a white lab coat and goggles. She picks up Spook and breaks his neck." A single tear crept from the corner of Caddy's closed eye. "Spook is dead," she whispered.

Robert wanted to reach out and touch her shoulder, check that she was all right, but he knew it might break her trance and then they would never know what had happened next.

He stroked the mouse, who was climbing about on the bedspread. Not dead at all, but perfectly fine and alive, though cold to the touch.

Caddy took another breath. "Professor Milksop is stepping through a far door at the back of the lab. It's marked with a picture of an ouroboros snake and the words: *Reanimation Lab. Danger! Keep Out!*

"The professor holds the dead Spook in her hands." Caddy clutched Dane's fingers tighter in her own. "You follow her, Dane…you follow her through that door…"

"What's on the other side?" Dane asked, his words fraught with agitation.

"Music," Caddy said. "Strange ghostly opera music, playing from a phonograph. And Miss Buckle, adjusting a machine that looks like an electrical engine. It has a snake stamped into the metal plate on its front." She paused, her eyes flicking wildly behind her closed lids, as if she was looking around an imaginary room.

"Your aunt places Spook before the lens of the machine. Then she and Miss Buckle walk to a lead-lined observation booth on the far side of the room. Your aunt's in that booth now. She flicks a switch on a panel and the machine turns on." Caddy gasped.

Whatever she was seeing, Robert realized, it wasn't good.

"Crackling blue rays come out of the four lenses on the front of the machine," she said. "They're twisting together in a circle, like writhing snakes." She shivered. "The rays wind their way around Spook, and his body begins to jiggle and dance. Then he totters to his feet, standing up slowly, and opens his eyes."

"Stop!" Dane pulled his hands away from her. His eyes glistened with tears. "I can recall the rest now."

"You can?" Caddy blinked away her trance and stared at him.

"Yes," he whispered. "The lightning. It crackled from the machine and hit me. And I…I *died*."

Nobody spoke.

That last word seemed to hang in the air, echoing ominously around the room.

Everyone waited for someone else to speak.

No one quite knew what to say. The shock of it had stunned each of them to silence.

Lily stared at Spook, and at Dane. She couldn't quite believe that both of them had died, and yet here they were, alive as day. Brought back from the dead, just like she had once been. If it had been the case for Spook, it must've been the case for Dane too.

"There's more…" Caddy blurted. "I see more… The blue bolts of lightning…they burst out of the lab and run wild around the rest of the submarine base. They kill everyone. Your parents too, Dane. I…I'm sorry."

"It's my fault." Dane was wracked with sobs; he wiped snot from his face. "I opened that door. I couldn't let my stupid aunt be… I wanted to see what she was up to in that lab of hers, and because of that, because of me, her dumb machine killed everyone on that base. Everyone, including me…including my folks."

Robert felt sick. "No," he said. "It's not your fault." He knew what it was like to lose someone and feel that you were to blame. "It was your aunt who did that."

"Robert's right," Lily said. She was shivering too, from the weight of it. The whole room felt heavy and charged. "Your aunt's the one to blame for everything that happened down there. It's her fault for making such a machine in the first place…an engine that deals out life and death."

"The thing I can't understand," Dane said, "is, if my aunt's machine could reanimate me and Spook, bring us both back to life, then why didn't she use it to save *everyone*? Why didn't she bring them *all* back to life, after they'd died in that awful accident? *Why?*" He twisted wildly towards them, his breathing shallow and desperate.

"I don't know," Caddy said sadly. "But I can look again, if you like."

She took his hands anew, only this time she did not shut her eyes – she didn't need to, as she still had the vision of what had happened to him trapped inside her. A memory so ugly and vivid that she could see it clear as day.

"Your aunt couldn't save them," she said finally. "She moved everyone into the lab to try, but her machine was broken. The Ouroboros Diamond inside it had fractured from all that power flowing through it when it brought you back to life, Dane, and so the machine wouldn't work on anyone else. To make it work again, your aunt knew she'd need to find an identical stone. So she took you and then fled from the scene of her crime, back up to the surface to look for one."

"That must be why she came to this hotel," Lily said. "Because there was someone here with another one of those diamonds."

Quietly, Dane picked up Spook and hugged the mouse to his chest. "Really, I knew all that," he said. "In my heart of hearts it was still there, I just chose to forget it. To block everything out, because it was too unbearable."

"You were right to," Lily said. "If that's what you needed to do to feel better."

"Just like you're right to remember it now," Robert added. "It's the next step to healing. To recovery."

"I suppose." Dane dried his eyes and stroked Spook, who was nuzzling his palm to comfort him. "Anything else?" he asked Caddy. "Are the spirits telling you anything else about my future? Does it get better?"

"You want me to look a third time?" Caddy asked, unsure.

"Yeah." Dane nodded.

"I should warn you," she told him. "The future isn't always better, or more certain than the past."

"Please," he replied. "You gotta do it..."

"All right," she said, her face full of uncertainty. She took his hands for a third and final time and repeated the words to take her into a trance, while her eyes flickered rapidly behind her closed lids.

As she drifted deeper, a shiver of panic spread through her, like ripples from a pebble dropped in a becalmed sea. Robert saw the colour drain from her face. Soon her skin was beaded with sweat that plastered her hair to her skull and she struggled for each breath, her body thrashing about like she was drowning. Finally she seemed to reach a place of stillness.

Then she opened her mouth and spoke to Dane once more, in a deep and raspy voice that sounded nothing like her own:

"At twelve o'clock on New Year's Eve, you will wake the dead."

Dane choked.

Lily gasped.

Robert felt a dry gulp fill the back of his throat.

Outside the nursery, Malkin barked three times.

Quickly and quietly, the fox slipped in through the narrow gap in the bedroom door, and stared up at them, his black eyes wide and his ears pinned back with worry. His brush swept about crazily as he spoke in a whispered warning.

"Someone's coming!"

CHAPTER 10

Everyone froze and listened.

Malkin was right. Footsteps were coming up the hall, fast approaching the suite.

"Professor Milksop," Robert whispered. "We have to go."

There wasn't much time left for discussion. Lily spoke in a muted hush, putting her case to Dane. "We want to help you, Dane, but we can't leave you here with your aunt and Miss Buckle on your own, not after all we've discovered. We can get you out. Tell the police that you're being held prisoner here, but we need your agreement."

"No." Dane shook his head, his eyes glittering with tears. "Not yet. I gotta speak to my aunt first, find out what happened to my parents and all them others from her own mouth. Hear about their...*deaths*." That last word came out in a choke. "I gotta talk to Miss Buckle too, persuade her that doing my aunt's bidding ain't helping. She's my nurse, she's supposed to take care of me."

His speech was interrupted by loud cursing and rattling of the key in the main door. The professor was trying to unlock it. The trouble was, Lily had picked the lock so it was already open.

"I'm sure Miss Buckle will help you, if you ask her, Dane," Robert whispered quickly. "Mechanicals don't understand everything humans do, but they always protect them. She'll be on your side if you explain your situation – that your aunt's done you wrong and doesn't have your best interests at heart."

Robert's speech seemed to have sparked an idea in Dane; his eyes glistened with a slim sliver of hope.

"We'll come back soon," Lily whispered to Dane. "Meantime, we'll try to find out more. Now we have to go, before we're caught."

But it was already too late. Outside, Professor Milksop was stomping about the lounge.

Lily peered round the edge of the door trying to see what she was doing…

The professor had found the stilled Miss Buckle. She took a key from her pocket and slowly began to wind the mechanical up again.

Lily knew it took at least twelve good turns of the key to get a mechanical's cogs going, and probably more for a mech as vast as Miss Buckle. It wouldn't give them much time, but perhaps it was enough.

"Is there another way out of here?" she asked Dane.

"Over the balcony?" Dane suggested, nodding at the corner of his room. "It's locked but you probably have the key on that ring there."

"Of course!" said Lily. "The balcony! Just like ours!" She pulled back the curtains and there were the same French doors that led to the same modest balcony. Their own balcony stood just beyond the edge of Dane's, further off along the wall.

Robert unlocked the French doors with the keys and ushered everyone through. He was last to leave and as he did so, he peeped back worriedly at Dane through the closing door.

By the time he turned, Lily had already strung Malkin over her shoulders and was climbing over the balcony's snow-topped balustrade.

Caddy stood nervously by, watching the pair of them.

Robert stepped in beside her and surveyed the drop.

It was a long way down, at least far enough to break a lot of bones, if not every one of them. And the gap between the two balconies was further than it had seemed at first glance too. Robert estimated it to be about four feet. A metal drainpipe ran down the wall halfway across.

Lily took a hold of the drainpipe and shook it.

It didn't move, fixed solidly to the wall.

"Surely you're not thinking to cling onto that?" Robert hissed.

"Surely she is!" Malkin said.

"There's no time!" Lily shifted her feet on the edge of the balustrade, clasped the drainpipe with both hands and swung herself and Malkin across the gap.

Caddy went next. As she climbed over, she glanced nervously down between her feet.

Lily seized her hand and pulled her across.

"Now you, Robert," Caddy whispered.

"All right," Robert muttered. "Give me a second."

There had to be another way…

He peered back through the window, and, at that moment the lights in Dane's room flicked on. Through the gap in the curtains, Robert saw the shadows of Professor Milksop and Miss Buckle march into the room.

He held his breath hoping that, from the inside, the half-drawn curtains and the bright reflections of the room in the glass might hide his presence on the balcony.

"Why are all the doors unlocked?" Professor Milksop demanded of Dane.

"I-I dunno," Dane stammered. He wasn't very convincing.

"Liar!" Professor Milksop snapped. "Where are the keys?"

Robert gulped. He'd left the keys in the lock!

Miss Buckle blinked slowly. "Professor," she said. "It's probably my fault. Maybe I forgot them when I wound down?"

"No," the professor answered. "Someone took 'em." She stalked around the room. "Someone's been here. Who was it? Where are they?" she asked Dane.

"No one," Dane replied, but his guilty glance at the balcony gave the game away.

"Aha!" Professor Milksop strode towards the glass doors, behind which Robert was hidden. "What are these doing here?" She had found the keys. She pulled them from the lock.

Robert shrunk back from her eyeline. He felt queasy about the climb to come, but he knew there was no other way to escape now without the professor seeing him. He hugged the brick wall and stared over the edge. It was a long way down if he fell. His guts writhed and dropped into the soles of his shoes as the French doors behind him creaked open ominously.

"Come on, Robert!" Lily and Caddy called hurriedly to him from the balcony on the other side.

It was now or never.

Robert climbed over the balustrade and leaped for the drainpipe.

Its fixings creaked and cracked as he snatched at it. One of the bindings started pulling loose from the wall.

There was nothing for it…

He jumped.

Lily grasped his hand and he pulled himself across the remaining gap, just as the frozen section of drainpipe snapped away and toppled into the street below.

Robert flopped over their balcony's balustrade and Lily hauled him to safety.

"That was close," she whispered, dusting the snow off his front.

His pulse was still pounding as Professor Milksop stepped out onto the balcony he'd just left.

"Good evening!" Lily called over to her casually. "We were just looking at the view."

"The stars are incredible at this time of year, don't you think?" Caddy added.

Robert couldn't say anything. He still hadn't caught his breath. Malkin, too, wisely stayed quiet, pretending to be just an ordinary fox-fur ruff.

Professor Milksop's eyes bulged and she gave them a suspicious look. She twisted round and headed back into room one hundred.

Lily sighed with relief. The professor hadn't lingered long enough to notice the scuffed snow on her balcony, nor the broken drainpipe.

Back in their own room and safe and warm once more, they shook the snow from their shoes and the panic from their limbs and flopped down on their beds, waiting for their pulses to return to normal and their hearts to stop pounding so hard.

They'd barely recovered before there was a knock at the front door of the suite. Malkin hadn't even had time to climb down from around Lily's neck.

Lily felt sick. Surely this was Miss Buckle and Professor Milksop, come to enquire why Lily, Caddy and Robert had been in their room? She took in Robert and Caddy's frightened faces. They looked just as worried as she felt.

"Which one of us should get it?" Caddy whispered.

"I will," Robert said.

"No, I will," Lily said. "It ought to be me." She stood

and walked uneasily through the living room and down the long dark passage to the room's front door.

Her hands shook as she reached out to turn the handle. Fearfully, she inched the door open and peered around its side…

She let out a sigh of relief.

It was only Papa and Selena.

Selena clutched a thick bundle of papers in her gloved hands. "Why," she declared, when she saw Lily. "You look white as a sheet!"

"Are you all right?" Papa asked, frowning at his daughter.

"I…I…" Lily stuttered. Then she snapped, "Why didn't you use the key?"

"There's only one and you have it, you silly sausage! Why are *you* wearing Malkin around your neck?"

"It's my new role as Lily's fox-fur ruff," Malkin snarled sarcastically. "Though I don't think I add much to her ensemble."

"We have good news," Selena announced, brushing past them both.

"What's that?" Caddy said. She and Robert had crept out of the bedroom to join everyone.

"Thanks to John, we've renewed our certified documents." Selena put down her papers and took off her coat. "It means we can stay in America for another six months."

"We just have to go and collect the permit tomorrow morning, signed and stamped," Papa said, taking off his own coat and hanging it along with his hat on the hatstand in the corner.

"Plus," Selena added, "we're looking into what I would have to do if Caddy and I were to stay here permanently. I have a few more forms to fill out in that regard. I must take them back after New Year, but the wheels are in motion...so to speak." She stared around at everyone. "What do you think? Isn't it marvellous?"

They gave muted grunts in response.

"Don't everyone cheer at once!" Selena snapped, upset. "What on earth have you been up to? Why does everyone look so glum?"

"Nothing," Robert, Lily and Caddy said together, practically in unison.

Each of them pasted on a smile, but beneath the surface, their hearts were still heavy with the implication of their meeting with Dane and all they had discovered.

"Well," Selena said, huffily. "*You* lot may have more important things on your mind, but I for one think this news deserves some type of celebration."

Half an hour later, in the hotel's Tea Lounge, Selena had ordered high tea and chocolate fondant cakes for everyone in their party.

The rest of the room was packed with hotel guests, sat around at various tables, enjoying the teatime selection of scones, beautifully glazed petit fours and perfectly cut sandwiches.

As they waited for their tea to arrive, Papa and Selena chatted quietly over the considerable pile of embassy paperwork Selena was required to fill in. Lily, Robert and Caddy played a game of rummy. It helped to keep their brains busy and distract them from the ghastly revelations of the last hour. Malkin wasn't with them. He'd decided to stay in the suite this time, pleading a rest, and claiming he didn't want them getting him in any more trouble.

While Robert and Caddy dealt a new hand, Lily thought about everything that had happened earlier. She'd been stunned by Caddy's visions, but she didn't doubt that what Robert's sister had seen in her trance was true.

Lily realized something else: both Dane and she herself had died and been brought back by science, only to discover they'd lost someone. And they'd both tried to block what had happened to them from their minds.

Lily was sure that was why she'd instinctively felt that connection to Dane when she'd first met him.

But it was Caddy's shocking revelation that Dane was going to wake the dead at twelve o'clock on New Year's Eve that worried at her more than anything. It came and went in nauseous waves that she could do nothing about, pestering her like an unscratchable itch.

If Caddy was right, then something horrifying was due to happen in two days' time. Lily wondered if they should finally tell Papa and Selena what had been going on. She'd have to pick the right moment so as not to scare them half out of their wits with what she and the others had found out.

"After we collect Selena and Caddy's stamped permit tomorrow," Papa was saying, "we should go to the Grand Central Depot and get train tickets for our onward journey on the third of January."

"Good idea," Selena chirruped. "We want to beat the holiday rush and the station might be closed on New Year's Eve." She laid aside her forms as a pile of delicious-looking cakes arrived on a three-tier cake stand. The stand was packed with scones, pastries and buns. The waiter put a large silver teapot down on a doily beside it. "Why, this all looks simply marvellous!" Selena said, handing around the cups and plates. "I don't think

I've ever had such a tea!"

Lily picked up a gorgeously glazed pastry. It should've tasted delicious, but when she tried it, the disquieting unease that was shored up inside her dried each bite until it felt like she was eating cardboard.

"I don't know why everyone's behaving like it's a funeral," Selena said, tucking into a chocolate éclair. "It's good news! Caddy and I will be coming on to Boston with you!"

"And to Harvard," Papa added. "In fact," he said, smiling at Robert, "your mother and sister are going to be joining us for the rest of our stay!"

For Robert's sake, Lily was glad to hear that Selena and Caddy were coming with them to Boston. But she couldn't shake her worries about Dane and the fact that, whether he had spoken to them or not, by now Matilda Milksop and Miss Buckle would both know that she, Robert, Caddy and Malkin had been in their suite.

She scanned the room for the professor and spotted her just at that moment entering the Tea Lounge through the far door. As usual she had her wooden case clasped in her hand, but in her other angry fist she gripped her set of keys.

Lily and Robert watched her warily.

The professor gave them a grim little nod, as if to say,

I'm coming for you. Then she marched over and plonked the keys down in the centre of their white tablecloth.

"Your kids were in my suite earlier. I found these where they shouldn't have been."

"What the devil?" Papa cried.

"You heard me," Professor Milksop snapped. "They broke in."

Lily, Robert and Caddy tensed in the knowledge that the news of their antics in room one hundred were about to revealed.

Only, not quite yet. For, just then, a loud scream in the hallway interrupted everything.

Miss Alcilia Child burst through the double doors on the near side of the room, her arms flung up in the air in alarm.

"My necklace!" she screamed, now clutching at her neck. "The Milksop mechanical's just stolen my diamond necklace!"

CHAPTER 11

Whatever Matilda Milksop had been about to say to Papa and Selena about their children breaking into her room, it was swept aside by the chaos of Miss Child's accusation and the arrival of the police ten minutes later.

The chief inspector's name was George Tedesko, which he announced to the whole Tea Lounge. He wore a formal coat covered in brass buttons and badges. And when he removed his cap, Lily saw that he was a rather elderly man, with short white hair that receded over his temples and a salt and pepper beard that was cut square across his chin in a blunt line. His eyes were sparkling blue and had, she thought, a serious and attentive quality behind their gaze.

"No one's leaving till we're done speaking with you," the inspector said to everyone. "Seems a mechanical named Miss Buckle is responsible for the theft of a very valuable diamond necklace belonging to Miss Child here. Since then, this mechanical's vanished from the hotel." He paused to let that sink in. "Now, in a moment, my assistant, Lieutenant Drumpf, will come round and take names to find out what you know about these things. Those we don't talk with tonight can expect us to call at your room for an interview in the morning."

Lily watched Matilda Milksop. She'd snatched up her keys and sloped off to the nearest free table. She seemed flustered by the sudden arrival of the police, and kept glancing at the wooden case that was still handcuffed to her wrist. Lily wondered if she'd put Miss Buckle up to the robbery. Maybe that's why she'd burst into the Tea Lounge and made such a scene at their table in the first place – as a distraction and alibi for herself.

She peeped over at Miss Aleilia Child, who was seated on a daybed in the corner of the room, being fanned with a menu by one of the waiting staff and talking loudly in an operatic voice to Lieutenant Drumpf, a short, pug-faced man in a plainer uniform, about her ordeal.

"I can't believe it! I've never been robbed before – and

by a mechanical, of all people. I thought they weren't supposed to do that sort of thing. I tried to talk her out of it, but she was frighteningly strong, and since she's not my mechanical, I couldn't stop her. She even apologized to me as she took the diamond! Called me Ma'am and everything, as if she was put up to the whole deal and it was distasteful to her... As if it weren't her fault!" She paused and took a breath, like she was singing. "In my opinion, someone else put that mechanical up to it. Most likely her mistress, Professor Milksop. She asked me if the Ouroboros Diamond was for sale only this morning. And, I just remembered...when we first met, two years ago – at some sorta singing event I did for the Shadowsea Corporation – she showed a great interest in my diamond necklace."

That was the newspaper article Miss Child was referring to! Lily leaned in close. She was so busy eavesdropping, she almost forgot to check what the inspector was up to. She searched the room for him and saw he was making his way across the lounge, interviewing each table of guests in turn. Many of them seemed quite incensed at his interruption of their afternoon tea, but no one caused a scene.

Lily imagined being spoken to by the police was an intimidating prospect for the bulk of them, but not for her and Robert. They'd met a lot of police officers in their time. Earlier that summer, on the case of Jack Door, it had been Chief Inspector Fisk of Scotland Yard, and then in Paris in the autumn, Commandant Oiseau of the French police had interviewed them in regard to the criminal activities of the owners of the Skycircus.

So Lily was perfectly prepared to answer anything put to them by the New York Police Department and to give her opinion on who she thought the person behind the diamond robbery really was. She felt she knew enough to suggest that, in all likelihood, as Miss Child had just hypothesized, it was Professor Milksop who had put Miss Buckle up to the robbery. Even though there was no way Lily could prove it outright, she was sure the professor needed the diamond to make her Ouroboros machine work again.

Lily decided she would also take the opportunity to tell the police what she had learned about Matilda Milksop's actions on the Shadowsea from Caddy's vision, despite her promise to Dane to do nothing of the sort. It would back up her story of why the woman had asked her mechanical to steal the diamond. Things were moving fast now, and it would be best to let the police know all they had learned to stop anything else from happening. Papa and Selena would be shocked to hear what Lily,

Robert and Caddy had been up to, but Lily had been planning to tell them sooner or later anyway.

Eventually, the inspector approached them.

"Am I correct in assuming you are the Hartman and Townsend families, in room ninety-nine?" he asked, looking at the hotel guestbook in his hand.

"Yes," Papa said, answering for everyone.

"What do you know about this mechanical Miss Buckle and her theft of the Ouroboros Diamond?"

"Nothing that I'm aware of," Papa said. "If the mechanical did it, then I don't see what it has to do with us."

"Mechanicals have no free will," the inspector said. "Someone must've put her up to it."

"What about her owner, Professor Milksop?" Selena said, butting in, before Lily had the chance to suggest it herself.

"We're looking into that." The inspector glanced over at where Professor Milksop was sat. "But, until we've gathered more evidence, we have to consider a range of possibilities. Now, where were you at the time of the theft?" he asked.

"In here having tea, of course," Selena said.

"We all were." Papa swept his hand around the rest of them. He was being politeness itself, but Lily could detect a slight bristle in his voice. This was how he spoke when he was cross. "Are you suggesting that we're suspects?"

"I'm not suggesting anything," Inspector Tedesko replied gruffly. "Merely making enquiries."

"Only about the robbery?" Robert asked. "Or anything suspicious?"

"Anything suspicious," the inspector said. "We'll decide if it's relevant to the robbery."

"Then we *do* know something," Lily said. "It's about Professor Matilda Milksop. She was using Miss Buckle to keep her nephew Dane prisoner in their room."

"Oh, come now, Lily," Papa said. "That's not true. We've seen her nephew. He came down to dinner the other night. He's just ill." He smiled reassuringly at the inspector. "My daughter has a rather overactive imagination, Sir, fuelled by an abundance of penny dreadfuls."

"It *is* true," Lily snapped. "Dane said so." She pulled Dane's note from her pocket and showed it to Papa and the inspector.

"This seems more of a prank than anything else," the inspector said when he'd finished reading the message. "Nothing for us to concern ourselves with."

"It has *everything* for you to concern yourself with," Lily said. "Please, just speak with Professor Milksop about it."

The inspector beckoned over his assistant. "Fetch Matilda Milksop, will you." Then he looked around at the various empty pots of tea and coffee and the half-eaten cakes at each table. "Oh, and, Lieutenant Drumpf, while you're at it, can you ask the staff to fetch me a cup of coffee, and maybe one of those little chocolate-finger puff-cakes? They look rather tasty, and seems like there's plenty to go round."

Lily watched, relieved, as Lieutenant Drumpf brought Dane's aunt to their table, before wandering off once again to see about the inspector's cake and coffee.

"These kids say you're keeping your nephew against his will. And that Miss Buckle was his jailer," the inspector said to her. "That true?"

"My nephew's ill," Professor Milksop said. "Needs his bed rest. That's why he stays in our suite. And yeah, Buckle's his nurse. She's always behaved appropriately in that capacity. Far as I'm aware, that's not a crime, and she ain't never done anything criminal before...that I know of," she added, staring hard at Lily, Robert and Caddy. "These kids, Inspector, they don't know zip about me, or my family! They just took it upon themselves to spy on us."

"You're lying," Robert said. "You *are* keeping your nephew prisoner. And Miss Buckle was helping you, before she ran off with the diamond. Dane told us so."

Matilda Milksop snorted. "Why in tarnation would I keep my nephew prisoner?"

"So he won't tell anyone you were reanimating mice and you killed his parents and him and everyone else on the Shadowsea Base in the process," Robert said, all in a rush.

"And so he won't tell anyone that you brought him back to life too," Lily said.

"Or that on New Year's Eve he'll wake the dead himself," Caddy added.

"Mice! Murder! Waking the dead!" Professor Milksop snapped. "In all my days, I ain't never heard such garbage. Anything else you'd like to try and pin on me? Nope?" She didn't wait for an answer. "Trash, is what it is! I've done nothing wrong."

"It's not trash," Robert said, "Caddy saw your crimes in a vision. She saw everything that happened on the Shadowsea Submarine Base before you left it. And now she's seen what will happen in the future as well."

Papa and Selena were listening, aghast. It was plain they barely knew what to make of these revelations. They were coming so thick and fast that Lily could see they were having trouble taking them in. The inspector too. They needed the inspector to believe them more than anyone!

"What do you mean she 'saw' it in a vision?" he asked sceptically.

"I'm a medium," Caddy explained, handing the inspector one of her cards.

"You've had these visions before, have you?" the inspector said after reading it.

"All the time," Caddy said.

"But she has occasionally been wrong about a few of them in the past," John said.

Caddy frowned at her mother.

"Although not recently," Selena added, taking her daughter's hand.

"Well, we don't want to go around accusing people of crimes on the strength of a vision," the inspector said doubtfully. "That seems rather rash."

"But they already did," Professor Milksop butted in.

"We saw Dane today," Lily protested. "He confirmed everything we've just said…at least the bits he could remember."

"There you go, you see?" Matilda Milksop said. "These kids've spent the entire afternoon putting crazy ideas in my nephew's head."

"How'd you speak with the boy if he's in bed and no one can visit with him?" the inspector asked Lily and the others, ignoring Matilda's interruptions.

"She broke into our suite, that's how," Professor Milksop said.

"That the truth?" the inspector asked.

"I…" Lily hesitated, flummoxed for once.

"Course it is," Matilda Milksop said, waving the keys around. "They took these from where I'd left them on the sideboard."

"Lily…?" Papa asked.

"We knocked and no one answered," Lily mumbled, turning red. "So we picked the lock, found her keys and…"

Papa's eyes went wide with alarm. "Lock-picking again, Lily?"

"That's not the important part," Lily insisted. "The important part is what Caddy saw when we spoke to Dane and what Dane said she's done…" She pointed at Professor Milksop.

"What *you've* done, you mean," Professor Milksop said. "That's probably why they broke in in the first place, not only to turn my nephew against me, but also to mess with Buckle's cogs and programming and suggest this robbery to her. I saw the Hartman girl looking at that diamond the other day. It's like I told you, Inspector, these kids are crooks, spies and robbers. If anyone here's mixed up in this diamond robbery, it's them."

"How dare you accuse my children of such things!" Selena said, standing up from her seat so she was face-to-face with Matilda Milksop.

The other guests in the lounge stared in alarm at this quickly escalating ruckus.

"And mine too," Papa added, joining Selena on her feet. "They may be a tad wild around the edges, but they are *not* crooks...or spies. And it was your mechanical who committed the robbery, Professor. If you ask me, you're making things up now to cover for yourself..."

"Making things up!" Professor Milksop snapped. "How about the bunch of trashy lies your kids just told about *me*?"

"ENOUGH!" The inspector put a hand between the grown-ups to keep them apart.

He would have barged his way between them, but at that moment one of the waiting staff arrived with his cup of coffee and éclair.

"Now..." He took a sip of coffee and a bite of cake before putting them both down carefully on the table. "I don't have time to stand around here and listen to you folks rubbing each other up the wrong way all night, I have an *actual* crime to solve. In my humble opinion, it'd be better if you settled your differences calmly, amongst yourselves."

"But don't you see?" Lily said frustratedly. "It's all connected."

"No, Miss, I do not. Now get back to your rooms. I don't want to hear any more unfounded accusations from anyone."

At the inspector's dismissal, Professor Milksop left, relieved. Lily watched her head for the door. She was probably in a hurry to check on her nephew...

"What about Dane Milksop?" Lily asked the inspector as they gathered up their things to leave too. "You have to promise to speak with him."

The inspector sighed and took another sip of coffee. "I don't need this kinda grief, Miss. It's nearly New Year's...I'm supposed to be on half-day holiday tomorrow. What time is it?" he asked Lieutenant Drumpf, who'd just arrived back from interviewing the last of the guests at the other tables.

Lieutenant Drumpf took out his pocket watch. "Six o'clock, Sir. We've still got the crime scene to get to tonight before you go."

"Then let's do that." The inspector gathered up his coat and tipped his hat to Lily, Robert and Caddy. "I'll speak with this Dane Milksop tomorrow. If he's really being held prisoner by his aunt against his will and his parents can't be contacted, then I suppose that will be a case for child services, but I doubt if it has anything to do with my robbery."

And with that, he strode off, leaving the three of them seething angrily and with rather a lot to explain to Papa and Selena.

Lily couldn't sleep that night for thinking about everything that had happened. The diamond robbery, and meeting Dane. What they'd learned from Caddy's visions and Dane's memories about his life on the Shadowsea; how his parents had died on that submarine base and how awful he must feel about that.

They'd spent the whole evening trying to explain the rest of the details to Papa and Selena back in the suite after the unprecedented accusations that had taken place in the Tea Lounge.

Papa and Selena had been shocked when they had once again gone over their account of events and of Caddy's revelations, but all they could do was promise to reiterate them to the police tomorrow in a more sober way. They would try to impress on the inspector how accurate Caddy's prophecies had been in the past, and hope that he took note of what they said in order to broaden his investigation.

Otherwise, Papa suggested that the best course of action was for Lily, Robert and Caddy, and especially Malkin, to stay out of the way of the Milksops for the rest of the holiday.

Especially if Professor Milksop was involved in the diamond robbery and this group of undiscovered murders that Caddy's visions suggested. It was the police's job to investigate all that, he said, not theirs, and anyway he did not want any more scenes with her.

Just recalling that last part made Lily very cross.

She got up and put on her slippers and dressing gown, and, taking care not to wake the others, sneaked over to the French doors, opening them to get a breath of fresh air. As she did so, she glimpsed something strange over the balustrade and stepped out onto the balcony to get a better view…

Down below, the street was grey and bare, except for one figure stood opposite. Lily supposed it was too cold now for most people to be out. The frosty branches of the trees stretched upwards, making cracks in the black shell of the sky. Snow fell gently through the lamplight, coating the slushy sidewalk in a blanket of white.

Lily stared harder at the figure standing in the shadows where they thought they couldn't be seen, peering through the branches of the trees. It was a woman

– practically the only thing visible of her was her dark dress and shiny black patent-leather shoes. Her face was hidden by the brim of her feathered hat, but something about the tilt of her head suggested she was gazing upwards. At their window, Lily realized with a start. Waiting for something.

Or could it be the Milksops' suite next door she was staring at?

There was something odd about her.

For a while, Lily couldn't work out what it was. Then she did…

It was so cold outside that Lily should have been able to see the clouds of the woman's breath. But she could not.

The woman was not breathing.

At the next door balcony, behind the French doors and closed curtains of room one hundred, there were three brief flashes of light as if someone had turned the room lights on and off again very quickly in succession. In each brief glow, Lily saw that the woman wore something round her neck.

A glinting blue jewel.

The Ouroboros Diamond.

It was Miss Buckle!

The mechanical nursemaid had not seen Lily, but she

had seen the signal that she had evidently been waiting for, for she turned and walked away along the street.

Lily stood there, shivering and trying to process what it all meant. When Miss Buckle had finally disappeared into the gloom, she crept quietly back to her bed.

She laid her head back on the pillow and thought about the many moving parts of this mystery. There were so many balls in the air, so many pieces of the puzzle and she still couldn't quite see how they fitted together, nor – most importantly – what they should do next to help Dane.

She shut her eyes and tried to will herself to sleep, and eventually, with the tick of her heart and the slow breathing of the others echoing in her ears, she was carried off by dreams.

CHAPTER 12

Robert woke early the next morning feeling like he was on the cusp of some strange revelation, but when he opened his eyes it was gone.

He sat up and rubbed his face. Today was the thirtieth of December – the day before New Year's Eve. Tomorrow Caddy's prophecy about Dane waking the dead would come to pass, unless the police could stop it.

"You will wake the dead." He whispered the line softly to himself.

It had sounded so crazy and alarming when Caddy had said it to Dane, but, repeating it out loud now, Robert didn't doubt she'd seen a future truth.

The first time he and Lily had met Caddy, she had

straight away divined one of Lily's deepest secrets. How Lily's mother, who'd loved her very much, had given Lily a present of a unique gold ammonite she'd found while fossil hunting.

That was the first piece of true insight Caddy received from the spirits, and, as far as Robert knew, she'd rarely been wrong in her visions and prophecies since. Which made this latest revelation about Dane all the more worrying.

He got up and took his clothes to the bathroom, shivering as he dressed and washed his face, then combed his hair in the mirror. As they did everyday, his unruly curls sprang back into place as soon as he'd finished brushing them.

Finally feeling more ready for the day ahead, Robert returned to the room to find Lily and Caddy already up and dressed. Lily was winding Malkin and Caddy was looking over the papers they had collected about Dane.

"Morning," Robert said, giving them a nervous grin. "How did everyone sleep?"

"Awfully," Caddy said. "I re-dreamed my vision, over and over again, throughout the night, and every time I woke up I thought of Dane."

"Me too." Robert shook his head. "I kept thinking about how fearful he looked when you revealed what you'd seen happening down on that submarine. And then his face when you told him that his parents had died down there, and the dangers you'd foreseen in his own future." He shuddered, thinking of his own father, gone too.

"We've all lost people," Caddy said.

"We could've helped him," Lily agreed sadly, "but we didn't really even have the time to speak to him properly about any of it. That's what was so...upsetting." She finished winding Malkin. "And it's your prophecy, Caddy, that worries me the most. What does it mean for Dane...? He...he doesn't seem the sort of person who would do something so disturbing and atrocious."

"Perhaps his aunt will coerce him into it?" Malkin suggested. "After all, we already think she may have had a hand in the diamond robbery."

"I feel like we should try and see him again this morning, if we can," Caddy said. "If only to comfort him and to tell him that, on a few rare occasions, the spirits have been wrong in their predictions."

"That will be hard," Lily said, "given that he's going to be speaking to the inspector today and hopefully telling him all the bad things his aunt has done."

"I hope they arrest Matilda Milksop for everything that happened on the Shadowsea," Robert said. "And for stealing that diamond… Miss Buckle may have been the one who committed that crime, but I just know Matilda Milksop put her up to it."

"It seems likely," Malkin said. "I mean, if I were Matilda Milksop and I needed to steal an Ouroboros Diamond to repair my engine – a machine that could both kill people and bring them back to life – then that's what I would do."

Lily stared moodily out of the window. Finally she spoke again. "I saw Miss Buckle stood beneath a tree, opposite the hotel, at midnight last night, after you had all gone to bed."

"What was she doing?" Caddy asked, shocked.

"Looking up at the Milksops' window, waiting for a signal."

Robert gasped. "See? We're right. She did steal the diamond on Matilda Milksop's orders. What happened then?"

Lily turned back to them. "Then someone in the room flashed the light on and off three times. And Miss Buckle walked off down the street."

"Where did she go?" Caddy asked.

"I don't know," Lily said. "She just disappeared into the night. But one thing I did see was that she had that diamond necklace around her neck."

"Lily, you have to tell the police this as soon as possible," Caddy said.

"Not until we've spoken with Dane," Lily said. "First I want to see what more he knows and whether he's all right."

"It's a horrible situation," Robert said. "I'm still not sure how the pieces fit together. But, with this new information about Miss Buckle, I believe even more that everything that Caddy saw yesterday is true."

"Me too," Lily said. "It seems clear to me that Professor Milksop has planned for Miss Buckle to bring her the diamond when the fuss around the robbery dies down. She still wants to repair her machine so she can use it again."

Robert nodded. "And I think that somehow she's going to force Dane to help her," he said. "Isn't that what Caddy's prophecy suggests?"

"Help her do what?" Malkin asked.

"Kill people?" Lily suggested with a horrible shiver. "Like she did on the Shadowsea. Or wake the dead? Like she woke Dane and Spook."

"Why would anyone want to do that?" Robert said. The others had no answers, but it was a chilling thought. Robert gave a shiver, then pushed those worries aside.

No, the police would interview Dane this morning

and he would tell them the truth about his aunt. And then they would put a stop to whatever she was up to. Hopefully Inspector Tedesko would recover the diamond from wherever Matilda Milksop and Miss Buckle had stashed it, and have them both arrested. Dane would be free and this would all be over. That was the only way things could end, surely? It was certainly not the holiday they'd planned. None of them had expected to find themselves embroiled in such an alarming mystery, yet again...but here they were.

Matilda Milksop was present at breakfast but Dane was not. Nevertheless, the screen that they usually ate behind was still up, which was probably a good thing for her, as it hid her from the prying eyes of the other guests and staff. The theft of the Ouroboros Diamond was all any of them seemed to be talking about.

The story of the diamond robbery was even the lead article in *The New York Daily Cog*, which Papa had brought to the table. Robert, Lily and Caddy read about it as they drank their tea and ate their toast, while Selena and Papa conversed quietly.

NEW YORK DAILY COG

ROGUE MECHANICAL STEALS PRICELESS OUROBOROS DIAMOND

NYC Early Edition , December 30, 1897   All today's news!

Miss Aleilia Child, opera singer at the Met, has been robbed in her room at the Murray Hill Hotel. A mechanical named Miss Buckle, who was staying in the hotel to care for a sick boy, broke in and ripped the priceless Ouroboros Diamond from Miss Child's neck and left by jumping out of the window. Miss Child was distraught and immediately summoned the police.

That was all Robert could take in – he knew the rest and, besides, there was another article underneath it which had caught his attention.

RADIO SILENCE FROM SHADOWSEA SUBMARINE BASE

Families of crew working on the Shadowsea submarine are worried that they've heard nothing from their relatives since two weeks before Christmas. None of them returned for the holidays. Leading enquiries into what has happened is Mrs Miriam Milksop, mother of Professor Milksop, and her brother Mr Daniel Milksop, and grandmother to Daniel's son Dane, who is the only child living aboard the Shadowsea. All are missing, along with Dane's mother Lucille and the rest of the crew. Miriam Milksop will lead a delegation to meet the project's financier Mr Nathaniel Shadowsea, at his office in Manhattan on New Year's Eve, to try to find out what has happened to their relatives on his submarine base.

Beneath this was a picture of a determined-looking woman with grey hair and a pleasant, friendly-looking face. She was holding up the picture from the same yellowing article that Lily had in her pocket, showing the entire Milksop family, along with Mr Shadowsea and Miss Aleilia Child, standing on the dock with the president as the first modules of the submarine base were being built.

Dane hadn't mentioned his grandmother Miriam when they'd spoken. But his memory had been such a muddle that Robert wondered if the boy even remembered her?

They needed to go up to the Milksops' suite and speak with him again, to tell him about this new discovery and find out what had happened between Professor Milksop and Miss Buckle after they left him yesterday. Perhaps he knew why the mechanical nursemaid had stolen the diamond... Even though they had agreed last night that they would wait for the inspector to talk to Dane first, now, in the cold light of morning, Robert felt as if they couldn't wait that long. Dane was their friend and he'd appealed for their help, and now they deserved answers as much as he did. They should probably go straight away to see him, while Matilda Milksop was still eating her breakfast behind the screen.

Robert nodded to Lily and Caddy. They all stood up, Lily carrying her basket with Malkin inside.

"We've finished breakfast," she said. "May we be excused?"

Papa glanced up from the morning papers. "All right," he replied. "But Selena and I have decided that you should keep out of the way of those Milksops from now on. It's just as we told you last night. We don't want to get mixed up in any of these matters to do with the diamond and Dane and so on, especially not now the police are involved. So tell me you won't bother them any more, Lily."

Lily bit her lip.

"Promise?" John said.

"All right," Lily said at last. "I promise we won't bother the Milksops."

Robert wondered if she really meant it, after all they'd been through?

"And you two?" Selena said, looking pointedly at Caddy and Robert.

"We promise too," Robert told her, his guts squirming as he said so.

Caddy nodded grimly.

"Good," Papa said. "Then let that be an end to it. Now you may go." He took out his pocket watch and consulted it. "Your mother and I have to head out to the embassy again this morning to collect her stamped visa. You lot should probably stay here in the hotel again, but be ready after that to set off for the train station."

Robert peered over at Matilda Milksop one last time as they left the dining room and saw that one of the mechanical waiters was bringing her a folded message on a silver tray.

He, Caddy and Lily stole quickly from the room before Professor Milksop had time to open it.

On the way up to their suite, Robert whispered to Lily, "How could you promise that?"

"Promise what?" she asked.

"That we wouldn't carry on investigating the Milksops."

"That's not what I promised at all," Lily said. "I promised we wouldn't bother them. And we won't. We'll be so subtle that Matilda Milksop won't even know we're still looking into her crimes, and nor will the police."

Having said that, she walked straight past their own door and on to room one hundred.

"We'll have to work fast if we want to get into the room and see Dane again before the professor returns," Lily said, as she once again got out her lock picks. She'd just put the first pick in the lock when there was an almighty smash from inside the room. Quick as she could, Lily jimmied the lock.

They wrenched the door open just in time to see Miss Buckle dragging Dane out onto the balcony. She was wearing the same outfit Lily had seen her in last night when she had stood outside the hotel looking up at this very room! Snow was spilling in through the French doors and melting on the carpet. Dane screamed as Miss Buckle hiked him up onto the balustrade.

Lily, Robert, Caddy and Malkin ran across the room towards him.

But they were too late. Lily's heart ticked wildly as Miss Buckle jumped up beside Dane, and, taking him under her free arm, leaped into the snowy sky, her long coat flapping like a cape behind her. With a crash, she landed on top of the snow-capped roof of an electrical-wagon parked in the street.

As Lily and the others peered over the balcony's edge, Miss Buckle leaned down and picked up her hat, which had come flying off in her jump. She dusted the snow from its rim and put it on her head, then, calm as you like, she hopped down onto the sidewalk and, carrying Dane in her arms, clattered off down the empty road so fast it almost seemed as if she was dodging between the falling snowflakes.

"Quick!" cried Lily. "After her!"

They ran back out into the corridor and took the stairs two at a time down to the ground-floor lobby, smashing into Inspector Tedesko and Lieutenant Drumpf, who were just arriving to recommence their interviews with the rest of the hotel guests about the stolen diamond.

"Miss Buckle's taken Dane!" Lily shouted at the inspector as she skidded past him, heading out through the swinging entrance doors. Malkin, Caddy and Robert rushed along behind her. Robert threw a look over his shoulder at the shocked inspector and lieutenant as they quickly gathered themselves together and followed in their wake.

Lily bounded down the red carpeted steps, past the mechanical doorman, asleep in his box, and skidded out onto the avenue. She stared up and down the long frosted walkways, between the blizzard of falling flakes, searching for Miss Buckle and Dane, but the nursemaid and the boy had already gone.

They had vanished entirely in the stark white street.

Lily cursed and caught her breath as the others joined her. The cold was already drying the sweat on her back. The sprint down the stairs had tangled Caddy's hair even worse than usual and given Robert a sharp stitch.

He gave a sigh. "We lost her then? Maybe the inspector and his men can track them down?"

Lily looked at the elderly inspector puffing his way after them, assisted by his lieutenant, who was making a face like he was sucking a wasp. "I doubt it," she said.

"What did you see?" the inspector called out wheezily. "Who was that you were chasing?"

"Miss Buckle," Robert said. "She's taken Dane."

"Kidnapped him!" Caddy added, still in shock.

"Sprang from the window like a lone wolf," Malkin yipped.

"The outfit she had on was the same one she was wearing last night," Lily said.

"What do you mean, last night?" the inspector asked.

"I saw her at midnight standing outside the hotel," Lily said. "She was across the street, watching the Milksops' room." Lily pointed at the corner where Miss Buckle had stood. "Then someone inside the room flashed a light on and off three times, as if they were signalling something to her."

"A secret signal?" The inspector scratched his head. "And then this villainous mech returned to the scene of the crime, to commit more atrocities. How interesting." He turned to his assistant who was searching in his pockets to retrieve a notebook. "Write all this down,

Drumpf, and take a statement from each of these kids. I'll call the station from the hotel telephone and tell 'em to revise the police bulletin we put out on Miss Buckle with these new details."

Lily didn't hold out much hope for that. Since they'd first arrived last night, the police had seemed at least three steps behind everyone else.

As the inspector walked back up the hotel steps, Professor Milksop tumbled out of the entrance blocking his way. She was still carrying the wooden case with the Ouroboros snake stamped on the side, and in her other hand she clasped what looked like a note. It must've been the message she'd received at breakfast.

"Dane's gone!" Professor Milksop cried. "I've been up to the room and he's been taken!" Then she saw Robert, Lily, Caddy and Malkin, and pointed them out to Inspector Tedesko. "Arrest those Hartman kids, Inspector! They're responsible for this new atrocity too, I'd wager!"

"More likely you are," Lily said. She stared around Lieutenant Drumpf's shoulder at Professor Milksop standing three steps above her. "Those flashing lights I told you about, Inspector… They must've been to tell Miss Buckle to come back and break in this morning and take Dane."

"Lies!" Matilda Milksop cried. "This girl's a liar! See this note, Inspector." She waved the paper at him. "I just got it. Only a kid would be stupid enough to write a threatening note like this, all cut outta newspaper letters!"

The inspector took the note from her. His eyes widened in alarm as he read what was written on it. "I don't think any of this is a child's doing, Ma'am," he said at last. "It seems pretty serious."

Professor Milksop glared daggers at Lily and she snatched the note back from the inspector's grip. "She's involved somehow. I know it. I bet she's informed on me to whoever's running this racket. Probably put them up to it!" Suddenly she clutched the message to her temple. Her legs buckled beneath her and she collapsed onto the red stair carpet, fainting dead away.

Lily couldn't decide if this pathetic scene was for real or whether Professor Milksop was faking it. The inspector looked sceptical too. Nevertheless, he waved at his assistant and then at the mechanical porter who'd finally arrived.

"Fetch some smelling salts," he ordered, and they both hurried off into the hotel. Meanwhile, he kneeled beside Professor Milksop, put her in the recovery position and checked her pulse.

Several minutes passed.

"Clank it all!" the inspector said angrily. "What's taking them so long? You stay with her and make sure she's all right," he told Robert, Lily and Caddy, and then he got up and strode back into the lobby, searching for Lieutenant Drumpf and the hotel porter.

Robert and Caddy crouched next to Professor Milksop. Lily put her basket on the floor and joined them.

Now that the inspector had gone, Malkin nudged Professor Milksop with his nose, but she didn't move. "Well," he said, "what do you know! I think she's really fainted. Probably the stress of telling all those big fat porkies to the police."

"Maybe she panicked that the truth is finally going to come out," Robert said.

Lily noticed something else. The note Professor Milksop had been clasping had dropped to the floor when the inspector had moved her.

She picked it up, and examined it. Just like the professor had said, it was made up of letters cut from random newspaper headlines, which made it impossible to tell who'd written it. Some of the cut-out letters were yellowing around the edges. She glanced around to see that the inspector had still not returned and then, quickly, read the note aloud to everyone.

Professor, IF YOU WANT TO seE YOUr NEpHEW AGAin YOU MUst HAND OveR YOUR Ouroboros EnGINe AS RANsOM

"What's ransom?" Caddy asked, confused.

"It's where kidnappers exchange a person they've taken for something they really want," Lily explained. "They're trying to use Dane as a bargaining chip to get the engine."

Robert read out the rest of the message: "At midday today be waiting in the hotel lobby. We will telephone with further instructions for the ransom swap. Do as we say or your nephew Dane will not be returned alive."

Caddy shivered when he'd finished. "I thought mechanicals didn't have free will, so why is Miss Buckle threatening to hurt Dane to try and get Matilda Milksop's machine?" she asked. "Surely it's of no use to her? And what will happen to Dane in all of this?"

"I don't know," Lily admitted. "Maybe she's working for someone else, who instructed her to do it? Either way, Dane's obviously in even more trouble than we knew…" Her brow knitted with this new worrisome concern. "I suppose this means there could be someone else involved in this kidnap and ransom that we're not even aware of yet."

She was right, Robert realized, there could be. But if Miss Buckle wasn't working alone, and she wasn't working with Matilda Milksop as they'd first thought, then who else could have ordered Dane's kidnapping? And what would that mean for Caddy's prediction about him waking the dead? None of them could answer any of these questions, not without more information about this terrifying new development.

Just then, they heard a noise behind them. Inspector Tedesko was returning. Robert stuffed the note back into Matilda Milksop's fist.

"Professor Milksop!" Inspector Tedesko called as he kneeled down beside her and waved the smelling salts under her nose.

Finally Professor Milksop woke and the inspector helped her up, the wooden case still handcuffed to her wrist. Lily, Robert and Caddy followed them inside, keeping their distance. As they entered the lobby, a bell cut through the chaos. It was the telephone on the reception desk.

The receptionist picked it up. "Hello?"

She put her hand over the receiver and called to the

inspector and Professor Milksop, who was leaning woozily against him, her free hand clutching her temple.

"It's for you, Professor. I'm not clear who it is, but they say they've got another message for you."

Lily felt a jolt of shock run through her. It had to be the kidnappers on the line!

Matilda Milksop went white as a sheet and glanced at the clock above the desk.

Its hands pointed exactly at twelve o'clock, just like the kidnappers had said.

"Should I take it?" she asked the inspector.

"I think you should," the inspector replied. "Do you feel well enough to?"

Matilda Milksop nodded.

Lily and the others watched as the inspector helped her over to the bank of telephones and signalled to the receptionist to transfer the kidnapper's call.

The inspector installed himself in the second booth next to Matilda, so that he would be able to listen in.

Lily, Robert and Caddy scanned the lobby. Lily knew there was no question they needed to hear this converstaion as well.

"Come on," she said, pulling the others behind the Christmas tree right next to the phone box, hoping to hear what was being said.

In his booth, Inspector Tedesko held up two fingers behind the glass to indicate to the receptionist to patch the call through to both lines. Then he picked up the phone and put his hand over the receiver, before giving the signal to Matilda to answer the call...

CHAPTER 13

Lily could see Professor Milksop through the glass door of the telephone booth, talking to whoever was on the other end of the line and writing down various instructions on the pad beside the phone. But frustratingly, from where they were hiding behind the Christmas tree, she couldn't hear what the professor was saying. The door to the phone booth was closed and the glass in it was thick enough to block out all sound. Lily couldn't even try to read Professor Milksop's lips, for the woman had bent away from them to talk into the receiver.

As she watched, Matilda hung up the receiver. Then she ripped the top sheet of paper from the pad and put it in her pocket before walking out of the booth.

Now the call was over, Inspector Tedesko pulled Matilda into a quiet corner to strategize. Lily signalled to Robert and Caddy to sneak in closer and eavesdrop on them. Unfortunately, when she and the others stepped out from behind the Christmas tree, they found that the inspector's assistant had arrived and was waiting for him nearby. If they tried to get any closer, Lily knew they would be clocked by the man.

After a while, Inspector Tedesko and Matilda Milksop finished their conversation. The inspector called over Lieutenant Drumpf and together they synchronized their watches.

As she leaned in, Lily heard the inspector say the words *three-thirty*, though she didn't know what this was in relation to, and then the pair of them took the elevator with the professor up to the third floor.

"Clank it!" Robert said. "We missed the call completely. We don't know what they're planning or where the ransom swap is."

"Wait!" Caddy cried. "I've had an idea!"

She grabbed the others and pulled them across the marble floor and into the first booth, where Matilda Milksop had taken the call from the kidnappers.

When they were all squeezed in tight, she picked up

the telephone pad and pencil from where they lay on a wooden shelf.

"What are you doing?" Robert asked.

"I saw this in the spy book you gave me," she explained. "All you do is…" She rubbed the pencil over the top sheet of the pad and ghostly writing began to appear as she revealed the indentation of Professor Milksop's notes from the page above.

When Caddy had finished, the entire message was revealed in white inverted words that stood out from the grey of the pencil shading. She read it aloud.

Meet Grand Central Depot.
New York Central and Hudson River Railroad
Platform 9.
4 p.m. this evening.

"That must be where and when the ransom exchange is going to take place," Lily said. "That time we overheard – three-thirty – must be when they're heading over there."

She couldn't believe that Professor Milksop had agreed to give up her invention so easily. "I don't understand it," she told the others. "Yesterday, Dane told us the professor was trying to buy the Ouroboros Diamond herself so she could fix her engine, and now she's going to exchange that Ouroboros Engine for her nephew. It doesn't even seem as if she particularly likes Dane, so why is she going through with this ransom swap? She'll lose her valuable machine."

"Perhaps she's just doing it for the police," Robert said. "To keep up appearances. She can't let anyone know what her machine really does or she would be arrested. You know, the Grand Central Depot is only one block over from here," he went on. "We have to be there for the ransom swap."

"How are we going to manage that?" Caddy asked. "Ma and John won't let us out alone."

"We'll take them with us," Lily said. "I'll tell them we heard that the inside of the station is an amazing tourist attraction and that we're dying to see it, especially the steam trains. Papa is mad for those. He's bound to agree. He wanted to buy train tickets for our onward trip next week anyway."

"Great idea!" Robert said. "When we get there, we can ditch John and Ma in the main lobby and make our way to where the exchange is going down."

"And then," said Lily, "we can find out who the kidnappers really are and help the police rescue Dane!" As she said that, she saw something white sprint across the carpet towards them.

It was Spook, Dane's pet mouse.

The boy had left it behind and it had sneaked through the hotel and found them.

Robert picked Spook up, cupping him in his hand. The mouse felt cold and strange. Its heart wasn't beating, like Robert's did, nor did it clank, like a mechanical's would, or tick-tock somewhere in between, like the hybrid noises Lily's heart made. It was as if Spook radiated life, but at the same time was not alive. Robert put the mouse in his coat pocket, where he thought it would be comfortable. He vowed to return Spook to Dane when they found him.

Just then he spotted Papa and Selena coming through the hotel entrance, returned from their second visit to the embassy to collect Selena's stamped permit. Luckily, they had quite missed all the morning's excitement and Lily thought it best not to tell them what had happened in case they thought she, Robert and Caddy had broken their earlier promise about not getting involved.

Over a late lunch of minute steak with French fried potatoes, Lily reminded Papa and Selena of their plan to go and buy their tickets for the onward trip to Boston that afternoon.

"I don't know," Papa said, staring out the dining-room window at the large and constant flakes falling heavily in the street. "It looks rather inclement now. Perhaps we should leave it until tomorrow?"

"But the station might be closed tomorrow," Lily said desperately. "For New Year's Eve."

"Please, Professor Hartman!" Caddy pleaded. "I haven't had a chance to see any of the city yet. A little snow shouldn't stop us, not if we're wrapped up warm."

"It would be a good chance to admire the Grand Central Depot while we're not in a rush," Robert added, persuasively. "We could have a look at the trains."

"Hmm," Papa replied. "What do you think?" he asked Selena.

"It is only one block away," Selena said. "And the children do deserve an outing. A walk in the snow might be nice."

"I suppose," Papa agreed. "I am very interested to see what kind of stock they're running on each of the lines, especially what kind of foul-weather gear the locomotives are fitted with. What time would you like to leave for the station?" he asked them.

"How about at three o'clock?" Lily suggested.

And so it was agreed.

Back in the suite, Lily and her friends put on their hats, gloves and coats and assembled the things they thought might be useful for spying on a ransom swap:

Caddy packed her book on spy craft in her day bag.

Lily wound the tiger-striped scarf around her neck and secreted her lock picks, magnifying glass and pocket watch about her blouson – she was sure that one item or another would come in handy.

Robert put on his cap and packed the compass John had given him in his da's coat, next to Spook. Finally he hung Selena's binoculars around his neck. They sat across his chest, just below the Moonlocket which was nestled beneath his shirt.

Malkin didn't bring anything because he didn't have any pockets, not even in the new winter jacket Mrs Rust had knitted him, and now that he had noticed as much he complained about it, loudly, as Lily stuffed him away into the basket.

That was it then – they were ready to sneak off from

Papa and Selena and follow the Milksops and the police. Ready to trail Miss Buckle, or the kidnapper, or whoever ended up with the machine, and finally find out what they were up to and stop them. So, with Papa and Selena, and barely half an hour before Lily knew that Matilda Milksop and the police would be due to leave themselves, they set out for Grand Central Depot.

CHAPTER 14

Robert shivered and huffed out a cloud of warm air. He pushed his cap back on his head and stared up at the humongous snow-capped shape of New York's Grand Central Depot. He could feel Spook scrabbling about in the pocket of his da's jacket beside his compass. The little mouse poked its head out and Robert put a hand over it to keep him still.

Despite all his current anxieties, Robert couldn't help marvelling at the station. He'd never seen the like. The building was far bigger than any of the rail or airship terminals he'd visited before, and he'd seen quite a few, in London, Manchester, Liverpool and Paris, not to mention the Staten Island Airstation, where they had first docked in New York.

This building dwarfed them all. From the roof sprouted six large towers topped with round domes coated in snow. Each bore a Stars-and-Stripes flag that flapped back and forth between the blizzard of snowflakes. On each of the three towers above the south entrance the name of a different railroad was printed:

NEW YORK CENTRAL AND
HUDSON RIVER R.R.

NEW YORK AND HARLEM R.R.

NEW YORK and NEW HAVEN R.R.

Robert was finding it all too confusing, with these three different lines and entrances. "Which one is the ransom swap on again?" he whispered to Lily.

Lily pulled the phone-box note from her coat pocket and consulted it. "New York Central and Hudson River Railroad. Platform nine," she whispered back.

"That's the entrance beneath the tower on the left," Caddy said.

"According to your *Appleton's Guide*," Selena said, interrupting their whisperings to read from the book that she was carrying, "this entire terminal was designed by John B. Snook and first opened in 1871. Each railroad has its own separate lines, waiting room, ticket office and depot."

"Interesting," said Papa. "So where do we need to go to buy our tickets?"

Selena checked the guidebook again. "We want the New York and Harlem Railroad. It's beneath the biggest tower, the one right in the centre with the clock on." She pointed at it, and she and Papa set off walking in that direction across the slushy street filled with steam-wagons.

Lily checked her pocket watch. "Three-twenty," she whispered. "The ransom swap is at four, and Professor Milksop and the police will be on their way to the station right now."

"If they're not here already," Malkin growled from within Lily's basket.

Robert, Caddy and Lily crossed the street in John and Selena's wake and followed them up to the entranceway in the central tower that led to the New York and Harlem Railroad.

"We need to get away from Papa and your ma as soon as possible," Lily said as they stepped through the swing doors into the lobby. "Then we nip across to the next line and look for the ransom swap."

But John had already found a line of ticket booths along the side wall, where a row of mechanical men and women wearing the train company's livery sat taking money and dispensing tickets. He and Selena joined the queue at the nearest window. Robert and the others stood behind them, clapping their gloved hands together in the cold and impatiently waiting for the best moment to sneak off.

The queue was moving forward quickly and John was nearly at the front.

Selena took out her purse. "I'm happy to pay for our tickets."

"There's really no need," John said.

"Weather warning!" called the guard in the booth. "Last trains out of New York are in an hour." He pointed at a clock above his window, which read three twenty-five. "After that, all service is suspended on account of the incoming blizzard."

"Oh, but we don't intend to travel today," Papa said, checking the noticeboard for fares and counting the money out of his wallet. "We're purchasing advance tickets. For the third of January."

Lily nudged Robert's and Caddy's arms.

"We have to go now if we're to catch the police and the professor arriving for the ransom swap."

"I can't see them anywhere from down here, in my sedan chair," Malkin grumbled from his basket.

"It's on another line, Malkin," Robert whispered. Then to Caddy he said, "Tell them you need the toilet."

"All right." Caddy tugged at her ma's sleeve. She was at the ticket window with John.

"I need the bathroom," Caddy told her.

"Can't it wait?" Selena asked agitatedly.

"I'm desperate," Caddy said, hopping about.

"All right then. Go."

"But all of you together!" John added nervously. "Be careful and don't get lost… And be sure to meet us back here in five minutes!"

As the two adults turned back to the ticket seller, the three children – Robert with Spook in his pocket, and Lily carrying Malkin's basket – slipped away towards the front of the station.

As soon as they were out of sight of Selena and John, Malkin popped his head out of Lily's basket. "Oh, thank goodness," he said. "I couldn't spend another second hidden in there beneath that blanket. At least this way I can see what's going on." He glanced at Robert's pocket. "I expect Spook would say the same if he could talk."

"But he can't," Robert said. The mouse wasn't

scrabbling around any more in his pocket. He hoped it had fallen asleep.

"Looks like it's going to be a bad storm," Caddy said, turning up her coat collar as they stepped out of the main door into heavy snowfall and ran towards the entrance for the New York Central and Hudson River Railroad beneath the left clock tower.

As they hustled their way through the crowds, an electrical hansom cab pulled up right in front of them, and Professor Matilda Milksop stepped down from it. She was wrapped in a thick winter overcoat and a heavy fur hat, carrying the wooden case in her gloved hands.

Lily shrank into her tiger scarf and Robert quickly pulled down his cap, but the professor was in such a rush she hadn't clocked them. Lucky they'd seen her, as she would have been hard to spot otherwise, in all the crowds.

A moment later another cab pulled up and Inspector Tedesko and Lieutenant Drumpf got out. The pair looked very different out of their uniforms. They were both now dressed in plain clothes to try and blend in. Flanking them were four officers – squat, heavy-set bruisers also dressed plainly too. When they thought no one was looking, they would nod to each other or make little hand signals to let their buddies know what position they were going to take up.

Robert couldn't help but wonder that no one else outside the station seemed to notice them. He made sure to point them out to Lily. "Best to hang back a little," he whispered to her. "We don't want to be seen."

"They might think you're the kidnappers," Malkin said.

"I don't think so," Lily said. "Grown-ups really never pay attention to children in these types of situations."

To be on the safe side though, she ushered Malkin back down in the basket. If anything was going to draw attention to them, it would be the fact that they were walking along with a talking mechanical fox.

They followed Professor Milksop and the police officers through the entranceway and across the concourse of the New York Central and Hudson River Railroad, taking care to hang back so as not to be seen.

The police and the professor passed through a waiting room where high marble arched doorways led out to the platforms on one side and a porched entrance led out to the street on the other side.

Rows of long wooden pew-like benches, each at least thirty feet in length, spanned the centre of the space. At them sat men in top hats and bowlers and women in long skirts, shawls and bonnets, clutching their luggage, handbags, parcels, or in some cases a baby.

Others read newspapers or talked distractedly to their children.

Matilda Milksop and the police officers headed for a doorway marked *Platforms 5 to 9* on the far side. Nervously, Robert, Lily and Caddy crossed the waiting room and stepped through behind them.

On the far side of the doorway, a guard stopped them. "Only ticketed passengers on the platforms, please. And no mechanimals," he said, staring at Lily's basket.

"But…I…we…we don't have tickets," Lily said, hurriedly. Over his shoulder, she could see Matilda Milksop and the police heading towards platform nine and the ransom swap.

"Come on," said someone behind them. "Out of the way, we need to get through!"

There was nothing for it, they would have to make a scene.

Lily plucked Malkin from the basket and dropped him on the ground.

Malkin growled and snarled at the passengers, snapping at their legs and feet. The passengers danced about, shouting in consternation. One woman let out a loud scream as Malkin skidded beneath her skirt and out the other side, dashing for the platform.

The rest of them were all up in arms, looking about

everywhere, unsure what was going on. "Calm down!" the guard cried chaotically, waving his hands and a bunch of torn tickets at them. Robert, Lily and Caddy meanwhile had slipped past him.

They walked along between the platforms, searching for platform nine. Robert surveyed each row of seats and every nook they passed for evidence of the kidnappers or Miss Buckle, but there was none.

Despite the imminent warning of dangerous and deteriorating weather, the station was busy with people waiting for the last trains. When they finally arrived at platform nine, they found Matilda Milksop was only a minute or two ahead of them, already walking down the platform's length.

Lily beckoned to Robert and the others, and they huddled together behind a railway sign so they wouldn't be seen.

"We'll walk down the platform, on the opposite side to Professor Milksop," Lily said. "That way the central columns and signs will keep us hidden. Don't look across her way and don't make eye contact. We don't want to be seen by her, or by the criminal – whoever that is – or the undercover police. The most important thing is that we don't interrupt whatever's going to happen. If the detectives don't foil the whole thing, once we're sure Dane's safe, we'll just follow the criminal and grab the case from them ourselves."

They strolled slowly up the length of the platform and sat down on a seat where they could see Matilda Milksop without being in her direct eyeline. Malkin slinked in last, darting along between the lamp posts, signs and benches that sprouted along the platform. When he finally arrived at their bench, he scrabbled under the seat beneath Robert and Lily.

Robert pulled his cap down low over his eyes and Lily and Caddy shrank into their scarves and collars, while they watched the inspector and the lieutenant and the rest of the undercover officers position themselves around the platform and at the entranceway.

Then they waited…

After a short while, Lily checked her pocket watch. Three fifty-five.

TOOOOOT! TOOOOOT!

The sudden whistle of an arriving train made her jump. She raised her head to see clacking wheels cutting through a cloud of steam that was billowing along the track, as a locomotive with a string of carriages pulled in where Matilda was waiting.

"FINAL STOP! NEW YORK CENTRAL DEPOT!" came a shout from the train.

Over the rim of her scarf, Lily glimpsed the conductor's silhouette. The man was leaning out of the open door of the goods van, hanging onto a handrail.

"FINAL STOP, LADIES AND GENTS!" he called again, jumping down onto the platform. "NEW YORK CENTRAL DEEEEEEEE-POT!"

The train ground to a halt and all the doors along its sides swung open. Passengers barged down onto the platform and immediately their shapes became jumbled up in the steam and smoke that was billowing from the engine.

There was no way any one person could be picked out from another. Whoever had planned the swap here knew what they were doing. It was the perfect place to sneak up on someone.

When the smoke and crowds finally drifted off, Lily saw that a woman with an odd gait was approaching the bench where Matilda sat. A boy was with her.

Robert pushed back his cap and took a quick darting glance at both suspects through his binoculars. The woman was Miss Buckle, disguised as a commuter in a long coat and broad-brimmed hat. She stood in the middle of the icy concourse with the Ouroboros

Diamond half-hidden beneath the scarf around her neck. *How brazen of her,* Robert thought.

The boy was Dane. He seemed scared, his face even paler than usual. He was shaking and he peered about as if he had no idea what was going on or where he was.

For a second Miss Buckle's head flicked round. Robert thought she'd caught a glint of the lenses. He felt a horrible chill of cold sweat drip down the back of his neck.

The mechanical signalled to Dane to wait further down the platform. Dane stood, watching her worriedly and fidgeting around. Why didn't he run? Was he too scared?

"Dane!" Professor Milksop called out to him from her seat, but he didn't answer. Was he just confused as to what was going on?

Miss Buckle walked over to the bench where her former owner sat and, towering over her, began to speak. Unfortunately, they were too far away for Lily and the others to hear what was being said.

Frustrated, Lily got up quietly and sneaked a little closer, taking cover behind a pillar. Her friends followed. The professor and the mechanical nursemaid were still speaking, and now Lily and the others could hear every word.

"I'm sorry to have do this, Professor, especially after our time working together, but I'm afraid I have to ask you to give me the Ouroboros Engine." Miss Buckle clenched a fist around the professor's handcuffs and wrenched at them, until, with a snap, the links broke apart. Then, with a studied force, she prised the case from the professor's vice-like grip.

"Stop her!" Professor Milksop yelled, jumping from her seat. At that, the inspector and the rest of the plain-clothes police officers suddenly converged on the exchange.

But Miss Buckle was ready for them.

"Afternoon, Inspector, Lieutenant, detectives, I'm afraid I haven't time to talk right now. I've orders to carry out." She swung around, making a beeline across the platform back towards Dane, before she scooped him up under her free arm and ran at superhuman speed down the platform.

Lily, Robert, Caddy and Malkin leaped into action, chasing after her, as did Professor Milksop and the police. Professor Milksop was screaming something about the case and her nephew but her words were drowned out by the stationmaster blowing his whistle.

PHHHHEEEEEP! PHHHHEEEEEP!

Steam puffed from the train's chimney stack. It was about to depart.

Inspector Tedesko, Lieutenant Drumpf and the rest of the plain-clothes police officers were speeding along the platform after Miss Buckle, just behind Lily, Robert, Caddy and Malkin.

"Get out of the way!" the lieutenant yelled angrily at them.

But Lily, Caddy and Malkin didn't stop, and neither did Robert. The binoculars bumped heavily against his chest.

"Come along, Dane, we must cross the rails," he heard Miss Buckle say.

She threw Dane over her shoulder, clasping the case beneath him. Dane kicked his feet, beating them against her metal chest, but she ignored him, jumped down from the platform and ran along the track.

The two nearest detectives were about to follow, when…

TOOOOOOOT! a train whistle screamed.

Another arriving locomotive hurtled down the track.

Miss Buckle pulled Dane and the case out of its way and sprung up onto the opposite platform in one great superhuman leap, her skirts flying, revealing mechanical legs beneath. Still carrying the case under one arm and Dane under the other, she seemed to say something to him, before running for the end of the platform and the exit beyond, pushing shrieking passengers out of the way.

Lieutenant Drumpf, Inspector Tedesko, Matilda Milksop and the other police officers jogged breathlessly around the end of the platform, trying to reach where Miss Buckle and Dane had just been, but they were too slow and out of shape – there was no way they would catch them.

Lily, Robert, Caddy and Malkin, though, were faster. They followed Miss Buckle as she carried Dane and the case out of the main entrance and back onto the street in front of the station, where the snow was falling thick and fast. Malkin had almost caught up to Miss Buckle, who, despite being weighed down with Dane and the case, was speedier than any of them on her mechanical legs.

Robert glimpsed her taking a flight of covered stairs two at a time and then thrusting through a turnstile to a raised railway platform above the street. Malkin sprinted after her, his little leg pistons pumping. Lily, Robert and Caddy, flagging now, stumbled up the icy stairs behind them and pushed through the turnstile at the top.

They ran past a mechanical guard in a ticket booth and on to a southbound platform, where a steam train of two long passenger carriages, a goods van, a tender and a locomotive was waiting. Its engine chuffed eagerly, ready to depart.

"STOP!" the guard yelled from behind them. "THAT TRAIN'S OUT OF SERVICE!"

It was true. The carriage windows were all dark.

Miss Buckle ignored the guard's shouts. She was halfway down the length of the second carriage. She had Dane by the hand, rather than under her arm and was pulling him forward roughly. Holding the wooden case by its handle in her other fist, she opened a door, pushed Dane onto the train and stepped aboard herself.

The engine whistled and released a head of steam, then lurched forward, starting to pull the cars off slowly. Robert, Lily, Caddy and Malkin skidded along the platform, desperately chasing after it, snow streaming in their faces.

The moving train was speeding up, going almost as fast as they were. Already most of it had passed, but Robert managed to grab the handle of a door and throw it open.

He climbed aboard and quick as flash, Malkin leaped in after him, and with his teeth, helped Robert pull Lily and Caddy up behind them.

Lily peered out the open doorway at the guard, running along the platform of the receding station. He was screaming as loud as he could, blowing his pocket-whistle.

"EMERGENCY!" *PHHHHEEEEEP!* "STOWAWAYS ABOARD!" *PHHHHEEEEEP!* "EMERGENCY!" *PHHHHEEEEEP!* "STOP THE TRAIN!"

The train driver and fireman must not have heard him over the loud clack of the locomotive's wheels, or the hiss of their fire and the huff of the engine, for the train kept moving, heading off down the line, to who knew where.

They were alone in the city now, leaving Papa and Selena and even the police and Matilda far behind. All alone chasing a dangerous mechanical who'd committed robbery, kidnapped their friend, jumped with him from a third-floor window, stolen a dangerous electrical device, clambered across train tracks to escape the police and hitched a lift on an out of service train... Who knew what else she was capable of?

Robert suddenly felt quite vulnerable, but whatever happened, they couldn't lose sight of the machine, nor of Dane. Not if they wanted to rescue him and stop Caddy's prophecy.

CHAPTER 15

Lily, Robert, Malkin and Caddy walked through the empty, dark carriage of the out-of-service train, as it chuffed along the raised track. Between the gusts of smoke billowing from the chimney of the locomotive, the snowy night sky and the roofs and high windows of city blocks were just visible, streaming by.

Finally they arrived at the door to the other car, which Miss Buckle and Dane were in.

Lily could see their silhouettes through the dusty frame of the door glass, sitting at the far end of that carriage. Robert took a quick look at them through his binoculars.

Miss Buckle, in her big hat, was reclining calmly next

to Dane, with the wooden case containing the engine balanced on her lap. She hadn't seen them.

Quickly, Lily beckoned to the others and they huddled together, ducking beneath the window in the carriage door. Spook poked his head out of Robert's pocket, as if he was listening too.

"We need a plan," Lily said. "How are we going to get to Dane?"

"Should we just go up to them?" Caddy asked tentatively, glancing over Robert's shoulder at Miss Buckle. "Try to reason with Miss Buckle? Take the case and Dane away?"

"That won't work," Malkin said. "She seems far beyond reason. And there's no one here behind us, to back us up."

"She'll probably try to make a break for it if we approach her directly," Robert said. "And you saw how fast she was at the station. She outran all those policemen. I don't even think we'd have caught her if she hadn't slowed down to get on this train."

"Plus, she's strong and fearless." Lily stared sideways through the window at Miss Buckle with a shiver. "She doesn't seem intimidated by anyone, least of all humans."

"Precisely," Malkin said. "Whoever's instructions she's obeying, she intends to see them through. She's not going to do what we say just because we ask her nicely. We need to come up with a better ruse than that!"

"I think the only solution is to try and sneak up on them," Lily said at last, mainly because she couldn't think of anything better.

So, they crouched down and as stealthily as they could, opened the sliding door between the two adjacent carriages. Then the four of them slid through one by one and hid behind the nearest row of seats.

Miss Buckle was talking to Dane very loudly and her voice echoed down the length of the empty car. "Are you sitting comfortably?" she asked Dane, his hand tight in her grasp.

"Yes, thank you," Dane said quietly. He was sat next to Miss Buckle, shivering with distress – too anxious, it seemed, to do anything but agree.

Seat by seat, Lily, Robert, Caddy and Malkin crept closer to the pair of them in the dark, until they were only one row away from where their friend and the mechanical were sat.

They paused there while Lily tried to think what to do next.

She waited, but any idea was a long time coming...

Suddenly Caddy shielded her mouth with a gloved hand.

"I think…" she whispered. "I'm going to…sneez—"

"Stifle it!" Robert whispered urgently.

Caddy did, and it came out in a low cough.

But it made no difference. Miss Buckle had heard.

She stood up and was staring right at them, her face contorted with anger. She picked up her case and dragged Dane from his seat along the last few feet of the rattling carriage, glancing back over her shoulder as she departed.

"What should we do now?" Robert asked, hurriedly.

Lily gritted her teeth. "We don't really have a choice. We have to follow."

"Try not to lose her under any circumstances," Malkin advised. "If you need me to run ahead again, I will." The hackles on the back of his neck were raised and he stood growling at Lily's side.

It made Lily feel a little more confident about facing down the mechanical woman if it came to that. She motioned to Robert and Caddy and they set out in pursuit of Miss Buckle as she lugged Dane and the wooden case down the last leg of the swaying carriage.

They were getting closer.

Miss Buckle had more to contend with, pulling Dane and the case along.

The clattering of the train tangled Lily's nerves. Now that Dane had seen them, she couldn't figure out why he wasn't crying out. Perhaps he was scared of the mechanical woman? Had she threatened him to make him keep quiet? He kept glancing over his shoulder at them, his troubled face filled with worry.

"Keep moving, please, Master Milksop," Miss Buckle told him forcefully. Her loud and urgent words carried down the empty carriage. "We must keep moving."

"Please don't…" Dane murmured to her. He spoke so quietly, Lily had to strain to hear him over the clatter of the carriage. "Please let me just…" He said something else, but his voice was drowned out by a blast of the engine releasing excess steam.

Robert held Caddy's hand in his. His other fist was clenched at his side. Spook scrabbled in his pocket – the mouse must have been reacting to Robert's nervous heartbeat, which pounded in his chest and stopped him from even thinking straight. He no longer knew if trailing Miss Buckle had been a good idea, but he supposed they had no choice if they wanted to stop the machine getting into the wrong hands and rescue Dane.

Miss Buckle had reached the end of the carriage. She thrust Dane and the case in front of her and tried the door.

It was locked.

She yanked hard on the handle and it came away in her hand. Frustrated, she tossed it along the carriage floor, smashed the glass window and reached through to open the door from the outside.

But there was no escape, only a blank wall of wood in front of her: the doorless snowy side of the goods carriage.

Robert, Lily, Malkin and Caddy pushed past the last row of seats towards her.

Miss Buckle was cornered now, her eyes flashing around wildly.

"Be careful!" Dane hissed worriedly at them. "She might do anything!"

Lily ignored his warning and the fear coursing through her. With Malkin stalking out in front, she and the others stepped closer to Dane and Miss Buckle.

"Dane!" she said, trying to keep her voice from wavering. "Don't panic, we're here to help you. Miss Buckle, you must do as I say. You've nowhere else to go. I'm a human. Mechanicals always obey humans. Now let him go!"

"And hand over the case!" Robert added, trying to imitate the confidence in Lily's voice.

Miss Buckle shook her head. "I'm sorry, Miss Hartman, Master Townsend, I'm afraid I can't do that. I have orders from my master." Her eyes glowed red and threatening.

Lily shivered with dread.

Robert flinched.

Malkin growled at Miss Buckle.

"Please!" Dane implored, staring at Miss Buckle and then glancing worriedly at Lily and the others. "Don't hurt them… Don't do that. They're my friends…" The words were gabbled and mixed up with anxiety.

At Dane's begging, Miss Buckle seemed to change her mind.

"All right," she said. "Come along then, Master Milksop. A slight detour, I'm afraid." She kicked the door open wider, picked up the case once more and dragged it and Dane through the doorway, pushing them up a ladder that ran up the narrow gap on the outside of the carriage onto the roof of the train.

Lily rushed over and peered after them. Cold snow and wind and smoke and the scream of the steam engine blasted in through the open doorway, tearing at her face. She narrowed her eyes against all of it.

Miss Buckle had Dane grasped under one arm and the case somehow slung across her back. She was climbing one-handed. She reached the roof and dragged Dane and the case up onto it.

KER-SCREEK, KER-SCREEK! screamed the wheels of the train.

Lily swung herself out of the carriage and, balancing one foot on the jiggling buffers, reached for the ladder herself, with her free hand.

"What are you doing?" Robert cried, as he, Caddy and Malkin clustered in the doorway around her.

"Going after them!" Lily shouted back. "We can't lose sight of her. She has the machine and Dane."

"Wait!" he cried again. "You're not going up *there* alone, are you?"

Lily clung tightly to the first rung of the ladder. "I'm not alone, I'll have you." She began to climb upwards, rung by rung, her scarf streaming out behind her, bracing herself with each step against the tug of the ferocious snow-filled wind.

Robert gave a loud sigh. He yanked his binoculars from around his neck and looped them over Caddy's head. "Take care of these. And of Spook…" He scooped the little mouse from his pocket and handed it over to her too. "I have to go after Lily."

"Be careful!" Caddy cried tearfully.

"Don't do anything stupid!" Malkin yapped. "…Or stupider, anyway! And don't worry about your sister, I'll look after her!"

"Thanks," Robert said pulling his cap down tight over his ears.

Here we go again, he thought as he grasped the bottom of the ladder and swung through the broken doorway, climbing behind Lily as quickly and carefully as he could.

A few rungs above him, Lily's scarf and coat billowed out, like snow-spattered flags. Why did he always end up doing this? Following her into ever more dangerous and life-threatening situations?

Lily reached the top of the ladder. She poked her head up to peer along the frosted roof. Robert joined her, squeezing onto the same rung.

Black smoke from the steam engine streamed over the top of the goods van and billowed past her, strafing across the top of the two carriages they'd just walked through. For a moment it dispersed and Robert saw Miss Buckle, pulling the case and a screaming Dane along the icy surface, heading back towards the rear of the train.

"Come on," Lily muttered in his ear. "They're getting away."

She climbed onto the roof and pulled him up beside her.

Crouching and clinging to the slippery surface as well as they could, the pair of them followed Dane and Miss Buckle, the other way, down the length of the train.

Robert felt giddy. The train's shake was more pronounced up here and the smog made it difficult to keep the mechanical and the boy in sight.

Snow and cold wind blasted in Lily's face and the sooty steam from the locomotive swept around her like a column of fog. Her scarf pulled against her face as the end of it thrashed about behind her.

Robert took a quick peep over the edge of the carriage. The train was speeding high above the city on a metal gangway. Houses swept past as the cars sped southwards. This wasn't how he had expected to see New York, that's for sure!

A dizzy swirl of vertigo suddenly shivered through him, threatening to topple him over the edge. He snatched onto Lily's arm, took a deep breath and tried to steady himself. "Never mind airships and drainpipes," he shouted. "This is the worst climb we've *ever taken*."

"We can't let Miss Buckle get away," Lily screamed over the clatter of the rails, pointing along the rooftop.

Robert glanced up. The mechanical and Dane were already over halfway down the train. Miss Buckle, with her metallic feet, had crossed over to the roof of the next car, dragging a tearful Dane and the battered wooden case along beside her.

Robert and Lily struggled on after them. Beneath the rim of his cap, snowflakes stuck to Robert's eyelashes and melted into his eyes. In a blur of terror and snow and ragged crab-like steps they followed Miss Buckle and Dane along the juddering top of the rear carriage. As they neared the end of the car, there was a horrible screeching noise of the steam-brakes and the train ground to a sudden halt.

Robert and Lily tipped over backwards and had to grab onto a rail that ran along the roof's edge to stop themselves from toppling off altogether.

When Lily looked up again, peering through the smog, Miss Buckle had barely wavered, but Dane seemed to be pleading with her, snot running from his nose and tears streaming down his face.

Miss Buckle cricked her head to one side, as if she was considering what he was saying.

Then suddenly she seemed to make a decision and, ignoring Dane's pleas, she grasped him tighter to her and jumped from the end of the train.

CHAPTER 16

Lily and Robert clambered to their feet and scuttled and slid along the stilled carriage roof towards the spot where Miss Buckle and Dane had jumped from.

Lily glanced over the edge and saw the mechanical holding Dane in her arms and running along the frozen elevated rails behind the train, back the way they'd come, towards a fork in the track which swung off to the south.

"Quick!" Lily shouted. "We mustn't let her take him away!"

But she could barely breathe. The pain of the chase cut through her like a knife, and the Cogheart ticked wildly in her chest.

She and Robert clambered down the ladder at the

back of the train and dropped onto the track, just as Caddy and Malkin burst through the rear door of the end carriage in a flash of orange and green and grey. Caddy had Robert's binoculars around her neck and Spook still clasped in her hand. Her face was shot through with dread, but there was a glimmer of determination there too.

"Where did Miss Buckle go?" she cried.

"Down that branch line," Robert panted, pointing it out, clutching at his chest with his free hand.

Malkin hopped onto the track, and Caddy started to climb down after him.

"Wait!" she said. "Is it safe?"

"I hope so," Robert said taking her hand. "It's not electrified and there'll be no more trains in this weather."

"Shouldn't we go find the driver and fireman?" Caddy asked, but just as she said this, the train started up again with a shudder and pulled off, disappearing round the bend, behind a high-rise tenement block, making for the next station.

Now they were truly alone on the tracks.

Lily wound her scarf tight once more and stared off down the line. She could still just about see Miss Buckle with Dane up ahead. The pair of them were lit in flashes by the bright electric lamps that arced over the railway on its raised gantries. They had to follow. There was too much at stake to let the mechanical go. Lily took a deep breath and steeled herself to run on. "Come on," she shouted at the others. "Let's get them!"

Somehow, they all found the energy to continue in pursuit of their new friend.

"This is worse than a cross-country run and wild goose chase put together," Malkin grumbled as they vaulted the wide spaces between the railway sleepers.

Caddy huffed and puffed and Robert clutched at the stitch in his chest. Lily found her shoes slipping with each step, the frosted surface was treacherous enough to turn an ankle. She could see the street far below through the gaps but tried not to think about what would happen if she fell through one of them.

She shot a glance over at Robert. He had a far worse fear of heights than her. Beneath his cap, his face was frozen with anxiety, but he ran alongside her keeping pace, as did the other two.

If they didn't catch up to Miss Buckle and grab Dane and the machine, then they had no idea what she might do. She had certainly shown no regard for Dane on the train, and Lily remembered the flash of red in her eyes earlier. Worse than that, tomorrow – according to Caddy's prophecy – Dane was due to wake the dead.

The thought was horrifying – they just couldn't let it happen.

Malkin sniffed at the tracks like a bloodhound, determined to track the scent of the mechanical woman in case they lost sight of her. Lily could see the lights of the Brooklyn Bridge in the distance and Miss Buckle running fast towards it. Still dragging Dane and the case with her, she slowed suddenly at the next curve in the track and looked round.

"We've nearly caught them!" Caddy shouted.

But then the mechanical woman soared over the edge of the bridge, carrying Dane and the case in her arms.

They ran to where she had been, but their quarry had disappeared.

"How are we going to ever find out where they're going now?" Lily cried exasperatedly, the last glimmer of hope inside her guttering away.

"Look," Caddy said. "Miss Buckle dropped something." She crouched down and snatched up a piece of paper that was flapping against the edge of the railway track before it could fly away.

Hope soared in Lily at the sight of it. A clue – perhaps their chase had not been in vain?

The three of them crouched down beside Caddy, crowding round the note to see what it said. The writing was so spidery-thin it was almost impossible to read in the darkness.

"Maybe we need your magnifying glass, Lily?" Malkin suggested.

Lily got it out and, shaking with cold, the four of them peered closer at the note.

It was some kind of list.

1. Ouroboros Diamond

2. Dane

3. Ouroboros Engine

4. Warehouse

5. Diving Belle

6.

7.

Items six and seven were indistinguishable. The snow had melted the words away, so that they had become black ink blots. Robert concentrated on points four and five instead, for those were the two things they knew nothing about.

"Warehouse," Lily said.

"She's going to a warehouse?" Robert suggested.

"But where-oh-where is it?" Malkin said. "This where-house?"

"And what's a *Diving Belle*?" Caddy asked, her teeth chattering.

"Who knows," Robert said. "We'll need another clue to throw a little more light on the situation, I reckon."

Just as he said this, a literal bright light suddenly appeared around the corner and pointed straight at them. It was so glaring it almost blinded them. And it was coming closer at great speed, accompanied by a SCREECH of a train whistle. Puffing fast up the tracks towards them.

Another train!

Lily stuffed the note in her pocket and glanced to the right. There was a second elevated track running alongside them, just a few feet away, a narrow gap between them.

"We have to get onto that line!" she shouted above the horrible echo of the whistle, pulling Robert and Caddy to their feet. "ALL TOGETHER..."

Malkin had already vaulted the gap before she'd finished speaking. "Come on," he called to all of them. "Hurry up, slowcoaches!"

Lily took Caddy's gloved hand and Robert's and pulled them both to the edge.

"I-I can't," Caddy said.

The train was almost on them now, steam billowing around it.

"JUMP!" Lily screamed and they leaped across the rails, stumbling over the sleepers on the other track.

Lily's heart ticked wildly in her head – or was that the screaming clack of the train wheels as they whooshed past, the screech of whistling wind and the huff of the chimney?

The train had missed them by inches. Lily found herself shakily clinging onto the others as she watched the locomotive disappear into the distance.

"We made it!" Robert said, breaking free from Lily's grip and hugging her and Caddy to him. Caddy was shivering, clasping Spook protectively in her free hand.

Slowly, Lily brushed the soot and snow from her clothes. A sharp stitch pulsed beneath her ribcage and the cold, which the heat of the chase and the excitement of finding the note had kept at bay, suddenly closed in on her compounding into a wave of tiredness. Caddy's knee was grazed and jewelled with scarlet pinpricks of blood. Robert was still out of breath. Malkin, as one might expect, was fine – his new green Christmas coat was smeared with coal dust, but he didn't seem to mind that.

The important thing was they had survived. The night seemed even blacker after the brightness of the train's lamps, but they couldn't just give up, not when they'd come so far. They had the note after all: it was a new clue. If only they could work out what it meant.

The four of them hobbled along the tracks, searching for somewhere to descend. Buildings crowded in along the rails up ahead, their distant windows throwing vague ghostly lights, but there were no stations or stairways down to the street.

Lily dried the sweat and meltwater from her face with the end of her scarf, though the wind blew more snow at her ceaselessly. By now Papa and Selena would be really concerned. They had probably reported them missing to one of the many police officers in the Grand Central Depot. Lily felt sick that she had made her father worry again, especially after all he had been through – all they'd both been through – in the last year.

"I can't believe that Miss Buckle got away," Caddy said, putting Spook in her pocket.

"She's almost a super-mech," Robert said. "Regular mechanicals aren't usually that strong."

"We'll get more from that note and find out where

she's going when we see it under a proper light," Lily said. "I'm sure of it."

"I have a more pressing concern," Caddy said in a worried tone, looking around at the dimly lit track. "I think we might be lost."

"How is that possible?" Malkin asked. "It's a straight track that goes north and south."

"No," Robert said, taking his compass out of his pocket and looking at it. "I think she's right. We're travelling west to east."

They had reached a siding. Robert motioned to the others and they stepped onto it to take a moment to get their bearings.

Lily wondered how on earth they were going to get back. The cold was encroaching into her shoes and her thoughts. Her toes were so frozen it felt like they might fall off. How could they have been so stupid? Getting involved in Dane's problems had only left them here, lost in the dark in a foreign city in the snow. Lily wished she had never heard of the boy. If he had never contacted them with his note, they would be safe in the hotel now, not going through this. She shook that thought away. No, he was their friend, and they'd promised to help him no matter what. They couldn't break a promise like that. It was just the cold and searing tiredness making her think such things.

"We could be on any line by now," Robert said. "Who knows in this blizzard?"

"Perhaps it's better to keep going forward rather than turn back?" Caddy suggested, when suddenly, on the far side of the track, a figure appeared through the fog. With a shiver, Lily understood the person must have been following and listening to them for some time.

Could it be Miss Buckle, come back for her note? But if so, she no longer had the case or Dane with her. Lily wondered in horror what she had done with them. She felt another rush of guilt for her previous anger at Dane – he needed their help.

The figure vaulted the tracks and came closer. It was a lot shorter than Lily had first thought – barely taller than them, in fact.

As the snow eased a little, Lily saw it was a girl who looked to be around their own age, all wrapped up in layers of torn clothing. She wore a large men's herringbone jacket over the top and a scarf wrapped around her neck with more holes than wool. Instead of gloves she wore socks on her hands like mittens, and she had wound an old piece of material around her head like a hat to ward off the pinch of the cold.

The girl took something from her pocket – a box – and flipped its lid. There was a crackle and a flame appeared from the box, lighting up her face. Beneath her shadowy makeshift hat, an eyepatch hid one eye and a familiar cherubic grin dimpled her cheeks. Kid Wink!

"What in tarnation are you guys doing here?" she asked.

"It's a long story," Lily said, joyfully. She hadn't imagined she'd find anyone else wandering this snowy railway siding, let alone Kid Wink.

"Tell me on the way." Kid Wink snapped her Wonderlite shut and plunged them all into darkness... but not despair, for now they had found her, they knew they were going to be all right.

Robert was just as pleased as Lily to bump into Kid Wink – it was such a relief to have someone leading them who knew the way.

Only, what was the way? Where *were* they going...? Apart from the note, they had no clues left and their plan to help Dane was coming apart at the seams.

"Where are you taking us?" he asked.

"Where were you trying to get to?" she replied.

"We don't know! We're lost," Caddy admitted.

"We were following Miss Buckle," Lily explained. "That's Dane's nursemaid, who stole the Ouroboros Diamond and kidnapped him. She's got the professor's wooden case too. It has a dangerous machine in it. We need to get back to the hotel and tell the police where we lost her and show them the note we found, so they can track her down."

"You won't get back there tonight," Kid Wink said. "Not in this clanking snow. Blizzard's closing in. The city'll be on lockdown. Best you come with me."

"Where?" Lily asked incredulously. Kid Wink still hadn't explained why she was on the rails.

"Home," the girl said. "This is the quickest way. Trains are stopped because of the snow now. You can spend the night with us there, if you like?"

"How far is it?" Caddy asked with a shiver.

"Only a step or two up the track." Kid Wink pointed away into the fog and darkness. "It's warm and cosy, and there's food. Then I can get you back to the hotel at first light tomorrow." She ducked under a red-and-white striped wooden barricade that was blocking her path and beckoned Robert and the others to follow. The snowy track beyond was mangled and patched with rusty rivets.

As they walked, Lily, Robert and Caddy told Kid Wink all they had discovered in the past few days about Dane and his parents and what had happened to them on the Shadowsea Base. Then they told her about Professor Milksop, and finally about Miss Buckle and the diamond robbery and kidnap. It was quite the tale, Lily observed, telling it out loud for the first time since they'd spoken about it to the police inspector.

Kid Wink listened, but her focus was mostly on navigating the slippery, elevated terrain of the rail track.

They had just got to telling her what had happened that morning – how they'd read the ransom note, uncovered the phone message from the kidnappers and contrived to follow Professor Milksop and the police to the ransom swap – when an abandoned rail car appeared up ahead. It had a single smoking chimney, and snow was melting off its roof, falling in mushy lumps onto the track.

"All right," Kid Wink said, interrupting their story, "here we are… This is my place."

"Wow!" Caddy said.

"Bow-wow-WOW!" Malkin added.

"You really live in *there*?" Robert asked incredulously.

The railway carriage must've been standing on the siding for a long time, for there were wooden sleepers wedged against it and, beneath its hat of snow, its sides were scribbled with graffiti. The ivy growing round the car's wheels was starting to engulf the undercarriage.

"Of course!" Kid Wink said. "Don't you recall nothin'? I told you the first time we met."

"I thought you were joking," Robert replied. "I didn't think you actually…" He trailed off.

"He means he didn't think you lived in an *actual* railway carriage," Lily finished for him.

"Well, I do." Kid Wink stepped up onto the rear platform and knocked on the car's door.

After a moment, a voice inside called out: "Password?"

"Cloudscraper Express!" Kid Wink said and, as an aside to everyone, she added, "That's what we named our train, because we're the Cloudscrapers."

A dusty window in the carriage door slid down, and a boy peered out. Lily recognized him too. "You're the elevator boy from the hotel!"

"Hey, Kid," the elevator boy said, ignoring her. "You're back!"

"Hey, Rails," Kid Wink said. "Course I'm back! Got some pals with me. You wanna meet them?"

Rails gave a broken grin. "Met 'em already."

"This guy's Rails," Kid said. "Also known as Will."

"Railroad Will," Rails added. "Named for Railroad Bill. I love that guy. He's my hero. The Cloudscrapers call me Rails for short."

"We don't need your life story," Kid griped. "Just let us in before we freeze to death! It's colder than an arctic icebox out here."

Rails pulled the door open. "You're late, Kid," he said, standing aside for her. "We was wondering what'd happened to you."

"Never thought to come looking though, did ya?" Kid said, barging past him.

Rails shook his head. "Nuh-uh. No way. Not in this blizzard."

Kid Wink shook her head, then beckoned to Robert, Lily, Caddy and Malkin. "Come on in!" she said. "Or are you waiting for a formal invitation?"

Lily flicked a glance at the others, who stood shivering and wet beside her in the doorway. She clasped her damp scarf and coat around her, and one by one they stepped through the door.

CHAPTER 17

The warm scent of fresh baking bread hit Robert as he, Lily, Caddy and Malkin gathered beside Kid Wink and Rails in the train carriage's rear section. It smelled delicious and Robert felt relieved to have finally come in from the cold.

Malkin did too. "Thank clank for that!" the fox said. "If we'd stayed out there a moment longer, my cogs would have frozen stiff. This coat Mrs Rust knitted does nothing to keep out the tocking frost and neither does my own fur."

Kid Wink chuckled. "You really need bear-thick fur to brave December in New York! Come this way…" She led them past a pair of closed side doors, which must've once been used to get on and off at stations. A coat rack stuffed with thick winter coats was fixed to the wooden wall in front of them. Kid Wink took off her coat and hung it on one of the free hooks. Robert did the same and the others followed suit.

A corridor ran down the right-hand side of the carriage, with a row of sliding doors suggesting several separate modest compartments. Robert guessed that the car must have once been used for long-distance travel. "Do you two live here alone?" he asked Rails and Kid Wink.

"No," Rails said. "There's six of us kids all together."

"But no grown-ups?" Caddy asked.

Kid Wink shook her head. "We do fine without 'em."

"We don't." Robert thought of how worried his ma and John must be about them. "We need to get back to our folks," he said, clutching the Moonlocket around his neck.

"Tomorrow, like I told you," Kid said.

"One of us might try to get a message through tonight?" Rails suggested. "We could get across town a heck of a lot faster than the fox or these kids."

Kid Wink shook her head. "It's too dangerous in this weather." She smiled at Robert and the others. "We'll have to save any special messages for when I take you back in the morning."

"The morning…" Caddy said, her voice quavering.

"Everything'll be fine, I promise," Kid Wink soothed. "Now, come sit by the stove and melt the ice off yourselves." She pulled open a door to a compact and comfy compartment, where a proper iron pot-bellied stove crackled with warmth, its chimney sticking out through the train roof. More railway children sat on the padded seats all around it, chatting in their strange New York accents.

"Lily, Robert, Caddy. This is…Parsons, Maze, Spoons and Curly." Kid Wink waved at each of the Cloudscrapers in turn. Robert had trouble keeping track of who was who.

"Hey!" Each Cloudscraper gave a little nod of greeting. They didn't seem much interested in the new arrivals and quickly returned to their conversation.

"And this is Malkin," Kid Wink said, as, lastly, the fox stepped into the cabin.

At that the Cloudscrapers' eyes all lit up. They hopped from their seats and gathered round the mechanimal, cooing and stroking his head and ears and ruff.

"Is this the mech-fox you told us about, who's staying at the hotel?" one of the Cloudscrapers asked. He was a short boy with glasses, who Robert thought might be Parsons.

"The very one," Malkin told the Cloudscrapers.

"He speaks!" the Cloudscrapers cried in delighted unison.

"I told you he spoke, you bunch of dopes," Kid Wink said. "You knew that."

"I didn't," the one who might be Maze said.

"I guess I never expected a fox to speak to me," added a Cloudscraper who was definitely Curly, for his hair was curlier than Robert's.

Maze giggled. "You never expected to meet a mechanimal full stop! Not in your lifetime."

"That's what you told me too, Curly!" a girl Cloudscraper, who Robert thought was Spoons, shouted, butting in.

Malkin was delighted with their attention and introduced himself personally to each and every one of them by licking their palms and fingers. When all the Cloudscrapers had finished stroking him, he settled down in the warmest spot in the room, on the floor beside the stove.

"So these guys are staying with us?" Parsons asked when the introductions were over.

"Only till the blizzard stops," Kid Wink said. "Then they'll be on their way back to the hotel." She turned to Robert and the others. "You never finished telling me your story," she said. "How did you end up on the track?"

"The track!" Spoons said. "Never walk the track! It's dangerous. Could kill ya."

"It's true," Maze said. "I seen plenty of folks walk that line and get themselves smashed like broken eggs. What were you doing on the track, anyways?"

"Looking for someone," Lily said.

"Who?" Parsons asked.

"Dane – a boy who was kidnapped from the hotel by a mechanical called Miss Buckle," Lily said.

"We made a promise to help him," Malkin explained.

"Yeah, well, like I said," Kid Wink replied, "best leave it till morning. Neither you nor the police could do anything more for him tonight. Besides, we heard the police earlier outside Murray Hill Hotel. Even with what you have to tell 'em, they ain't got no new clues to go on."

It was then that Robert remembered Miss Buckle's note. "But we do," he said. "Read the note out to everyone, Lil."

"It's a list," Lily told them as she took the note from her pocket and read it aloud to the Cloudscrapers. "Number one is: 'Ouroboros Diamond' – that's the diamond Miss Buckle stole from the hotel," she explained. "Two is 'Dane' – that's our friend, who she kidnapped. Three is: 'Ouroboros Engine' – that's the machine in the suitcase Miss Buckle stole. Four is: *'Warehouse'* – but we don't know what that means. Five: *'Diving Belle'* – we don't know what that means either, but maybe one of you does? There are two more points at the end, but they're smudged and unreadable so of no use."

"Do any of you know what *Diving Belle* might mean?" Caddy asked the Cloudscrapers.

They shrugged and shook their heads. None of them did.

"Sounds like some kinda thing you might find down the docks?" Kid Wink suggested.

"It does…" Robert said. He thought for a moment. "I could swear I've heard the name somewhere before."

"Me too," Lily said.

And then she remembered. It was in the yellowed newspaper article they'd found about the Shadowsea Submarine Base. She'd kept it in her other pocket just in case they needed it. She quickly pulled it out. The paper was soggy – wet from the snow that had seeped through to the lining of her coat. But, luckily, the article was still in one piece.

She smoothed it out carefully and held it close to the stove to dry before reading it out to everyone:

"'Mr Nathaniel Shadowsea, Professor Matilda Milksop and guests…on the dockside of the Shadowsea Warehouse near

Battery Park... A submersible named the Diving Belle *will be used to take down supplies needed for the work...*' That's it. The *Diving Belle*. It's at the Shadowsea Warehouse, in Battery Park."

"We think Miss Buckle is working for other people," Robert said. "This must be where she's going to meet them."

"Well, that ain't so far," Maze said.

"At the bottom of Broadway," Rails added.

"Which is about twelve blocks west from here," Parsons said.

"Be quicker to take East Broadway," Spoons corrected. "That way's maybe an hour's walk."

"On a good day!" Curly added, glancing at the snow on the window.

"We'll have to tell the police all this tomorrow when we hand the note over to them," Robert said.

"There isn't time for that!" Caddy said suddenly. "We have to go there ourselves as soon as possible."

"What do you mean?" Robert asked.

"Don't you remember? Because Dane's going to wake the dead at twelve o'clock tomorrow. That could mean midday or midnight. We need to find him and get him back before then to make sure the prophecy won't come true."

"What do you mean, wake the dead?" Kid Wink asked in shock.

And Robert realized that, although they'd told the Cloudscrapers everything else, they'd forgotten to tell them about Caddy's prophecy. So he and Lily and Caddy took it in turns to tell the kids the story of Dane's past and what Caddy had seen of his future...

How Matilda Milksop had invented a life and death machine. How the machine accidentally electrocuted everyone on the Shadowsea Base, including Dane and his parents, when she and her mechanical assistant, Miss Buckle, were trying to reanimate a mouse. How the pair had used the machine to reanimate Dane, but in doing so had broken the Ouroboros Diamond at its centre, and how the professor had come to New York to get another one to make it work again, not knowing that kidnappers were planning to take the diamond, Dane and the machine to use for their own purposes.

They explained how they had received a note from Dane and how that had ended up getting them and then Caddy involved. And they finished up with the diamond robbery and kidnap, and then all that had happened today – the failed ransom swap that they'd been witness to, and the chase that happened barely an hour ago. Finally they got to where they'd met Kid Wink on the branch line.

The Cloudscrapers listened to everything with interest, for though they'd heard bits and pieces about the robbery of the Ouroboros Diamond and Matilda Milksop and her nephew from those of their group that worked at the Murray Hill Hotel, the rest of the details of the story were entirely new to them.

"Well," Rails said, when they were finally finished, "I don't like to hear of kids in trouble, and your pal Dane sounds like he's in real deep. What d'you need us to do?"

"Someone needs to take us to Battery Park first thing in the morning when this weather has cleared," Lily said.

"The hotel would be better," Malkin said. "John and Selena will be up in room ninety-nine, waiting out the storm, worried sick about us and wondering where we've got to."

"I know that, Malkin," Lily said. "But this is more important. We need to find this Shadowsea Warehouse and the *Diving Belle* as soon as possible. The rest of you can go to the hotel and tell my papa and Robert's ma, and the police that we're safe…"

"For the moment," Malkin grumbled.

"And where we intend to go," Lily continued, ignoring him.

"When you see the police," Robert added, "ask for Inspector Tedesko."

"What'll you do at the warehouse?" Curly asked.

"Rescue Dane and get the diamond back," Lily said.

"We have to destroy the machine too," Caddy said.

"Good idea," Kid Wink said. "How?"

"We haven't really thought that far ahead," Robert admitted.

"Lily never does," Malkin added, from his seat beside the stove. "She's not a natural planner. Likes to live life by the seat of her pants, you might say."

"Details are for grown-ups," Lily said. "We'll work something out. The most important thing is to stop Dane from waking the dead, free him and hand everything else over to the police."

"Along with all the information about Matilda Milksop," Robert said. "She committed a crime down on the Shadowsea Base, and once the police speak with Dane he can prove it."

"Well, that seems like a plan to me," Kid Wink said. "Whatever way we can help, we will. But tonight, you should rest up and recover in readiness for it. Now, I was thinking...how about some dinner?"

Dinner did sound good to Robert. As Kid Wink showed them to the dining cabin, the amazing smells wafting along the length of the passage made his stomach rumble.

The train appeared to be an old sleeper carriage with

fold-down bunks in each room. The rest of the carriage was pleasantly decorated, the walls painted in bright colours. It felt snug and warm, just like a proper home. And, just like a proper home, each of the compartments had been decorated differently. The first compartment was obviously Kid Wink's room, for it was filled with inventions similar to her Wonderlite. The following five looked like they each belonged to a different Cloudscraper kid. Only the seventh was a spare compartment, still laid out as it originally would've been on the sleeper train, with three fold-down berths made up with sheets, blankets and pillows.

"You can sleep here tonight," Kid Wink said.

"Where did you get all these?" Lily asked, fingering the thick woollen blanket.

"The hotel throws them out when they get a few holes in," Kid Wink explained. "They're still good, so we liberate them from the garbage. That's how we got most of the things for the Cloudscraper Express."

The final compartment in the carriage contained the promised meal. The space had been converted into a dining room with a table placed down the middle between the two rows of seats, and Parsons and Maze were busily laying out dinner. There was roast turkey, cranberry sauce, boiled ham, turnips, beets, winter squash and mince pies – a second Christmas dinner in the most unlikely of places!

As they ate, Robert, Lily and Caddy took it in turns to tell the kids about their lives back in Britain; even Malkin piped in every now and then from his spot under the table. Lily was shocked to realize that some of the kids knew who she was. They had read about her story in the *New York Daily Cog*, and though they had questions for her, somehow she didn't seem to mind them asking.

When she had finished speaking, the kids told them all about their own lives in New York and what it had been like growing up on the Lower East Side.

"We were all living in tenements or on the streets, in stairwells and hallways," Rails said, "before we found this unwanted rail carriage."

"And made it our home," Curly added.

"Ain't no one gonna take it from us now," Parsons said. "Not even the IRT."

"Squatter's rights," Spoons said.

"Besides, it's the best for us," Maze admitted. "There's more light and air up here than in them tenement apartments and a clank of a lot less cold than down on the streets."

"They're right," Kid Wink said. "And, what's more, we don't have to stump up rent for no landlord. We have a home of our own and we can invest every spare dime we get hold of saving for our futures." She flipped the Wonderlite around in her hand. It glistened in the light.

After they had eaten, it was time for bed. The other Cloudscrapers returned to their rooms and Kid Wink showed Robert, Lily, Caddy and Malkin back to the spare cabin.

"Goodnight," she said, before she shut the door. "I promise I'll wake you in the morning, first thing."

They each picked a bunk bed. Robert took the top bunk, Caddy the middle and Lily the bottom, by the door. Malkin lay over her feet like a furry hot water bottle.

"If we get out of this adventure in one piece," Lily told him, "I shall give you the honorary foot-warmer award, Malkin."

Caddy must've been tired from all the running, for she dropped off straight away with Spook beside her on the pillow. Her deep breathing carried through the darkness and felt soothing to Robert and Lily.

Outside the window, the snowstorm howled, rocking the carriage on its rails. The wind pawed with its cold fingers through the cracks in the carriage, fiddled angrily with the fixtures and fittings and rattled at the windows.

Tomorrow was New Year's Eve. Lily, Robert and Caddy (and probably Malkin as well, if Lily could sneak him along) were supposed to go out and celebrate with Papa and Selena. They had planned to watch the fireworks from the viewing platform at the Croton Reservoir. It was supposed to be a spectacular display to celebrate the joining of the five boroughs... Robert hoped they would be back in time to see it.

He curled up and pulled the blankets and sheets up around him. The last thing he thought about before he fell asleep was Dane locked up again somewhere, while Miss Buckle and whoever else made plans to use him to work the professor's machine: the Ouroboros Engine. If that happened, and Caddy's prophecy was correct, then, instead of a celebration, tomorrow would be the day when Dane woke the dead. That was a terrifying prospect, and whether it was at midday or midnight, they now had less than a day to stop it...

CHAPTER 18

Lily woke with a start. Grey light filtered through the snow-coated window of the railway carriage, illuminating the cabin and the rucked woollen blanket on her bed. Outside, the wind howled a gale and threw snow around in great white sheets, but inside the carriage was toasty and warm, the room listing like a gently rocking boat.

She sat up and looked at her watch.

It was ten in the morning. They had overslept.

Lily imagined Papa and Selena hadn't slept at all. They'd probably been up all night wondering where they were and worrying about them, lost in New York. At least they were safe, unlike Dane. The spirits in Caddy's vision hadn't been specific about whether the prophecy that Dane would wake the dead was to come true at midday or midnight, but if it was midday, then that meant they now had less than two hours to stop it. They had to find the Shadowsea Warehouse as soon as possible.

Lily set the alarm on her pocket watch to twelve, so it would ring out and alert them when time ran out. Then she shook Caddy and Robert awake and sat on the edge of her bed and wound Malkin with his winding key.

"Morning, all!" Malkin chirruped, as the cogs and springs inside him began to tick. "Look at this weather!" he said, as soon as he had shaken himself awake. "We should return to the hotel and John and Selena as soon as possible."

"You'd be better off waiting out this blizzard," said Kid Wink, who'd just arrived at the door. "It don't look like it's gonna stop anytime soon."

Lily shook her head and stared around at each of them. "No," she said. "I told you all last night, we have to rescue Dane. We need to stop the prophecy before the stroke of twelve. Kid Wink, you mentioned you knew how to get to the Shadowsea Warehouse. Do you?" she asked, as she, Robert and Caddy dressed and put on their shoes, and Caddy settled Spook comfortably once again in her pocket.

"I do," Kid Wink said. "I mean, not to the warehouse itself…but I know the rough area where it is."

"Then we should go right away," Lily said, grabbing her scarf and blouson from the rack and throwing them on.

Malkin gave her a disapproving look as he climbed into his own jacket, pulling it on with his teeth. He didn't like the fact that Lily was once again ignoring his advice, intent on running towards danger; but he didn't say anything more on the matter. She'd made her decision, though he'd tried twice to change her mind. Now there was too much at stake and too little time for him to argue any more with her about it.

The rest of the Cloudscrapers gathered round as Robert and Caddy put on their coats. "We're coming too," they chorused, putting on their own woolly hats and patched winter wear.

"You can't leave us behind," Maze said.

"Especially if you're going on an adventure," Spoons added.

"No." Kid Wink shook her head. "I'll take them alone. We'll move quicker the fewer we are. The rest of you, get to the downtown Telephone Exchange and put a call through to the Murray Hill Hotel and tell these kids' parents what's going on – they're in room ninety-nine.

Then call the New York City Police Department and tell the cops what's happening. Tell 'em they need to get to the Shadowsea Warehouse in Battery Park as quick as possible, before the Ouroboros Engine's activated and causes death and chaos. Tell 'em we'll meet 'em there and explain everything. And if you can't get through on the lines, split up and walk to both those places." She nodded at Robert, Lily, Caddy and Malkin. "Right. Let's go!"

The snow was falling heavily as Lily, Robert, Caddy, Malkin, Kid Wink and the rest of the Cloudscrapers climbed out of the run-down railroad carriage on the old abandoned IRT siding and headed along the line to a maintenance stairwell where they could descend. Beneath them, rows of houses and railings and low-rise buildings, signs and storefronts peeped out from beneath cold white blankets – an inclement arctic landscape peppered with elements of the city.

Down at street level, the road crackled with ice. It was empty of steam-hansoms and cabs, nor were there any trolley cars or overhead trains on the frozen rails. New York was a ghost town.

The rest of the Cloudscrapers headed for the Telephone Exchange, while Kid Wink set off leading Lily,

Caddy, Malkin and Robert in the direction of Battery Park and the Shadowsea Warehouse.

The wind raged, pulling at snow-covered signs and power lines, throwing stinging snowflakes into their eyes and making them shiver beneath their scarves.

"You sure you still want to take this path?" Kid Wink asked Lily as they walked.

Lily checked her watch again. Ten-thirty. They might only have an hour and a half left. If Dane was forced to use the Ouroboros Engine, they had no idea what it might do – they had to stop it before it got that far.

"We have to keep going," she said. "We have no choice."

"I'll take you the quickest route I can," Kid Wink said, a determined look on her face.

They walked on southwards across town. Malkin jittered in the cold. Beneath the green wool and his fur, his joints were starting to seize up. Caddy's feet kept disappearing beneath her, her boots crunching through snow already six inches deep. Spook peeked occasionally out from her pocket. Robert's lungs were freezing and when he exhaled each breath came out as thick as fog. He wondered nervously what they would find when they got to their destination.

Finally, after forty-five minutes, they caught a glimpse of Battery Park in the distance.

Robert pushed back his cap. Taking up his binoculars, he searched the park's vicinity, staring carefully at the various warehouses that clustered round the dockside behind it. They must be getting close because the view was similar to the photograph in the newspaper article.

Then, he spotted the furthest warehouse, partly hidden from view behind frosted trees and a high fence plastered with damp and discoloured posters. Where the fence met the sidewalk, great white dunes gathered.

Robert focused his binoculars in on the building itself. Weeds grew twiggily from the cloud of snow sat on its roof and its front wall was painted with two words. With a shiver, Robert read what they said:

"This is it," he said.
"Let me have a look," Lily said.
He handed the lenses to her.

"Are you sure they're in there?" Caddy asked, with a shiver.

"They have to be…" Lily stared at the building's dark windows through the lenses. They seemed to glare at the frozen river. For a brief second, she fancied she saw a face behind one. She focused in, and the figure's eyes flickered in the light and the face became familiar. "Oh, there's someone in there all right," she whispered grimly to the others.

"Who?" Kid Wink whispered.

"Miss Buckle." Lily ducked down out of view, pulling the others with her. When she peered through the binoculars again, the figure was gone. She didn't think the mechanical had seen her.

"If Miss Buckle's in there," Malkin said, "then her accomplices must be, as well as Dane and the device."

"Are there enough of us to take down the kidnappers on our own?" Kid Wink asked. "We don't even know how many there are?"

"Eleven twenty," Lily said, checking her pocket watch. "We've got just over half an hour until they might force Dane to use the Ouroboros Engine. And if he does, we'll be in danger too. So I don't think we have much choice."

"We should've brought my gang along," Kid Wink said.

251

Robert stared at her. "Where are the police?" he asked. "They should be here by now. Your friends were supposed to call them urgently."

"Perhaps they have other emergencies?" Malkin suggested.

"Or the lines are down," Kid Wink said. "If my Cloudscrapers have to walk to the police station and the hotel it'll take them a lot longer to get your message through."

"So what do we do now?" Caddy asked.

"Cut our losses and retreat?" Kid Wink suggested.

"No," Lily said. "We have to get closer. Perhaps fewer of us will be an advantage. We can hide more easily that way and we'll have stealth on our side."

Robert glanced at his sister. He was having second thoughts about bringing her along at all, especially if they went into the warehouse alone and things got risky. "I don't think you should come, Caddy," he said at last. "Kid Wink should take you back to the hotel. You'll be safer there, and Ma'll be so worried."

"Absolutely not," Caddy said. "Dane's my friend too. He's in real peril. I want to help you rescue him and see this through. I saw the vision, and I need to help stop it."

"I agree with Robert." Lily put a hand on Caddy's shoulder. "It's too dangerous. The best way you can help

Dane is to get back to the hotel with Kid Wink and make sure the police are on their way."

"I suppose," Caddy said.

"What about you?" Kid Wink asked Lily and Robert.

"We'll keep an eye on the place until the police arrive," Robert said.

"I'll make sure they don't do anything stupid while you're gone," Malkin told Caddy.

"In that case," Kid Wink told them, "I'd be glad to take your sister back to the hotel. But promise you won't take any unnecessary risks."

"I can't," Lily said. "Not if Dane's in trouble and not if the kidnappers try to use the Ouroboros Engine. Who knows what it might do. It could kill Dane again – or, worse, hurt even more people."

"Then, here…" Kid Wink pressed something into Lily's palm. "Take this. You might need it."

"Thanks," Lily said, staring down at the Wonderlite in surprise.

"No problem," Kid Wink said.

"Good luck!" Caddy said.

Kid Wink took her hand and the pair of them set off in the other direction.

Robert, Lily and Malkin watched them disappear around the corner.

"It's just us again," Robert said when they were gone.

"The three musketeers," Malkin said.

They were careful as they approached the building, keeping beneath the cover of the trees.

As they got closer, Malkin snorted and sniffed at the air. "I think I'm picking up Dane's scent," he growled softly. "And Miss Buckle's, but I can't smell anyone else."

"Maybe there isn't anyone else?" Lily suggested, with a twinge of hope. "Maybe it's just Miss Buckle, holed up in there with Dane on her own?"

"In which case," Malkin said, "with a little planning, we might be able to take her."

"Maybe." Robert stared nervously up at the warehouse window where Miss Buckle had been. He half-expected one of the other kidnappers they'd imagined to appear in the glass like a conjuring trick, but they did not.

Lily checked her pocket watch again. Eleven thirty.

"We should climb the fence," she said, stealing over to it and jumping up to try and reach its top. It was too high. The spaces between the slats had been wedged with shards of broken glass to stop precisely that.

She tried to get a foothold on the fence, but the ice

was too slippery and she slid back to the sidewalk. Malkin jerked out of her way and Robert grabbed her arm to stop her from falling over.

"Clanking clockwork!" she muttered, pulling the ends of her striped scarf out of the snow. "It's no use."

"Maybe it'll be lower round the back and we can get in there?" Robert said.

"Good idea," Malkin piped up. "I'll have a scout." He slunk away along the perimeter.

They waited, crouching low to the ground beneath the fence, so as not to be seen if anyone was watching.

The fox came back a few minutes later. "There's no easy way in, I'm afraid," he said. "The fence is as high and sturdy all the way round."

"Perhaps there's another entrance?" Robert suggested. Now that they had a problem to solve, the nerves in his belly had all but fluttered away.

"Perhaps there is," Lily said. She'd noticed something about one of the bill posters plastered against the boards near where they were standing. It was slightly loose, the edges flapping in the wind, as if air was somehow getting in behind it to lift it up. Lily wiped the snow from its surface with her hand and felt the wood shift beneath her fingers.

The boards pulled easily aside and the space between

them created a slanted makeshift doorway through the fence, almost as if someone had gained access this way before. "Ready?" she asked Robert and Malkin.

A dread of stepping into this new and strange place shivered momentarily through Robert, but they had to push forward and investigate. All the clues had led them here. He climbed through the gap in the fence first. Malkin slipped through next. Then Lily, who pulled herself in tight to squeeze through the hole. Her scarf caught on a loose nail as she pushed through, and she snagged one of her gloves trying to free it, but finally she was on the other side with them.

They were in a derelict yard full of weeds and brambles that ran along the inside of the fence, filled with abandoned parts of subs and diving machines. Everything was tangled together, with arms and pipes and random pieces of metal sticking out from the snow.

Lily, Robert and Malkin crouched behind a massive metal tube that looked like it should be underwater, and peered round its side carefully, in case anyone might see them.

A pathway led through the tangle to the back of the warehouse and a second path snaked downhill towards a pier and the river further off. At the end of the pier was a spidery crane, its arm stretched out above the frozen expanse of the Hudson River. Chained to the end of the crane's arm was a metal ball, large as an electrical-wagon, that hung over the frozen river, like a metal moon. It was a diving submersible with propellers extruding from the back and large ballast tanks attached to each side. There was a commodious hatch in both the top and the base. Robert put his binoculars up to his eyes and read the two words painted on the submersible's side:

"That's the submersible from the newspaper." Lily checked the time on her watch. "Quarter to twelve." She gave a shudder.

"I don't think we should venture any further alone," Malkin warned. "We ought to just keep an eye out and wait for Kid Wink, Caddy and the other Cloudscrapers to bring John and the police."

But as he said this, they saw Dane and Miss Buckle come out of the house and head down the path towards the pier. Miss Buckle had Dane's wrist grasped in one hand and the engine in its wooden case clasped in the other. Lily shivered. Somehow, they had to wrest that machine and Dane away from her.

Miss Buckle and Dane walked along the length of the wooden pier and stopped beside the hanging submersible.

"What are they doing?" Lily asked, confused.

"I don't know." Robert stared at them through his binoculars.

The mechanical nursemaid let go of Dane's arm, walked over to a control panel at the base of the crane and pressed various buttons.

The crane swung over the frozen river, lowering the spherical *Diving Belle* down alongside the pier, until it smacked through the ice with a loud *KERRRACK!* The frozen surface of the water fractured into pieces as sharp and jagged as broken glass.

Miss Buckle pressed another button on the control panel and the crane released the chains that had been holding the *Diving Belle* up in the air. They trailed across the ice, while the unmoored *Diving Belle* floated in the freezing water by the pier. Miss Buckle climbed onto a ladder that ran up the submersible's rounded metal side and threw open the roof hatch.

"I think they're going to try and get in it," Robert said.

"Come on," Lily said, "let's get a little closer."

"All right then," Robert said reluctantly.

He and Malkin followed Lily as she sneaked along the path towards the pier, keeping as low to the ground as possible. As they crept beneath the crane, the cold in its shadow made Robert shiver.

Miss Buckle was carefully lowering the engine in its case down on a rope into the submersible, all the time watching Dane to make sure he didn't run away.

When she was done, she beckoned to the boy and he clambered up the ladder beside her, then disappeared through the hatch and down inside the craft.

Miss Buckle waited until Dane was safely inside the submersible, then shut the hatch over him, turning its handle to lock it.

Robert, Lily and Malkin shrunk back fearfully as she climbed down to the pier and strode towards where they were hidden. They barely had time to duck behind one of the legs of the crane as she passed by.

"What do you think she's returned to the warehouse for?" Lily whispered when she'd caught her breath.

"Provisions?" Malkin suggested softly. "Or to get someone else?"

"I thought you said you didn't smell anyone else?" Lily said.

"I could be wrong."

"When do you think she'll be back?" Robert asked, watching Miss Buckle as she retreated through the snowy yard.

"I don't know." Lily checked the time. "But it's five to twelve, which means we only have a few minutes to rescue Dane and stop the prophecy, if it is meant to happen at midday." She dipped out from behind the crane's leg and slunk along the creaking wooden boards of the pier towards the *Diving Belle*.

Robert nodded to Malkin. They had no choice but to set off in pursuit.

By the time they'd caught up with Lily, she was already at the submersible. She slung Malkin around her shoulders with her scarf and climbed the metal ladder.

Robert followed close behind.

At the top, they struggled to unlock the heavy hatch. It took all their strength to throw it open.

They peered down into the interior of the craft.

Dane sat in the centre of the cabin in the pilot's seat behind the ship's wheel and a long bank of controls facing a pair of round portholes. Behind him were four empty passenger seats and behind those, row upon row of enormous square battery units screwed into the walls, and a box that housed the engine.

Dane seemed dazed, fidgeting nervously with his fingers, cupping his hands together and breaking them apart, as if he had Spook to play with.

But Spook wasn't there.

They were.

Dane's eyes went wide when he saw them. "What are you doing here?" he asked, his face filled with surprise. "I thought we lost you on the rails yesterday?"

"We're here to rescue you," Lily said. "Do you need help getting out?" Malkin hung around her neck as she climbed down the interior ladder into the submersible, before holding out a hand to Dane.

Robert followed her down clasping each cold rung. "Quick," he said. "Before Miss Buckle comes back." He expected Dane to spring from his seat and follow them to freedom. Instead the boy shook his head.

"I don't need rescuing."

The alarm on Lily's pocket watch rang. She silenced it.

"What…?" she asked, trailing off. She didn't understand.

But Robert had heard him well enough. He had a sudden sickening realization.

"I said, I don't need rescuing," Dane repeated.

"What about Miss Buckle? She kidnapped you and forced you down here…" Lily's voice was rising. "It's twelve o'clock…remember the prophecy! Don't you want to escape her? Hurry!"

Dane laughed. A strange faraway laugh. "Don't you see?" he said. "There are no kidnappers. Miss Buckle didn't steal the Ouroboros Diamond. I did. And she didn't kidnap me or plan the ransom swap. I did all that myself. And now, I'm going to raise the dead."

CHAPTER 19

Lily's insides squirmed and her certainty dropped away. She glanced at Malkin, who had jumped down from her shoulders, and Robert, standing beside him in the cabin of the *Diving Belle*. The pair of them were agog with disbelief and staring at Dane.

"But why?" Lily asked Dane at last. "Why do all this?"

"It was the only way I could get my hands on the Ouroboros Engine." Dane's eyes strayed to the professor's wooden case, safely stowed under the *Diving Belle's* control panel. "I wouldn't have been able to get near it otherwise. My aunt never trusted me. She always took her machine with her in that case whenever she left the room. And she kept it and me under lock and key."

"So that's why Miss Buckle was waiting in the street the other night?" Lily asked. "You signalled to her from the hotel room by flashing the lights."

"Correct," Dane replied. "After that, the rest of the plan was set in motion… I made the ransom note by cutting out the letters from the newspapers in the bottom of Spook's cage. Then, after I was taken, Miss Buckle disguised her voice and spoke to my aunt on the phone. With all that, we were able to persuade her that she should come to the ransom swap and give us her case with the machine. Our plan was always to come here so I could take the machine down in this submersible and make my way back to the Shadowsea Submarine Base. It was all going so well, until you followed us onto the train. Luckily we managed to lose you again…until now. I guess this means you're coming with us."

"What could you possibly want down there?" Lily asked, aghast.

"My parents," Dane said.

Robert gasped. "Caddy's prophecy…."

Lily felt a chill. Of course. "You plan to wake your parents?"

"Yes," Dane said. "I didn't recall or even realize that my aunt's machine might make that possible, not till I met Caddy. Until then I'd forgotten everything. It was her prompting that brought back my memory of my parents. I miss them so, so much." His voice broke with emotion and raw tears. "Then I realized if I had the Ouroboros Engine, I could save them, bring them back from the dead."

"I promise you, you can't," Lily said gently. "Life doesn't work that way. It's too late already. That's what the prophecy meant…it was a warning. Your parents, they've been…they've been gone too long to return as they were. To try to wake them would only be… dangerous."

She stepped across the metal floor of the cabin towards him. "We've all lost people, Dane. I lost my mama and Robert and Caddy lost their da. Everyone loses someone in the end, and everyone feels lost and marked by it, and wishes they could bring those people back. But you can't change the past. And you can't change the cycle of life, the creation and destruction. It happens to everyone, no matter what. All you can do is learn to live with it." Lily put her hand over his.

"Please, Dane," Robert said. "Think again. Come with us." He gave Lily a sideways glance and together they tried to take Dane's arms.

"NO!" Dane shouted, brushing them away. "I will change *everything*. I will bring my parents back. Now I have the Ouroboros Engine, I will control life and death! And you can't stop me!" He pushed them away angrily. "MISS BUCKLE!" he cried, glancing up at the hatch in the roof. "WHERE ARE YOU? I NEED YOUR HELP!"

Outside they heard a loud scream. Caddy's scream.

Malkin snarled and raised his hackles.

"LET GO OF ME!" Caddy's shouts were accompanied by the heavy tread of Miss Buckle's metal feet ringing on the side of the *Diving Belle*. "Don't be concerned, Master Milksop, I'm back!" Miss Buckle called. "And I've brought another friend of yours with me."

Robert and Lily glanced up in time to see the mechanical nurse dangle Caddy over the open roof hatch and drop her in.

Caddy tumbled into the *Diving Belle*, grasping the interior ladder just in time to stop herself falling.

She clung on, swinging back and forth until her feet found a rung, and then she climbed down the few feet to the floor. She stood in a daze, clinging onto the headrest of one of the seats, her hair a-tangle, her face twisted with horror.

"What are you doing here?" Robert cried desperately at his sister. "We told you to go back to the hotel."

"I ran away from Kid Wink and came to find you," Caddy said, wincing.

"Why?" Lily asked.

"You forgot Spook. I had to bring him for Dane." She held the mouse out to the boy, and for a moment Dane didn't know what to do. Then he reached out tentatively and took Spook.

"Thank you, Caddy," Dane said, stroking the mouse. "I've missed you, Spook. I was so cross when Miss Buckle forgot to bring you." He glared up at Miss Buckle.

"I told you how sorry I was about that, Master Milksop. But we couldn't go back to the hotel again, not if we didn't want to get caught."

"Well, Spook's here now," Dane said. "Back with me where he belongs. Soon everyone I've lost will be back with me," he finished quietly as he put the mouse in his pocket.

Caddy, who was listening, finally seemed to understand that Dane had planned everything all along. "It's you, isn't it? You did this?"

"That's right," Dane said. "Close the hatch, Miss Buckle!"

"As you wish." Miss Buckle descended the ladder and reached up and shut the hatch above her, screwing it tight. She loomed scarily over Robert, Lily, Caddy and Malkin.

"Buckle them in, Miss Buckle!"

"Aye aye, Sir." One by one, Miss Buckle forced the children into the row of passenger seats behind. Then she closed and locked a cross-shaped seat-belt strap with a complicated buckle over each of their chests. When she got to Malkin, she pushed him into the chair and looped the belt around his neck, tightening it like a lead to keep him from snapping at her.

Caddy was last. "Please…" she said, looking up at the mechanical woman as she was grappled by the arm and strapped into the final spare seat. "You can let us go, you know?"

"I'm sorry, Miss Townsend," Miss Buckle said. "I'm afraid I can't do that. We're on a tight schedule to meet the tide."

Dane laughed. "Don't try to appeal to her better nature. I reprogrammed her to obey only me."

"How?" Robert asked.

"It was easy. I switched a few cogs around. It helps that she knows I'm doing the right thing – trying to reverse what my aunt did to everyone down there." He peered through the porthole, out along the river to the shadowy sea beyond. "Yes, I've had to do a few bad deeds these last few days to finally be able to get there…" Dane wiped a hand across his face, visibly emotional. "But you couldn't call me evil, not like my aunt."

"I didn't," Lily said. She could see she needed to stay on his side, and Miss Buckle's, now that she, Robert, Caddy and Malkin were strapped into the *Diving Belle* with them. As soon as Miss Buckle looked away, Lily struggled, desperately trying to loosen her seatbelt.

Dane placed Spook in his lap and checked the instrument panel on the dashboard in front of him. The needles were all in the black: full battery levels.

He turned an ignition key hidden beneath the steering wheel and the *Diving Belle* thrummed to life, her whirring propellers cutting a swathe through the dark water. As Lily struggled to try and undo her seat belt, Dane flipped a switch on the control panel and the craft's high-beam electrical headlight snapped on.

"Let's go see the sea." Dane flipped a second switch and the submersible began its descent. Shards of ice broke off the sides of the ship and bubbles fled past the dark portholes as the metal capsule travelled deeper and deeper, down into the shadowy depths of the river and the Hudson Bay beyond, swallowed by the frost-cold and endless sea.

CHAPTER 20

Robert, Caddy, Lily and Malkin sat strapped into their seats in the cramped cabin of the *Diving Belle*. Miss Buckle loomed behind them.

It had taken Dane a few hours piloting the craft to reach the pale desert planes of the seabed. Particles of white sand blasted the window in sparkling clouds, as he changed direction, propelling the *Belle* forward and skimming them across the bare lunar landscape of the ocean floor.

More hours passed. Lily had no idea how many. Miss Buckle had strapped her in so tightly she couldn't reach her lock picks or her pocket watch. All she knew was it must be late afternoon by now…or early evening?

The truth was there was no way of telling down here. The most important thing was it was long past twelve and they were still travelling, which meant that there was only one more moment left, according to Caddy's prophecy, when Dane could wake the dead: midnight.

If they could somehow turn the sub around before then they were in with a chance. If not who knew what would happen down on the Shadowsea Submarine Base. Lily closed her eyes, not wanting to think of what had happened last time the engine had been used on the base. Then she shook her head, and glanced around at the others, strapped into their seats. Their outlines glowed in the dark, illuminated by a weak red light from a single bulb at the back of the cabin's interior. Surely if they worked together, communicated, they could come up with a plan?

Malkin stared stoically ahead, taking in the view.

Caddy was shaking, trying to remain calm.

Robert bit his lip and clenched his hands into fists. His ears had popped as soon as their craft had reached the bottom of the ocean, and now each sound seemed far-off and echoey. He watched as the dials and pressure gauges embedded in the dashboard in front of Dane flickered to and fro, charting the power levels in each of the *Belle*'s batteries. At first, he had thought of nothing but escape, but now they'd descended so far, he accepted that there was probably no turning back.

Through the portholes, Robert glimpsed strange-shaped fish, plankton, jellyfish and octopuses distorted by the water, appearing briefly outside the glass then disappearing again. Ghostly aliens of the deep. Soon the green water became so tenebrous it felt as if they had ventured into a distant cosmos. Only the electric lamp on the front of the *Diving Belle* guided them onwards into the infinite darkness.

"This is all my fault…" Caddy said suddenly. "If I hadn't come back to find you…we wouldn't be here."

"Don't be silly." Robert smiled at his sister. She wasn't to know this was how things would end up. She was only nine, after all. "You're not to blame for this, sprout. You did what you thought was right."

"But it wasn't," Caddy said. "And now we're trapped down here with Miss Buckle and Dane." She gave a sniffle. "He's going to try to use the Ouroboros Engine and wake the dead on that Shadowsea Base at midnight and there's nothing we can do to stop him. But it won't work," Caddy whimpered. Then she shouted at Dane, "If you turn on that machine, Dane, then bad things will happen. Remember the chaos and death it caused when

Professor Milksop used it? That's what the spirits were warning me of."

"I'm no more messing with the dead than my aunt was when she brought me back," Dane said. "No more than your father was, Lily, when he brought you back from certain death. They both did it. And I intend to do the same, except I'll be doing it for my parents."

"Caddy's right," Lily said. "It won't work. When my papa brought me back," she went on, "I was only gone for a moment. And the same when Professor Milksop brought you back. Your parents, they've been dead a long time, weeks and weeks. Think how dangerous it would be to try and bring them back now."

But Dane wasn't listening. He was busy piloting the ship, following the Darkwater Oceanic Trench, which had appeared in the ocean floor, and ran like a long deep scar for miles and miles, outside their ring of light.

Finally, after more hours travelling, they saw a hulking shape of the Shadowsea Submarine Base up ahead, balanced on the edge of an underwater cliff.

The base was round in shape, half balanced over the seabed, half balanced over the edge of the trench. Passageways, like spokes of a wheel, ran from the exterior rim to a hub at the centre that was topped with a tower. At the summit of the tower was a turbine that rotated slowly in the underwater currents emanating from the trench. To Robert, it looked like a humungous rusted windmill.

"We've arrived!" Dane's eyes glinted white in the shadowy cabin, as if some bright hope was shining out from inside him. He cut the power to an absolute minimum and edged the *Diving Belle* around the gigantic base, casting the searchlight across the curved walls, as if he was searching for something.

In the viewport, Robert saw that parts of the base were unfinished. The ties that bound it to the seabed were still under construction, fixed with rope and cable, in place of iron trusses. The base bobbed slightly in place, barely connected to the ocean floor.

At last the spotlight found what Dane was looking for – a pair of adjacent airlocks for docking submersibles with metal hoops extruding from them.

Dane manoeuvred the *Diving Belle* into a position where she might dock with the Shadowsea. He fiddled with a joystick on the control panel and a crane arm popped from a hatch on the base of the *Diving Belle* and sprang to life.

Pushing his seat over from the steering wheel, Dane

managed to turn the external arm outwards and open its claws. The arm grasped one of the metal hoops on the side of the Shadowsea and pulled them closer in, gradually aligning them with the pair of hatchways on the larger ship.

Using the arm as a lever, Dane directly aligned the hatch atop the *Belle* with the left-hand exterior hatch on the side of the Shadowsea. His arm shook with the stress of performing such a delicate manoeuvre. But, finally, they were lined up perfectly.

Then Dane pressed a button on the far side of the instrument panel and a metal tube extended from the side of the *Diving Belle* and clamped itself over the Shadowsea's hatch.

"What is that?" Caddy whispered to Robert.

"I think it must be the airlock," Robert replied, with a shiver. "It creates a passageway between this ship and the Shadowsea."

Dane flicked another switch on the dash and there was a humming sound. As the airlock began to expel water from its chamber, bubbles spun around the viewport windows, their edges laced in silver light from the headlamp's beam.

The external pressure-gauge indicator on the wall panel flickered encouragingly. Dane switched off the engines of the *Diving Belle* and the lights on the instrument binnacles blinked into darkness, leaving only the single weak red light from the interior lamp at the back of the cabin.

Dane turned to Lily, Robert, Caddy and Malkin. "Welcome to the Shadowsea," he said. His face glowed red and his voice brimmed with a crazy tinge of hysteria that made Robert draw back in horror. "Miss Buckle, make ready to go aboard!"

"Aye, Sir," Miss Buckle replied, and she reached out her long arms to undo the hatch to the airlock. There was a hiss as the rubber seals came loose and the door opened inwards.

Dane stepped past them towards the door. His eyes glistening with excitement, he signalled eagerly to Miss Buckle to bring the others.

With a shudder, Robert stared from beneath the rim of his cap at Lily's pale face and Caddy's and Malkin's concerned dark eyes. The mechanical nurse freed each of them in turn from their bonds and forced them from their seats, out through the hatch of the submersible into the rubber and metal passage of the airlock. Whatever horrible things were hidden on the other side of it, Robert knew with an unnerving certainty they would soon be revealed.

At the far end of the airlock was a barnacled wheel and a lever that opened the door into the Shadowsea Submarine Base. Slowly, Miss Buckle yanked the lever downwards then wrenched the heavy wheel anticlockwise. There was a screech as the stiff rusted wheel began to turn, followed by an ominous creak, as the door swung open, revealing a mouth-like entrance, cold, dark, still and uninviting.

Electric lights along the walls strobed on and off in sickly patterns and the smell of something unpleasant drifted from inside, as if the base had bad breath.

As Miss Buckle and Dane ushered them onwards through the door, the floor seemed to sway and shift beneath them. The binoculars swung around Robert's neck and the hairs on his arms pricked up. The movement and the stench gave the place a horrible living feel, as if they were walking into the metal guts of some monstrous angry sleeping whale. He had no idea what their final destination would be, but he knew in his heart that something horrific was destined to happen aboard this base.

CHAPTER 21

Lily placed her feet carefully on the shifting floor, stepping through the hatch into the submarine base. The smell of the place assaulted her. It stank worse than the London sewers. Stagnant water, damp mould, rotten fish and…something else… Rank and pungent, like overripe fruit mixed with the smell of rotting meat. The wretched stink wafted on a cold wind from deep inside the base and it took a moment for Lily to realize what it was…

The stench of death.

It made her want to gag.

She wrapped her scarf around her face, covering her nose and mouth.

"Come on! Keep moving." Dane hurried her, Robert, Caddy and Malkin further into the submarine base.

Lily surveyed Robert and Caddy in the pulsing light. A curl of disgust twitched on Robert's lips; a flash of horror in Caddy's eyes.

"I'm with you," she whispered to them both, giving them a comforting smile. She held up her crossed fingers. "When I give the signal, we throw water over Miss Buckle and the machine to short-circuit them, then we force Dane to take her and us back to the *Belle*."

Robert and Caddy both crossed their fingers to show they understood. Malkin, who was stood at their feet, wiggled his whiskers to show he'd heard too.

"Quiet!" snapped Miss Buckle. She was bringing up the rear, her hulking body blocking their escape, her right fist clutching the handle of the wooden case containing the Ouroboros Engine.

"You know, you could still take us back any time you liked and everything would be all right," Robert said to her and Dane.

"Not for me it won't," Dane replied, his face crumpled in pain. "My ma and pa died down here. I'm gonna revive them using the Ouroboros Engine. Because what's the point of such machines if you can't save the ones you love?"

Lily watched as Dane peered through dark doorways, at cabin rooms filled with overturned tables and chairs. She assumed he was looking for some semblance of his past life here, and part of her wanted to help him, but another part of her just wanted to escape this place as soon as possible. She was terrified of what they might find.

Something dripped on Lily's bare head. She glanced up at pipes running along the ceiling above. Water seeped from their rivets in a misty spray, sloshing over their shoes in places.

"This clanking place is worse than New York," Malkin snarled, padding through the shallow puddles. "Up there my cogs only threatened to freeze to a standstill from ice and snow. Down here they'll rust to a stop instead, from all this seawater."

"Hush, Malkin," Lily whispered. She picked him up and slung him round her neck to stop the water soaking through his fur and footpads.

Dane ignored their protestations and Miss Buckle, clanking along at the back of the line, merely ushered them onwards through the flooded corridors. With her long legs and thick metal body, she didn't need to be concerned about a little bit of water. She seemed strong as iron, but Lily still couldn't help hoping that the dampness might make her malfunction so they could grab Dane and sneak back past her.

The further they got into the tunnels, the more Lily's scars itched. The drift of the base was more prominent and pronounced here, and with each step the floor seemed to be shifting beneath them.

They passed the hub, where all the passages met. At the centre of it was a large generator that hummed and pulsed with electricity. The vents on its side groaned as if the whole thing was on its last legs.

Further on they happened upon a room filled with damp, bulbous diving suits that stank of the sea and heavy looking oxygen tanks. Beyond the tanks and suits they glimpsed a hatch leading towards the exterior of the ship. It was painted with a sign that read: AIRLOCK.

Then there was the abandoned galley kitchen – all the pots and pans and plates thrown about and smashed on the floor. Lily couldn't bear to think of what hideous things might've occurred in there, and she didn't want to stop and find out.

Robert secretly checked his compass, trying to get a sense of their direction. He hadn't been sure if it would work underwater, or with all the generators and magnets around, but it seemed to. They were heading south, it turned out. So, if they had to get back by themselves, he knew which way to head. He wondered what their final destination was, and how on earth he was going to get himself and his friends out of this petrifying predicament.

Finally, they reached a point where the entire passageway was flooded. Dane waded through the knee-deep water and swung around, examining the various options. "Which way?" he asked Miss Buckle.

"That one, Master Milksop," she said, indicating the right-hand passage. "The Reanimation Lab's down there."

They set off again. The strobing lights illuminated discoloured patches on the metallic walls, where barnacles and blisters of rust bloomed like flowers on the cross-beams and rivets. The smell worsened and the air in the corridor developed an unpleasant aftertaste, like when you drink stale water that has sat somewhere for a long time and there's a dusty, metallic tincture to it.

At last, they arrived at a room full of empty rodent cages.

"This is the place I saw in my vision," Caddy whispered to Lily and Robert.

The water in here barely rose above the level of their shoes, perhaps because the doors were made of such heavy metal and Professor Milksop had shut them when she left. At the far end of the cage-room was a lead door with a sign on the front that read:

REANIMATION LAB

DANGER! KEEP OUT!

Above those words was stamped a picture of an ouroboros snake, curled into a circle eating its own tail.

Dane pushed open the door and stepped through. Their hearts in their mouths, the others followed. Miss Buckle, ticking quietly, still carried the Ouroboros Engine.

The strobing lights revealed a space that was a nightmare to behold.

A metal table, cracked tiles and a bucket in the corner, an observation booth, and in the rest of the room, bodies. The bodies of the crew were strewn around the lab, as if they'd been dragged in here.

Lily's stomach heaved at the sight of them lying there. So many people... Each had worked on the Shadowsea, each had been someone's mother, father, brother or sister, and each of them was gone. She'd meant for them to try and make their escape here, while Dane and Miss Buckle were distracted, but the horror of what she saw pushed the idea right out of her head.

A sudden keen and sickening sense of her own mortality shot through her, and she put her hand on the wall to steady herself. Her knees shuddered and her legs felt brittle beneath her. The sharp shock of fragility that jolted through her seemed almost as if it might lift her off the ground.

She gazed weakly over at Robert and Caddy. Caddy was stiff with fright, her twiggy hair flattened against her head with sweat. Robert shook uncontrollably. Even Malkin round her neck shivered. Lily could feel the cogs beneath his fur all a-jitter. "We shouldn't be here," he spluttered. "This place is a tomb. Everyone's been dead for weeks."

"Ever since the accident," Robert said aghast. "When was that, Dane?"

Dane thought about it. "I-it was around Thanksgiving... all the folks down here were getting ready to celebrate. That was the day I named Spook, made a cart for him."

"That's over a month ago," Malkin said.

"Really?" Dane asked.

"Yes, really," Lily said.

It seemed as if Dane was finally listening to them. Taking in what they were saying. Or was it the state of the bodies that made him think about what he was doing? Desperately, tearfully, he searched the faces of the slumped figures. "Where are my parents?" he asked, holding Spook tight against his chest. "I can't see them."

"I know you think you can find them," Lily said softly. "But they're not here. Not really. They're just bodies. Your parents, everything that made them who they were, that's gone. But you have your memories of them," she gently added. "Good memories. Better memories than this…"

But finally, Dane spotted them. He fell to his knees beside them and clutched at their hands. He put his palm on each of their cheeks, but their skin was cold and grey. Their eyes vacant. "After the accident," he said sadly cradling their hands, "my aunt brought them in here to use the machine to try and revive them. She failed. Spook and I were her last successes before she decided to evacuate the base with her machine and pretend none of this ever happened. I wish it hadn't. And now I've a chance to right that." He wiped his eyes and, setting his parents' palms down carefully on the floor, he turned to Miss Buckle. "Set up the machine," he said.

"Yes, Master Milksop." Miss Buckle placed the wooden box on the table in the centre of the room and unlocked it with a key to reveal the Ouroboros Engine within. A silver box, peppered with valves and rubber-coated wires, all twisted snakelike together. The four lenses on the front of the engine reflected the room in their unflinching gaze.

With great difficulty, Dane dragged himself away from the bodies and stared at the engine. He clutched his head, as if he was trying to remember what had happened last time it was used. "If the machine worked on me," he said, "then it should work on my parents…" He trailed off.

"I-I'm not so sure." Lily stared uncomfortably at Dane's lost parents. Thin and skeletal, they no longer resembled the living people they must have once been. She thought then of her own ma, gone too. And of Papa and Selena, up on the surface. It had been more than twenty-four hours since she, Robert and Caddy had seen them. She hoped that Kid Wink and the other Cloudscrapers had told Papa where they were and that he and Selena and the police were looking for them now.

Papa had been right, as usual. They should never have got involved in any of this, none of them. But she couldn't help it – she had wanted to befriend Dane, to answer his plea for help. And despite all that had happened, she still did. She still thought there was a chance to change Dane's mind.

She couldn't let him turn the machine on, not after all Caddy's warnings about the dangers it would cause. Either it would kill Dane and her, Robert and Caddy. Or if it did wake the dead, she had no idea what they would become. Despite the sorrow she felt for Dane and what he was going through, she couldn't let that happen.

She held up her crossed fingers and nodded to Caddy and Robert to let them know that now was the time to fight back. Dane was about to start up the engine, when Lily took Malkin from round her neck and threw him towards the boy.

The fox bit hard on Dane's arm. While Dane was trying to fight him off, Lily threw her scarf around Miss Buckle to confuse her, and Robert grabbed the bucket from in the corner and scooped up water and threw it at the machine, trying to short-circuit its power. He threw a second bucket at Miss Buckle hoping it would still her clockwork, or interrupt her programming long enough for them to make an escape...but it did not.

Miss Buckle tore Lily's scarf away and shrugged the water off. Then she swung round and seized Caddy, grasping her by the neck.

Caddy kicked out. Robert rushed to try to wrestle her from Miss Buckle's grip.

Dane scrabbled over to the observation booth and, throwing the door open, he wrenched Malkin from his arm and cast him inside.

"Put them in there!" he shouted at Miss Buckle, who thrust Caddy through the doorway next and then Robert, slamming the door to imprison them both.

Lily saw that her friends were trapped. She hesitated, wondering what to do next. She was about to try and make a second solo attack when Miss Buckle loomed over her, her eyes glinting red once more and then she saw that all was hopeless.

She gave up and threw up her hands in surrender. Miss Buckle took her arm and led her to the observation booth, and when she opened its door, Lily stepped willingly into the room to join her friends.

Miss Buckle stood in the open doorway of the booth, arms folded, guarding the four of them, making sure they didn't try to escape and do anything else. Robert stared desperately past her, into the room, at Dane as he fiddled with the machine. "What time is it?" he asked Lily quietly.

Lily took out her pocket watch and flipped it open. "Quarter to twelve. Fifteen minutes to New Year's Eve."

Robert took his cap off and picked at its rim. "Fighting might have failed," he muttered. "But there's still persuasion. We've got fifteen minutes left to change Dane's mind."

He was right, Lily realized. There was still reason left to try.

"You don't need to go ahead with this, Dane," she called out desperately to him.

"Please don't," Caddy shouted, joining her. "Can't you see? What you're doing is wrong. It can only cause more death and destruction."

"We know how you feel, Dane," Robert chimed in. He took a shaky breath. "When my da died, it felt so unfair. I felt like John Hartman had the technology to save him, but he didn't. I couldn't understand that in Da's case, it was already too late. You can't bring someone back who's been dead that long. They're truly gone."

Lily felt a sudden heart-wrench at this. She hadn't seen it before, but it was true – if things had been different, maybe her papa could have saved Robert's da. But in the end it had been too late.

"Robert's right," Lily said to Dane. "With me and with you, there was only a brief window to save us. I don't know what'll happen if you try to use Professor Milksop's Ouroboros Engine to bring back people who've been dead for so long."

"It may not work," Caddy said. "Or worse, they might return as something else."

"Or it might hurt us all, Dane," Robert added.

Dane shook his head. "No," he shouted back at them, his voice shrill and jaggedly off-kilter. "None of that is true. I can bring my parents back just as they were. And then we'll be together. My aunt's engine will work. If it woke me, it can wake them. I think I remember how to set it up." He unwound a heavy-duty wire from the back of the machine and screwed the end of it onto some sort of power point nearby.

Through the porthole windows in the lab, Lily glimpsed the black ocean beyond, where the massive underwater turbine was spinning like a giant windmill. The deep-sea currents were still turning its metal sails, which meant it was still creating electrical energy.

Dane had nearly finished setting up the machine. He adjusted the lenses so that they were aimed directly at his parents. The last thing he did was walk over to Miss Buckle and to take the Ouroboros Diamond from the teeth of the snake necklace around her neck. Then he returned to the table and slotted the stone into a gap in the machine's interior workings.

"There," he said, his voice wavering. "The last piece of the puzzle. Now we just need to open a connection between the turbine and the machine to bring them back."

The boy paused, staring at the dead figures of his parents. Lily could see he was finally questioning his choices. Could he really return them to life? Would they be the same as he remembered if he did? Doubt filled his face.

"Don't do it, Dane," Lily called, her voice breaking with emotion.

"I can't turn back now," he said. "I have no choice. I have to get my parents back…"

He stepped past Miss Buckle and joined the four of them in the lead-lined observation booth, the only place safe from the electrical rays of the machine. Miss Buckle shut the heavy door and Dane turned a dial on a circuit board in front of him.

There was a crackle of energy and Lily heard a hum as the electrical current ran through the Ouroboros Engine. The lights in the room flickered ominously as more and more of the electrical current was diverted away from them into the machine.

"The circuit's working, Master Milksop," Miss Buckle said.

"I know," Dane replied happily. He flicked a switch on the board and in the reanimation lab beyond the lead wall, Lily heard the Ouroboros Engine come to life, as the power from the turbine outside flooded through the base's generator and into the circuits of the machine. Energy was pulsing through the device and it practically shivered on the table.

Dane pressed one last button on the control panel. Staring through the narrow glass observation window, Lily saw thin skeins of blue lightning flicker from the four lenses of the Ouroboros Engine and earth against the bodies of Dane's parents. But it didn't stop there. It spread to all the other bodies around the room, and back again to the machine. As the lightning crackled, the humming of the machine grew more violent, gathering strength.

"Cover your eyes," Dane advised. "Don't look directly at it. It's about to complete the process."

Lily, Robert and Caddy did as he'd commanded. Malkin was curled up at Lily's feet.

Even with her hands pressed over her screwed-up face and her back to the narrow slit of the window, Lily still saw the explosion sizzle like a tangle of snakes. Jagged slices of ghostly blue light flooded the control cabin, illuminating everything. They flashed across her retinas and sparked inside her mind – the briefest flash of the brightest storm she'd ever seen.

Lily scrunched her eyes tighter and felt the electrical energy from the Ouroboros Engine melt away and dissipate in a wave through the ship. Afterwards, she could still hear it hissing in her ears, a horrible static sizzling, like when you reached the end of a long-playing wax cylinder on the phonograph and the only sound left for the needle to pick up was scratches and dust.

She opened her eyes, and found she could see nothing.

At first she thought the sudden flash of light had blinded her, then she understood.

She was in real darkness. The power had been sucked away from the rest of the base by the machine and the lights had blown for good in the explosion.

A soft moaning was coming from somewhere outside the lead door of the observation booth. And creaking. Something was alive out there.

Many things… And they were moving about.

The moaning became a clamour, and gradually that clamouring got louder and louder.

"What is it?" Robert's voice whispered from a few feet away in the dark.

"I-I don't know." Lily felt about in her pocket for the Wonderlite Kid Wink had given her. Pulling it out, she opened the lid and flicked the flint. A flame sprang up at once, illuminating the booth. Lily saw the fear in the others' faces, gathered around her.

Dane's expression oscillated between trepidation and hope. "Do you think we did it?" he asked Miss Buckle, stroking Spook, who was squeaking worriedly in his hand.

"I'm not sure, Master Dane," Miss Buckle answered.

"You mean, do we think *you* did it?" Malkin corrected.

"He didn't," Caddy said softly. She turned and appealed to Lily. "He didn't do it, did he?"

"I-I'm not sure," Lily said. She held the flame of the Wonderlite up to the porthole window and motioned to the others to look too. Together they peered through the thick safety glass into the pitch-black lab…

It didn't seem as if anything was moving in there.

Lily held the Wonderlite up higher, pressing her nose right against the glass.

The others gathered closer, doing the same.

Vague shapes shifted in the blackness.

Something *was* moving…

"I can't…" Lily said. "I don't see—"

SMACK!

A bloated face smashed against the window, its mouth a gaping cavern. It gazed with wild fury through the glass.

Caddy shrieked in terror as more figures joined it, crowding in on the far side of the glass. The reanimated faces of the crew. Now revived.

"It worked!" Dane cried joyfully. "My parents must be in there too." He scrambled towards the door.

"Wait! Don't go out there!" Lily cried. "It might be dangerous."

But Dane wasn't listening. He pulled the door wide and raced into the lab. Cursing Dane's idiocy, and holding the Wonderlite aloft, Lily and the others hurried after him.

A handful of the corpses that had been lying on the floor mere moments ago were standing upright, clustered by the window to the observation room, swaying from side to side. They twisted slowly towards Lily and Dane, and stared at the flame of the Wonderlite.

The rest of the bodies, which were still strewn about on the lab's floor, now started to move too. Life rattled back into them, filling each body in turn, until one lifted a skin-and-bone arm…

The undead squirmed slowly, grasping at the floor as they clambered to their feet and joined their already upright friends.

Then, as one, the entire group began to shuffle towards the dancing flame of the Wonderlite.

Lily didn't know if it was that which was drawing them, or if it was the flickering flame of life inside her and Dane.

CHAPTER 22

Robert held his sister back as they watched the zombified corpses lurching about the laboratory. The submarine city had awoken. The slouching undead staggered about, knocking things off tables and bumping into walls. Their eyes were empty, and their mouths were open in hideous grimaces. Their hair was patched and moulting and their shrivelled skin clung to their bones, visible through the gaps in their torn and damp clothing.

Whatever they were, they were no longer human.

"The Ouroboros Engine's brought them back!" Dane cried. He slipped quickly between the swaying figures. None of them had the look of the real people they'd once been, and none of them seemed able to recognize him.

"Where are my folks?" he asked, his voice tight with despair as he searched for the spot where his parents had just been lying. "They were here."

At last, he found them, or at least the zombies who used to be them. They were almost indistinct from the others now, no longer his parents, except in memory. He tried to approach them, tried to put his arms wide around them for a hug, but instead they smacked against him, bouncing away as if he was no different to the wall or the table or anything else in the rest of the room. "W-what's the matter with them?" he asked, tearfully.

"They're all wrong," Robert muttered.

"They're not there," Lily whispered. "They haven't come back to life properly." She waved the Wonderlite at the zombie figures.

"They may have been woken from death," Malkin growled. "But that doesn't mean they're truly alive. Their bodies – their brains and organs – will have been dormant for so long that they can't possibly be the same as they were before. They haven't the capacity to think like humans. Nor like mechanicals. They're husks of their former selves…"

"I feared this," Caddy whispered. "It's what I was afraid of."

"I'd better recover the Ouroboros Engine, Master

Milksop." Miss Buckle stepped over to the table at the centre of the lab and began fiddling with the engine, undoing the leads to turn it off.

Dane was still trying to get the two zombies who were his parents to recognize him. But there was no light behind their eyes. Finally he gave up, holding them by their shoulders, one then the other.

"Why can't you see me?" he cried. "Why can't you see I'm here?"

Lily noticed that his parents' expressions were slowly changing, but not in the way Dane wanted. She could see a mindless agitation growing behind their eyes.

They raised their arms, their fingers twitching, but Lily pulled Dane away from them before they had a chance to grab him.

The rest of the zombie horde shuffled towards them, moaning angrily.

"What are they doing?" Robert cried.

"It's like a primitive defence mechanism," Malkin said.

"What have you done? You've made them angry!" Lily snapped at Dane.

The woken dead were lurching straight towards them.

"Back in the observation booth!" Caddy cried, and they all tumbled back inside, pushing the heavy door closed behind them.

Lily shielded the Wonderlite flame with her hand so only a dim glow slipped between her fingers, then they sat there, breathing heavily: Caddy tearfully hugging Robert, Lily clutching Malkin. Dane was holding Spook carefully in his shaking hand.

"Miss Buckle!" he cried suddenly. "We left her in the lab!"

Robert felt sick. He watched through the observation window. The reanimated zombies who had gathered just outside it stared at Miss Buckle, still going about her task unplugging the Ouroboros Engine and attempting to pack it away.

Something about her movement was slowly raising their ire. Lily held the Wonderlite to the window. In its flickering light, she and the others stared in horror as the tangled group of zombies approached the mechanical nursemaid, converging for the attack.

Miss Buckle stopped what she was doing and stood facing the horde. She was strong enough to throw the first few creatures off, but soon there were too many.

"Master Dane, help me, please!" Miss Buckle shouted in a strangled yell, turning this way and that, hitting out at them with her long arms. She could barely hold them off.

The zombies roared and raged, attacking her from all angles, showing no fear or care for the damage to her or themselves. The life in her seemed to fill them with embittered anger.

Lily and Dane and the others rushed to the heavy door, trying to pull it open again. To get out there. To help save her... But she was already engulfed in the angry swarm. Submerged beneath their enraged bodies and lost from sight, and before they could even get the door open, there came a monstrous, mechanical scream of distress.

Lily shuddered with horror. The Wonderlite shook in her hand. She gritted her teeth against the cries. To hear Miss Buckle howl like that was awful. The noise went on and on like the brakes on a steam-wagon, until Lily thought it might never end.

Suddenly, the yelling stopped, and when the zombified figures moved away, Miss Buckle was no more, reduced to a pile of broken machinery.

Lily's eyes smarted with tears as she stared in shock at the mess. Even though she had fought against them, even though they had been adversaries up until only a few minutes ago, Miss Buckle had only been trying to do the right thing by Dane, just like Lily's own mechanical friends did right by her. She didn't deserve such an awful end.

Robert glared appalled through the window at the scattered pieces of the mechanical. It was a ghastly way to go, but by now they could do nothing to save her. He shuddered, gripping his fingers tight into two tense fists. Was that what would happen to them if they tried to sneak past the zombies? Would they end up like that too? How were they ever going to get out of here in one piece?

Dane slumped down in the corner, his shoulders hunched and his body wracked with sobs. "Miss Buckle's dead," he wailed. "Destroyed. It's my fault. It's all my fault." He was pale, grinding his jaw, breathing hard. "But you, you pulled me to safety. You didn't have to, after the trouble I caused."

"It's what anyone would do," Lily muttered in shock. "What makes us human... What makes mechanicals too," she added sadly, thinking of poor Miss Buckle. "And hybrids. Anything that feels the pain of others." She wiped the sting from her eyes and stared out of the porthole at the wandering zombies.

They weren't human. And they didn't care. If she and her friends were to get out of here in one piece, they had to find a way to get past them.

"It was a mistake to come here," Dane said, stroking Spook, who was clasped in his hand. "Foolish to imagine I could bring my folks back and they'd be like they were before."

Robert felt a surge of anger. They'd told Dane that. Tried to stop him. Then he remembered his own da and how much he missed him. He would've given anything to see him one more time. His fingers found the Moonlocket round his neck. "You can never return to the past," he said. "Not really."

"I thought *I* could," Dane replied. "My aunt resurrected me and Spook and that makes us different." He stared with a frown at the little mouse and then at Caddy, who was stroking Malkin in her lap. "But you, Caddy, you saw the truth of it. And Robert and Malkin, you believed. And you, Lily, you *knew* that truth in your heart." He stared at her. "You came back from the dead too, didn't you? We're not like anyone else, you and I. Not like those creatures out there... Why are they that way? Why can't they remember?"

"Perhaps," Lily said, "forgetting is for the dead, and remembrance is for the living. Or perhaps the only reason we remember is because we were gone for such a short time. Perhaps it was the shock of coming back." She thought about that. "One thing I do know, if I hadn't seen my mama on the other side, if she hadn't reminded me of who I was, and to keep fighting, I don't think I would've returned to life. Your parents, Dane, if they could speak to you now, they'd say the same thing."

"I dunno why I came back," Dane said. "There's nothing special about me. Truth is, I've barely slept since I did. I'm afraid my dreams'll pull me into the afterlife. And, now that I see them, I'm afraid I'll turn into one of those creatures too." He brushed a hand across his face. "It must be horrible being half-alive, like that. Not quite gone. Craving the life you once had, but not being able to return to it."

"Yes," Lily agreed. "But whatever happened to us, it's not the same as what happened to them. We're alive and that's a privilege. We owe it to ourselves to keep on fighting for that life." She crouched beside Dane and took his hand, holding the Wonderlite up between them. "Hope is strong. And I…" She paused, and glanced at the others. "I mean, we…we've hope enough for you, and for everyone."

Dane smiled at her then, for the first time in a long time, but, even as she said it, Lily wondered if that small glimmer of hope they carried together would be enough.

CHAPTER 23

L ily sat in the semi-darkness with her back against
the door, holding the Wonderlite out in front of
her. Its flickering flame lit up the observation booth. She
listened in dread to the quiet groans and clanging as the
zombies bumped against the outside of the booth, while
she tried desperately to think of a plan to get them out of
there. She could hear the creatures' feet sloshing through
the water – it was beginning to pour into the lab. The base
must have started flooding faster since they'd arrived.
Perhaps their docking and entrance onto it had partially
broken the airlock, which could only be bad news.

Robert and Caddy were arguing quietly beside her.
Malkin gave them an occasional angry, panicked woof.

Dane sat further off, lost in his own thoughts.

Lily closed her eyes for a second. She drifted, then jolted awake. Whatever happened, no matter how late it got, she couldn't fall asleep. Not until they were all safely out of here and back at the surface. She had no idea how that could happen. "We need to come up with something," she told the others. "And soon."

"What time is it?" Robert asked.

Lily took out her pocket watch and flipped the lid. "Twelve-thirty."

"Half an hour into the New Year," Caddy said. "Happy New Year, everyone!"

"Oh, yes," Malkin snapped, grizzling at the ends of his green coat. "Happy New Year! We're only thirty minutes in and already the three of you have helped this idiot boy reanimate a set of vicious undead underwater zombies. Well done. Well done indeed, all of you. What a stellar start to eighteen-ninety-eight!"

"I'm not an idiot boy!" Dane complained.

"And we didn't help him raise the dead," Caddy said. "He was going to do that anyway."

"All right," Robert said. "Why don't we all just try to look on the bright side—"

"What bright side?" Malkin interrupted. "There is no bright side. There's just zombies."

"Well," Robert said, "I, for one, think that the year can probably only get better from here on in."

"Don't you mean worse?" Malkin growled.

"All right," said Lily. "That's enough. We're going to have to work together to get out of this one." She couldn't believe how much they were at each other's throats. Being down here did that to you, she had noticed. In the hours they had been underwater, it was as if a confusion had settled over her like a fog, and it felt like there was no day or night, just shadows and sea.

She still didn't know how they could get out of the observation room and back across the base to the *Diving Belle* without the zombies attacking them, but they would have to make a move soon if they wanted to beat the flooding.

Suddenly there was a far-off scratching and the screech of voices. The quiet chatter of the others on the far side of the room fell silent. They were listening too.

Then Lily heard a furious rattling.

Through the porthole she glimpsed the rotting form of a zombified figure. It was bent forward, trying the doorknob.

Lily jumped up and frantically checked the lock. They had locked the door, thank clank! The zombies wouldn't be getting in.

Caddy snuggled against Robert in the dark. "It's silly really," she said, her voice tinged with worry, "but just to be close to you feels like protection."

"Did you see that?" Lily whispered to everyone. "Something's happening. What are they doing?"

"Trying to open the door," Robert muttered.

"But that's impossible," Caddy said. "They're barely alive. How can they remember how to open doors?"

"Perhaps they're gathering their memories back," Malkin suggested. "Maybe their bodies have some residual recollection of moving around this place."

"Do you think that means they'll remember me after all?" Dane asked hopefully. "My parents..."

Robert shook his head. "I don't think so."

Lily spoke with urgency. "We need to get past them if we're to get back to the *Diving Belle* and make it to the surface before this entire ship floods." As she said this, she heard a *drip, drip, drip* in the room they were in.

They all looked up to see new trickles of water leaking in through the roof panels.

"If we don't find a way out of here soon past those crazed corpses," Lily said, "then we'll all drown."

"The *Diving Belle*'s right at the far end of the base," Robert replied. "We'll never get all that way with them chasing us."

"And if they catch us who knows what they'll do," Caddy said.

"Perhaps if we wait long enough, they'll wander off and we can make a break for it?" Dane suggested.

"The only way that's going to happen is if someone can create a distraction," Lily said, and she stared straight at Malkin.

"What are you looking at me for?" Malkin said.

"You're the perfect one to do that job," Lily said.

"Oh, no."

"Yes, you are," Robert said. "They can smell the life in us. They want it. But you, Malkin, you're the fastest and the smallest – they're less likely to notice you until you want them to."

"That mouse is smaller," Malkin said.

"He's not going anywhere." Dane clutched Spook to his chest.

"You're more intelligent than Spook is, Malkin," Lily told the fox. "You can sneak amongst them and they won't even notice you. Then, when you get further down the corridor, you can make a loud noise to draw them away."

"That's the stupidest plan I've ever heard," Malkin snapped. "And that's bearing in mind that you've involved me in some seriously stupid plans in the past – jumping out of airships, wading through sewers, sneaking around flying circuses full of scary clowns, and all at your behest. But, this, *this* is the dumbest plan of all. This plan really takes the dog biscuit."

"It's the only thing we can do," Lily told the fox. "We'll open the door really quickly and you must slip out. But remember, don't let them see you. You saw what they did to Miss Buckle."

"That's precisely why I'm not doing it," Malkin said. "Besides, the water's rising out there and you know I can't walk through it. It rusts my insides."

Before Lily could respond, Dane butted in. "It's all right," he said. "Maybe you won't have to."

They turned to see him fiddling with something in the corner. It was a box on the wall with a transmitter, a receiver and a numbered keypad.

"What is that?" Lily asked, holding up the Wonderlite and approaching him.

"It's the base's internal intercom," Dane explained. "To relay messages from one place to another. It's like a telephone only without an exchange. You can punch the number of the speaker you want your message to come out of and you can call any other point on the base."

"So?" Robert said, fiddling with his cap.

"So, those things are attracted to noise – maybe,

when they hear it, they'll go and investigate?"

"It's worth a try, I suppose," Lily said. "But does it still work?" She was thinking of the blown lights. "If the generator's down, won't it be out too?"

"Don't worry," Dane said. "There's an emergency power system. A smaller backup generator. It cuts out the lights so it can keep the comms and the life support systems running for as long as it can. I think that's what's happening, which means there's still some power."

"How long is 'as long as it can'?" Robert asked with a gulp.

Dane shrugged. He didn't know. He dialled a number on the keypad beneath the transmitter, then pressed the confirm button. The intercom let out a static hiss.

"See?" he said. "Now, everyone stand behind the door," he commanded. "As soon as they wander towards the sound, you're going to have to open it and we'll all make a run for it."

"Good idea," Lily said. "Let's do it."

Robert shook his head. "It won't be enough."

"Why not?" Dane asked.

"It'll only distract them as long as you're here to call into the machine. Once we leave the room the noise'll stop and the zombies will turn around and come straight back this way."

"Wait!" said Caddy. "I know how we can make it work."

She had found something else. A phonograph on a wheeled stand that was pushed into the corner. Beside it was a stack of wax cylinder records. Incongruously, one of them was even printed with a picture of Miss Aleilia Child. It must have been a recording of her singing!

Dane's eyes lit up. "Of course, I forgot those were here. Matilda used to play music to her test subjects, or to herself and Miss Buckle. They always loved listening to singing while they worked."

Caddy pushed the phonograph over to the intercom, and positioned its horn against the intercom transmitter. Then she loaded up one of the wax cylinders. Lily and the others watched as she started to wind the handle of the machine to make it work.

"Someone still needs to be here to hold down the button on the transmitter," Dane said.

"Not if we wedge it," Caddy said. "Everyone look around for something to do that with."

They all searched the room quickly. Lily found a first-aid box in the corner with a red cross on the front, which was full of splints and bandages. She took the longest splint she could find and wedged it against the button on the transmitter.

Meanwhile, Dane dialled in the number for one of the other speakers on another part of the base. Caddy had finished winding the phonograph. She placed the needle on the cylinder and, a moment later, the first strains of classical music echoed from far away on the other side of the ship, followed by Miss Child's operatic singing voice…

The zombies began to edge away from the glass porthole in the door, their heads snapping round as they searched for the source of the sound. Gradually, as the crackling record went on, the music grew louder. Slowly, the zombies twisted and shuffled off in the direction of the noise.

Robert watched with bated breath their dark shadows drifting away through the binoculars until they were all out of sight.

Lily's heartbeat was jagged in her throat. She peered around the door and waved the Wonderlite around, checking that the lab room beyond was really empty.

"Ready?" she asked the others, the word coming out in a hoarse whisper.

Caddy shook her head. "I-I don't know if I can go. I'm still scared."

"There's no choice," Robert said. "We have to take this chance to survive." He put a comforting arm around his sister's shoulder.

Dane hid Spook carefully away in his coat, while Lily picked Malkin up and draped him round her shoulders again so he wouldn't have to walk through the water outside. Then she opened the door and the six of them crept out into the lab.

It was empty. They could hear the zombies down at the end of the corridor, clamouring towards the music.

Lily started sloshing as quietly as she could through the water towards the door, but something hard bumped against her shoe. She held the Wonderlite down by the floor and felt around in the murk. The thing glinted beneath the surface. She pulled it out.

It was the Ouroboros Diamond, cracked from the energy that had passed through it, but somehow still in one piece.

Lily stuffed the diamond in her pocket, then rose and beckoned to the others.

"Come on!" she whispered. "Let's go."

They crept through the lab door and into the room beyond filled with empty cages. Lily couldn't see much, beyond the ring of the Wonderlite in the dark.

Out in the corridor she held it aloft and waved it around.

"Careful," Malkin growled. "Don't burn me with that!"

"I won't," Lily whispered. The flame from the

Wonderlite seemed to last for ever. She thanked her lucky stars that Kid Wink had given it to her earlier. She would recommend the thing to everyone once they got out of here… *If* they got out of here…

As they walked down the corridor, the ghostly strings of the orchestra and the voice of Miss Child echoed around them. Robert took out his compass and checked the needle. North. They were headed back in the right direction.

Lily wondered how long the phonograph recording would play for. Would it keep the zombies occupied, or would they realize it was a hoax? Wax cylinder recordings like that one usually only ran about five minutes. "Stay close, everyone," she whispered, and they moved as quickly and quietly along the corridor as they could.

They reached the end of the passage and passed the generator room at the hub of the base, where they heard different-sounding groans coming from within the walls. It must've been the complaints of the emergency generator.

"We'd best hurry," Lily said, holding the flame of the Wonderlite aloft to light their path as they waded through the knee-deep water, following the steady stream of chill stale air that wafted up the shifting passageway.

Finally, they arrived at a place where the passage

dropped sharply downward and the entire corridor in front of them was flooded like the surface of a lake.

"We're just going to have to keep going," Lily said. Clasping Malkin closer against her chest, she scrutinized the deep lake of seawater spread out across the passage in front of them. "It's the only way out of this mess."

She, Robert, Caddy and Dane, who'd put Spook in his breast pocket to keep him safe, waded deeper into the water. It reached much higher than when they'd walked this way before on the way to the lab – now it was at chest height. That meant the water was rising even faster than that time they'd been stuck in the London sewers. Why did they always seem to get into these pickles?

They rounded the next corner and Lily's heart sank. Ahead of them was a set of closed doors. Robert slammed against the door and shook it. It juddered, but refused to open. Something heavy must've washed against the other side and jammed it shut. "We have to go back," Lily exclaimed.

"And do what?" Robert asked.

"Find a different route," Lily replied. "There should be another way. The base is circular. There must be plenty of other passages that will still take us back to the *Diving Belle*."

"I don't think—" Malkin said.

"Hush!" cried Caddy over their discussion. Something was up…

Suddenly, Lily noticed that silence had descended on the ship. The music that had been wafting through the corridors had finished. And now it was gone, the only things they could hear were their own voices and the splashing water pouring in through the cracks above.

They waded back towards the point where the water had got deeper and climbed across a bulkhead to a shallower, dryer part of the corridor beside the central generator room.

Then Lily heard the undead, scrabbling closer.

Suddenly one appeared around the bend in the corridor. Its clothes were ragged and rotten. It held out its hands, clawing at the air with green and discoloured nails, and gave a hideous cry. Soon others lurched around the corner to join it. Their crumbling and decaying bodies crowded together to block the path, and Lily perceived with a giddy certainty that there was no way past them. The base swayed beneath her, the floor shifting under her feet. Was this it? The end of everything?

CHAPTER 24

The passage was blocked by deepening water and the tightly-jammed door in one direction, and by zombies in the other. What were they to do now? How would they get out of this? If only there was time to think, perhaps Robert could work something out.

One by one, the zombies began wading towards them. Robert peered at their angry faces, his pulse quickening. The zombies' eyes were shrouded in darkness, their mouths dragged open in terrifying breathless silent screams.

Lily glanced about. There was a room off this passage a bit further up, whose door was wedged ajar. "Quick!" She motioned towards the room. "In there."

They squeezed into the room, as the zombies closed in. "Now shut the door!" she commanded.

Robert goggled at her in alarm. "We'll be trapped," he protested. "With no way out!"

"It's all right," Lily said, with as much calm as she could muster. "I have a plan."

She pointed at the diving suits and oxygen tanks hanging on hooks in rows behind them. They were swaying slowly from side to side with the movement of the base. Robert suddenly remembered that they had passed this room and seen them on the way in. Lily must've recalled that and the airlock beyond the room. It was a way out! But only if they put on the diving suits and tanks and stepped into the ocean...

The zombies were still wading through the rising tide, down the corridor towards them, getting steadily closer. Robert, Caddy, Lily, Dane and Malkin all pushed against the door. It slowly ground closed against the knee-deep water, which sloshed the other way. They got it shut just in time.

The door had stopped the zombies, for now. There was an emergency lamp on the table, Lily's hands shook as she lit it with the Wonderlite. She tried to ignore the quavering dread inside her and focus instead on something practical.

"We have to get into these," she said, pulling down one of the diving suits and a tank from a hook. She nodded at the far door. "Then we'll step through the hatch, open the airlock, exit the ship and go around it on the outside," she explained as she hurriedly started to clamber into the diving suit.

Robert shook his head. "It's too dangerous. I can barely swim."

"Me neither," Caddy said. "We have to find another route."

"There isn't one," Lily said. "This is the only way back to the *Diving Belle*. We'll just have to swim together as best we can."

"We won't need to," Dane said, stuffing Spook deeper into his pockets. "There's a rail that runs along the outside of the Shadowsea. It was so the crew could clip themselves onto it while they were building the base, bolting the parts together. If each of us hooks our suit onto that rail we can pull ourselves safely around," he explained. "That way it won't matter if you can swim or not."

"I can't go," Malkin said. "Mechanical foxes don't do well underwater."

"We're not leaving you behind, Malkin," Robert said.

"Don't be concerned about me," Malkin replied with false bravado. "I'll be fine. I suppose this is goodbye." He gave a brave woof. "By all that ticks, it's been nice knowing you. If there's a space for mechanimals in the afterlife, I hope to meet you there."

"NO!" Lily said, her voice fierce. "You're coming with us. We'll tow you behind in a spare suit." She pulled one off its hooks and tightened the belt in its midriff to stop Malkin falling through into the feet. Then she placed him in the top half. It held him like a cradle, and Malkin stuck his head out of the fish bowl helmet, watching as Lily and the others climbed into their own suits. He looked mighty strange, held in the centre of the man-sized suit. It was lucky though that being a mechanimal, he didn't need an oxygen tank like the rest of them, because there wasn't one to spare.

The rest of them finished putting on their diving helmets and strapped the heavy tanks to their backs. There was a gauge that attached to the suit arm with a needle in it painted with luminous radium to glow in the dark, so you could see how much oxygen you had left. When they were finally all suited up, they struggled through the knee-deep water to the hatch at the far end, Lily dragging Malkin by the empty leg of his suit.

"This should lead to the airlock beyond this room that will take us out into the sea. But we have to be careful," Dane said. "We all need to open it together."

They climbed through into the airlock and closed the hatch to stop the room behind them flooding. Then Lily reached for the rusted lever on the hatch, but Robert tapped her on the shoulder.

"Wait!" Robert cried, the words echoing off the inside of his heavy metal helmet. "There's another problem!"

He could see Lily staring at him through the glass of both her helmet and his. She was frowning deeply. "What is it?" she asked.

"How are we going to get in at the other end? If we try to enter the *Diving Belle* directly from outside it'll be flooded with water before we can even climb aboard."

"Clank it, you're right!" Lily cursed. "We'll have to go back aboard the Shadowsea first and enter the *Belle* that way. Can we do that?" She looked to Dane.

Dane nodded. "There are two docking airlocks on that side of the Shadowsea, remember?" he said. "The one the *Diving Belle*'s attached to and a second, emergency airlock next to it. We can go in through that one. From there we'll be able to cross back into the *Diving Belle* the same way we left it, without flooding her..." he said, glancing at the leaks that were already filling the room they were in.

"That's if we're quick," Lily said. And she directed them all to the rusted lever once more.

It took all of Robert, Lily, Dane and Caddy's combined strength to push it downwards and open the door. Soon, they were engulfed in pitch-black water, as one by one, they struggled out the far hatch that led to the open sea…

Silence.

The deep water muffled all noise.

After the screeches and groans of the submarine city, Lily found the quiet a blessed relief.

They crawled through the darkness around the outside of the Shadowsea Submarine Base, clinging onto the maintenance bar and feeling their way along the curve of the walls in an anticlockwise direction.

Lily was out in front. She had tied Malkin's suit to hers with a length of rope before they'd swum through the hatch and now he floated behind her, bobbing along in his man-sized diving suit. Lily thought it was probably the first and only time she would be towing a mechanical fox deep-sea diving. She wished there was enough light to see him. She could sense the others behind her. Robert and Caddy, then Dane last, Spook snuggled somewhere in his suit. They inched along in line, heading back round to where the *Diving Belle* was docked on the Shadowsea's far side.

The going wasn't easy. The water pressing against their suits kept their movements slow and heavy, and the air inside Lily's helmet tasted warm and metallic, the atmosphere as thick as treacle.

As they rounded one section of the base, Lily jerked to a standstill.

The sea in front of them was filled with brightly glowing fishes, floating together in one vast group that seemed to go on for miles. Their luminous fins were bright as knives, their scales glowed like shimmering armour and their eyes sparkled like diamonds. The fish seemed identical, each one no bigger than her little finger, plain looking and as sharp and pointed as a piece of flint. As individuals Lily imagined they probably wouldn't be able to light up anything, but together, in their enormous school, the thousands of them glowed bright as the sky at night, shining like a field of shooting stars.

Lily's heart soared and she forgot her own predicament as she stared in wonder at the darting glowing fish. She had never seen anything quite so beautiful in all her life. They seemed almost miraculous. There were, she realized, greater things than herself and her friends in the wild corners of the world. Things to whom the water was not a danger, but home. Things that glowed with hope. Even in the darkest places, working together, life could find a way.

She looked to Malkin and Robert and the others bobbing behind her and gave them a grin through the glass of her diving helmet.

All of a sudden, Lily had an unexplained sensation of standing on the edge of a deep drop. She gazed down beneath her feet. There was the immense chasm of the Darkwater Trench, the abyss stretching out beneath her. The fish were floating above it in the current. Warning her and the others they had been going the wrong way! The *Diving Belle* was in the other direction! She held her hand up to Robert and the others, pointing back past the airlock the way they had come.

She saw a flash of terror on their faces in the faint bioluminescent light.

A moment later, the fish flickered away, leaving them in darkness once more.

They retraced their steps carefully, feeling their way once again in the dark. Lily was last in line now, and Dane at the other end of the pack was leading the way, taking them all in a clockwise direction this time. Soon the sensation of walking along a cliff edge disappeared and Lily knew she was back on safer ground. She recognized the feel of the airlock leading to the suit room as they passed it and realized they had been out here a long time, a little too long which meant…the oxygen!

Lily examined the oxygen gauge on her arm, the needle glowing in the dark. The tank was almost empty. Lily's pulse quickened in sickening terror at the thought of running out of air, as she imagined ending up as another body at the bottom of the ocean. She wished they hadn't wasted time going in the wrong direction. Now she only had about five minutes of air left. The other three must be in the same situation.

She mustn't panic, she realized, that would only make her use her oxygen up quicker. She tried to calm herself, taking slow deep breaths and concentrating on her path ahead in the dark.

Finally, with a wave of relief, she saw a faint red light up ahead.

Lily had never been so glad to see anything in her entire life.

It was the interior cabin lamp behind the *Diving Belle*'s porthole windows and it glowed like a weak sunset moon, leading them on.

Dane hastened towards it, and the others followed.

Step by step, the light from the lamp grew bigger. As Lily and the others approached it, she saw that the *Belle* had tipped sideways, and she realized that the base must have too. Its moorings were loosening. Lily glanced back over her shoulder to see that the entire base had shifted, drifted. Now more than half of it was perched over the edge of the Darkwater Trench. If it continued to fill with water, and drift as it was, soon the moorings would snap altogether and, with the entire thing weighed down with water, there would be nothing left to stop it tumbling into the deep-sea trench. They had to hurry, get away as soon as possible.

The needle of Lily's oxygen tank was nearly at zero now. She pushed the others forward, driving them faster towards their destination. Malkin floated behind her attached to the rope.

Finally, they arrived at the *Belle*'s window. Beside them was the hatch that led to the secondary airlock on this side of the Shadowsea base. With Dane, Robert and Caddy, Lily fought to open the hatch and they tumbled through into the airlock beyond, scrabbling around as water filled the chamber, they fought their way to their feet and pushed the hatch shut behind them, shutting the light and the open sea.

Lily pulled a lever and they waited as the room drained of water.

Then she wrestled off her helmet and breathed in the air in great cool gulps. The rest of them did the same. It was rancid, but at least it was breathable.

They struggled from their diving suits and threw

them to the floor. Caddy wiped her face and Lily pulled her tangled scarf from her suit, while Robert took his cap from his pocket and lodged it firmly back on his sweat-drenched head. Dane checked his jacket to see that Spook was still in his pocket and still all right.

"We made it in one piece," he said, brushing a clump of sweaty damp hair from his face and kissing Spook's nose.

The four of them helped Malkin, lifting him from the cradle of his improvised diving suit. The fox scrabbled out of his rubber, metal and glass prison, and sniffed disgustedly at the rest of the pile of discarded suits and helmets. "About clanking time that was over!" he complained in the darkness. "I *NEVER* want to go diving again!"

"Me neither," Caddy said.

"Nor me," Robert said, his teeth chattering.

But Lily only thought of her moment of grace with the fishes. She took the Wonderlite from her pocket, flipped the lid and spun the wheel. In a shower of sparks, the flame sprang to life once again. Even the trip through the water hadn't dampened its wick.

"At least those things won't be able to follow us here," Caddy said. "So we can take a breather."

"I don't think so," Robert said. "Did you see how much

the base was tipping? And how much it's been shifting about since we've been here? I reckon, with all the water it's taken on, it might be about to break free of its moorings."

"You noticed that too!" Lily said with a shudder.

Robert nodded. "We'd best hurry," he said. "I don't think we have much time."

With Dane's help, they opened the opposite door of the airlock and found themselves back in the corridor of the Shadowsea station, on the far side of the blocked door. Robert could see now that a fallen metal truss was wedged against it. Beyond it was the flooded passageway, and the trapped zombies. They'd had to make their way around the dangerous outside of the base to bypass all those hazards, but they wouldn't have got through any other way.

Lily held the Wonderlite out and surveyed their surroundings. There was no flooding here, only the few puddles of water they'd brought in with them through the airlock from the sea outside. The rest of the corridor was clean and dry and they were just a few feet down from where the *Diving Belle* was attached to the ship.

"Come on," Lily said, beckoning to the others.

Together they opened the door and stepped through into the *Belle*'s airlock passageway. Robert went first, followed by Caddy, Lily and Malkin. Dane hung back in the corridor, watching the others as they struggled to turn the lock on the *Belle*'s roof hatch. Finally, with Lily, Robert and Caddy yanking and pulling as one, and with a little help from Malkin's jaws, they got it open.

Malkin tumbled straight in, landing on the floor of the *Diving Belle*'s cabin like a cat. Robert went next, holding out his hand so that Caddy could follow behind him.

Lily waited at the hatchway for them all to get safely into the submersible. She looked back over her shoulder. Dane was still standing in the Shadowsea's corridor. It was almost as if he didn't want to leave.

"You next," Lily called out to him.

Dane glanced down at Spook in his hand and shook his head. "I'm not going."

"What?" Lily asked.

Dane peered down the dark corridor, back into the deep tunnels of the Shadowsea. "My parents are still here somewhere."

Lily put a hand on his shoulder. "You can't save them now," she said softly. "They really are gone."

"And I'm here. Still living. How is that fair?"

"I felt the same way when it happened to me," Lily said. "And the answer is: it isn't. It isn't fair. But it's how things are." She felt a little teary as she said it, thinking of her mama gone too, and Robert's da, and all that had come to pass since those great losses. "It's true, we get older, keep living. And you think they don't see all that, think they don't experience it with you. But they do, in here." She touched her heart. "The ones we've lost, they may be gone from the world, they may be gone from time, but they're eternal now. Their life is complete, but yours is not. There's so much more for you to see… Things no one else has seen yet. Luminous, shining, miraculous things."

"Like those fish…" Dane said. His eyes sparkled as he stroked Spook in his palm.

"And all kinds of other fantastical, amazing visions," Lily said. "We came back, Dane, and that's a gift – a blessing not many get. You can make your life anything you want it to be, once you decide to throw yourself in and live it to the full. That doesn't mean you have to forget the past, or those who lived there. The best way you can honour it, and them too, is to go on living." She took his arm. "Now come on. There's someone waiting for you, up in the world."

"Who?" Dane asked.

"Your grandmother," Lily said. "I read in the paper that she was looking for you."

"I think I remember her," Dane said slowly.

Then he climbed through the hatch into the airlock, and down into the *Diving Belle* and, with relief flooding through her heart, Lily followed him.

CHAPTER 25

When Lily hopped through into the *Diving Belle*, Dane was already at the controls. Malkin sat beside him, his tail thumping nervously on the floor.

Lily, Robert and Caddy slammed the roof hatch closed behind her and twisted the wheel to lock it shut.

Dane pulled the release lever so that the *Diving Belle* detached from the Shadowsea, then he locked the steering wheel dead ahead, and engaged the *Diving Belle*'s engines. When he was done, he reached into his pocket and put Spook beside him up on the dashboard, before reaching across to ruffle Malkin's ears.

Lily gripped Robert's hand tightly in her own, staring

through the porthole at the disappearing Shadowsea Submarine Base.

Water was pouring into it freely now and it would surely soon break free of its moorings and tip over into the Darkwater Trench. There was nothing anyone could do to stop that. Who knew what was down in that trench, or if the base would survive the fall intact. It was destined to sleep with the fishes and all the strange creatures at the bottom of the ocean. Sights no one in this life or any other had seen. Gone but not forgotten.

"I wish Miss Buckle could've made it out too," Dane said softly as the base floated further from view. "She didn't deserve an end like that. And neither did my parents. But thank you for saving me," Dane continued. "For helping me get out." He gave everyone a tiny smile. It was all he could muster, but it was enough for Lily to know that, despite everything, eventually he would be all right.

She put a hand on Dane's shoulder. "You asked for our help, remember. It was the first thing you said to me in the hotel. You must've believed there was hope when you did that. And you came to the right place, because none of us ever lets a friend down, do we?"

She grinned sideways at Robert and Caddy, who had put their hands on Dane's arm too. "We do not!"

Malkin said, answering for all of them, and offering Dane a paw.

Lily laughed. With everyone close together, she and Dane were engulfed in a warm hug.

Lily basked in it. The tension that she had felt wound up inside her heart like a watch spring the whole time she had been on the Shadowsea suddenly dissipated and she felt free again. Dane should never have tried to use the Ouroboros Engine. But Lily could see why he had. If someone had offered her the chance to bring her mama back, she knew she would've taken it too.

But you couldn't cheat death like that. Not Dane's way or Professor Milksop's. And not Papa's way either, at least not without a great cost. And you couldn't really turn back time. But that didn't mean you couldn't carry a part of the ones you loved with you. They were eternal, always at your side, in every decision you made and every choice you took, and in that way you would never truly lose them, and they would never truly lose you.

As the *Diving Belle* picked up speed, gliding away along the ocean floor, the five of them broke apart from each other and climbed into their seats and, with Dane at the helm and Spook by his side, they headed for home.

The journey wasn't easy. For many gruelling hours they worked together to pilot the *Diving Belle* back towards New York, the submersible gradually emptying the ballast tanks as it rose on a slow and steady upwards gradient.

According to Robert's calculations with his compass, and Dane's navigation points marked out on the oceanic map, they had less than an hour to go. They might finally reach home!

All of a sudden, the dials monitoring the *Diving Belle*'s battery strength dropped into the red zone.

"The power's running out, Dane. We have to surface at once," Robert cried. They had been so close! But they had no choice. If they continued on their course, the power would fail, and they would fall to the bottom of the ocean once more.

Dane pulled a lever and the ballast tanks began a full evacuation of water as the *Belle* powered upwards.

Lily stared through the porthole as the *Belle* broke the surface. The sea around them was choppy and as soon as they broke the surface, they were buffeted about in the circular cabin. The waves threw them this way and that and they drifted with no power to turn the rudder or steer by. Without their props to keep them afloat they had little chance; if they weren't rescued soon, then they would sink.

Malkin cowered beneath the control desk, which Dane was gripping with white knuckles, while Caddy clung onto the wall, and Lily and Robert held on tight to the ladder.

"I don't know how long I can keep her afloat in this storm," Dane said, scooping up a shivering Spook. "We need to send an emergency message. Does anyone know how to work the radio telegraph?"

"I do." Robert stumbled across the rolling floor to the ship's miniature radio telegraph transmitter and flicked the switch on its front. He supposed they could have tried to use it before, but he'd heard they usually only worked on the surface of the sea for submersibles, not during a dive.

As the machine sprang to life, Robert tapped in the international emergency signal with the finger pad: SOS. Normally you would add your latitude and longitude coordinates as well, but Robert didn't know what those were, so he left them off and just hoped that the message would be enough for someone to find them.

"Now what?" he asked, when he'd finished tapping in the letters.

"Now," Lily said, "we wait and hope that someone hears our signal and comes to the rescue."

"Then we aren't out of the woods yet?" Caddy asked.

Lily shook her head. "No," she said. "It doesn't seem like it."

It was true, Robert supposed, this could all still be the end of them. Lost at sea. "Maybe I should try the SOS signal again one more time, just in case," he suggested.

"Keep sending it out, until we get a reply," Dane said.

Robert kept it up. Tapping in the SOS over and over again as the waves tossed them from side to side...

After what seemed an age, the receiver lit up and beeped out a message in response. Robert translated the code as it came in: "'This is the USS *Swallowtail* of the New York City Lifeguard Patrol Airship Fleet. We are tracking your signal. We are nearby. What are your coordinates?'"

Lily, Malkin and Caddy looked elated, but when Robert turned to Dane, the boy looked pale with unease. "We won't be able to give our coordinates," he said. "The radar's not working."

"They'll never see us from the sky in this storm," Caddy said, the elation draining away from her face as fast as it had come.

Robert knew she was right. Without their coordinates, the life-ship might miss them totally, and if they didn't hurry then the waves battering against the side of the life-ship might pull the submersible back under the waves where they would sink and be lost for good with no chance of rescue.

"What can we do?" Lily asked Dane.

"I have an idea," Dane said, rooting through an emergency tool cupboard beneath the control panel. After a few minutes he pulled out a flare gun.

"The emergency flare!" Lily exclaimed. "Clank it! Why didn't I think of that? It would've been good against the zombies."

"But then we wouldn't have it to fire now," Caddy said.

"You're right," Lily said as Dane handed her the flare.

"You should do it," he said. "I get seasick."

With the flare gun tucked into the belt of her dress, Lily climbed the ladder to the external hatch. Robert, Caddy and Dane reached up and helped her push it open, while Malkin offered some encouraging barks from beneath the control panel desk.

Outside, mountainous rolling waves were breaking against the round metal crown of the sub. Lily crouched in the doorway and aimed the flare gun up to the grey sky above. Then she pulled the trigger.

The flare shot upwards in a bright arc of smoke and light.

Lily ducked back inside and watched it through one

of the viewports as it exploded into a sparkling red firework, like a flame against the sky. Afterwards it dropped, letting off a plume of red smoke that hung in the air above the *Diving Belle*.

Robert hoped that the USS *Swallowtail* would spot their marker soon, before the storm winds blew its smoke away.

Flecks of seawater broke over the crown of the sub and came tumbling in as Lily pulled the hatch closed and climbed back down into the iron belly of the sub. "Well," she said. "That's the flare gone. Let's hope they see it."

They waited, Robert desperately scanning the skies with his binoculars.

Minutes passed in horrible anticipation…

Then, over the clattering raindrops pounding on the roof of the *Diving Belle* and the waves crashing against her side, they heard another sound. The *THUP-THUP-THUP* of an airship propeller.

Through the uppermost viewport, they glimpsed a bright orange zep with USS SWALLOWTAIL - NYC *Lifeguard Patrol Airship* written on its balloon. It hovered in the air above them, buffeted this way and that by the wind.

Through his lenses, Robert saw the hatch in her side open and a man in a flying helmet, goggles and a yellow rubber windbreaker lean out. He began unfurling a rope ladder that was attached to the edge of the zep.

The chain-link ladder fell downwards and with a *CLUNK*, the bottom rung hit the metal roof of the *Diving Belle*.

"Quick," said Lily and she threw open the exit hatch once more and climbed up onto the roof. The others followed her. Robert pulled his cap down tight over his ears, and scrambled behind everyone, bringing up the rear.

By the time he got to the top of the *Diving Belle's* ladder, water was pouring in through the hatch opening and he had to fight against it. Lily took hold of his hand and pulled him out onto the submersible's roof.

"CLIMB!" she ordered over the gurgles and glugs of the sinking *Belle*, the roar of the wind and waves and the loud whirring of the zeppelin's props.

The binoculars swung heavily around Robert's neck. He stared upwards.

The others were already on the rope ladder, hauling themselves towards the USS *Swallowtail*. Caddy was first, carrying Malkin around her shoulders. She had almost reached the top of the chain ladder and the lifeguard was waiting in the gondola's open hatch to pull her aboard. Behind her was Dane, with Spook in his pocket.

Lily stepped onto the lowest rung, her striped scarf billowing like a flag in the spray. Robert joined her, clinging on tight to the ladder as it waved in the wind, and letting Lily take the lead up to the next rung.

Below him the *Diving Belle* was sinking beneath the waves. Its open hatch gurgled as it sucked in gallons of raging seawater. As he climbed, he wondered why everywhere they went they ended up somehow scaling ladders in and out of airships.

A few minutes later, he and Lily were at the entrance hatch to the *Swallowtail*. The others had already clambered inside. The lifeguard hauled Lily aboard and then him too.

The man pushed them down the corridor to join the others, and for the second time in the last few hours, Robert and Lily embraced everyone in relief.

They were all aboard and finally, properly safe.

The man rolled the ladder up and slammed the hatch shut. He pressed a button on the wall and a bell rang through the airship. It must've been the signal that the rescue was complete, for the airship took off from its hovering position. Through the window, Robert glimpsed the last porthole of the *Diving Belle* sink beneath the ocean. Then the zep's propellers change direction and, with a slow about-turn, it began to fly north.

"We've been searching everywhere for all of you," the man said as he draped blankets around them and escorted them through the corridors of the airship. "You were reported missing to the police two days ago by your parents. Then we got a lead on your location yesterday, after a bunch of kids who work at your hotel contacted the police. Your folks are just through here."

He brought them into a cabin where their parents were poised on the edge of their seats, nervously waiting, along with Kid Wink and Inspector Tedesko, and an older woman in a thick woollen coat.

Instantly, everyone sprang to their feet and rushed over to gather round them.

Papa barged past the others and grabbed Lily and Robert in an enormous bear hug. "Lily! Robert! You're alive! And Malkin, you're still ticking!" he said kissing them both on their cold cheeks and rubbing the mechanical fox underneath his chin.

"Thank goodness you're all all right!" Selena seized Caddy, squeezing her close, and then Robert, and then Lily…even adding Dane to the scrum for good measure.

"I'm so clanking pleased to see you!" Kid Wink babbled. "Happy eighteen-ninety-eight!" She took each of their hands in turn. "You missed the greatest ever New York New Year's fireworks show. Five boroughs' worth – they were amazing! But forget about that, I'm just glad you're safe!"

"It's mostly thanks to your invention." Lily took the Wonderlite from her pocket and passed it back to Kid Wink. "If we hadn't had this to shine a light in the darkness, I don't know how we would have survived."

Kid Wink grinned and flipped the Wonderlite over in her hand, its silver case glinting in the light. "Pretty swell, ain't it?"

"Sure is!" Dane said. "It lasted hours and hours. I don't reckon I could've created anything better myself, and I love inventions!"

"Thanks." Kid Wink stared at him. "Is that the kid from the hotel?" she whispered to Lily. "He looks different. Much...better."

"It is!" Lily said. "Dane Milksop, meet Kid Wink. She's the one to thank for there even being a ship here to rescue us!"

"Hey, Kid," said Dane, shaking her hand. Then he noticed the old woman, who was still seated at the back of the cabin, and his eyes suddenly went wide and his face lit up with memory and joy. "Grandmom?" he said. "Is that you?"

343

"It sure is, honey." The old lady stood slowly.

She put her arms around his shoulders, enfolding him and, as she did so, Dane burst into tears. "I forgot I had you, Grandmom. I forgot everyone."

"Well, I didn't forget you, Dane," she said. "Not for one moment." She brushed her lips against his forehead and when Dane took Spook from his pocket to show her, she gave the mouse a kiss on his nose too.

"What happened to you down there?" Selena asked, clasping Robert and Caddy tight. "You look terrible."

So Robert, Caddy, Lily and the others told their story, as briefly as they could, for they didn't want to scare the adults with the horror of what they had seen, and they knew that there would be more questions to answer later.

But they told the gist of it and when they arrived at the waking of the dead and the death of Miss Buckle, it elicited looks of alarm and upset from everyone present.

"It is a harrowing tale," said Inspector Tedesko when they'd finished. "An awful predicament, but thank goodness you escaped with your lives."

He shook Lily's, Robert's and each of their hands gratefully; even Malkin's paw. "You're darn brave, the lot of you. I'm only sorry we didn't believe your story in the first place, when it was just this young girl's vision and prophecy." He smiled at Caddy. "If we'd done as you'd

said back then, then none of this would've happened…"
He trailed off for a moment and gaped at them, horribly
embarrassed, but then brushed it away as if it was
nothing. "Still," he said, with somewhat false bonhomie.
"All's well that ends well, as your greatest poet was fond
of saying."

"Are you a fan?" Papa asked, beaming brightly. "I've
recently become interested in his works myself."

"Only the comedies," the inspector said. "You see,
I can't bear anything with a tragic ending! I prefer the
happy ones."

"Oh, I almost forgot." Lily pulled something from
her pocket. "I have Miss Child's diamond – it's a little
cracked, and the necklace is gone, lost at the bottom of
the ocean, but we managed to recover her stone."

The inspector took the gemstone from her and
examined it. "Thank you," he said. "I shall see that she
gets it, and, I am sure, when she does, she will be singing
your praises!"

"Goodness," said Papa. "In all the furore, I never
remembered to book tickets for her show!"

Lily, Robert, Malkin, Dane, Kid Wink and Caddy
crowded into the observation room of the USS *Swallowtail*

as the airship approached the city. Selena stood behind Robert and Caddy with her arms around them both. Papa had Lily by the hand and Malkin by the scruff of the neck.

Dane stood hugging his grandmom. She had come to the police as soon as she realized that Nathaniel Shadowsea had no answers about what had happened on his base. Then the police had taken Professor Matilda Milksop in for questioning a second time and the whole story about what had happened to Dane, his parents and everyone else down on the Shadowsea had broken wide open. Now Matilda was under arrest, awaiting trial, and the whole mess of the situation was beginning to be unravelled.

There would, of course, be lots more questions for Dane and Lily and the rest of them to answer about what had happened on the undersea base last night, what Professor Milksop's engine had done and what they'd seen, but for now they just stared out of the window at the view and beamed elatedly at one another, ecstatic to be alive.

Robert watched his ma and Caddy seated beside him – Caddy in particular. Since the start of this adventure she had felt like a true sister to him. Seeing her upset and comforting her had made him realize that perhaps she needed someone to look out for her, as well as their ma. He'd even started to think that maybe, when all this was over, he could stay here with her and Selena. But after all Lily and John had done for him, could he really do that?

Robert's eyes strayed over to Lily, her freckled face reflected in the glass filled with relief and joy. If he stayed in America, he would miss Lily so much, and Malkin and John too.

No, he didn't think he could do it. But perhaps, in the long run, there would be a way to keep everyone together, at least in his heart.

It was like Lily had told Dane, about his parents – about all those who were gone, like his da or her ma: just because you were apart from someone, just because you missed them, just because they were gone for a little while, or even for ever, it didn't mean that a part of them wasn't always with you in everything you chose to do.

As the airship began her descent through the clouds, Robert glimpsed New York City bobbing closer for the second time that Christmas holiday. The city felt almost as if it was floating towards him.

Like Selena and Caddy stood beside him, Robert had yet to really see all sides of it. But it was growing on him, and there was so much more of the city and the country that he wanted to take in. He was looking forward to exploring New York and Boston with his ma and sister while they were still here, and then, he would go back home to Brackenbridge with Lily and John. That was still his home, there with them, the place where he belonged, he reflected, as the airship sped on through the rainstorm, back towards New York.

CHAPTER 26

The next morning, quite soon after breakfast time, Lily finally began to feel like she had recovered a little from her ordeal. It was funny how a good night's sleep and some warm food and friendly company could turn things around.

Lily, Robert, Caddy and Malkin took the elevator up to the sixth floor to visit Dane and his grandmom in their new suite. The pair had been given a room at the hotel for free, after all that had happened. Today there was a different operator running the elevator and different maids cleaning the rooms, because Kid Wink and the rest of the Cloudscrapers had been rewarded with a week's paid leave to celebrate their part in securing the safe return of Dane, Robert, Lily, Caddy and Malkin.

When they arrived at room six hundred and one, they knocked three times and waited for Dane's grandmom to let them in. She was all smiles as she opened the door. And when Lily and the others stepped into the suite, they saw that much else was different too. The curtains were drawn back to let in the morning sun and this room felt less oppressive and somehow lighter than room one hundred where Dane had been shut up by Professor Milksop.

Dane was sat at the table in the sitting room, dressed in a new suit. Spook was curled up asleep on the tabletop, while Dane busily worked on a set of sculptures and inventions with the tools his grandmom had bought for him. He'd placed a photograph of his parents on the mantelpiece, beside a photograph of him with his grandmom that she'd brought with her from home. So he was surrounded by family.

"How did you sleep last night?" Lily asked him.

Dane smiled. "Better than in a long time," he said. "I'm still sad. Still missing my parents. I'll never forget 'em, but at least now I don't think that it should've been me instead."

Lily thought of the conversation she had had with Papa a year ago that had been almost the same.

"I've realized something from this whole adventure," Dane said to her. "Somehow I've resigned myself to all that has happened." He paused and stroked the little mouse's ears as he surveyed them all. "I know now that the past can't be changed. It was my mistake to think everything could be put back to how it was. All that's gone."

"Gone but not forgotten," Robert said. "You can remember your folks and try to do things that make them proud. And you can grieve for them and miss them. But you can also live on and, with them always in your heart, go out into the world and find out what the future has to offer."

"I like that," Dane's grandmom said happily. "It's a good philosophy. I've been so glad to have Dane back unharmed after losing my son and daughter-in-law. He has the good of each of them in him, just like you do with your folks, and that's how we carry that good on." She pursed her lips and stepped to a bell rope in the corner that called the concierge. "Now then, if you're not full from your breakfasts already, I thought we might send for room service and ask them to bring us some cake and tea?"

Later, when they returned to their own suite, they found John and Selena sat together talking by the fire and playing cards.

"Your father's been teaching me whist!" Selena said as they entered. "It's the first time in years I've picked up a pack of cards and not been asked to tell someone's fortune with them!"

Papa chuckled. "Come on, all of you," he said. "Why don't you join us?"

So Lily, Robert and Caddy crowded together on the settee, beside the two of them in their chairs, and Papa dealt them all in to the next hand. Malkin, meanwhile, lay down as close to the fire as he could and proceeded to get beneath everyone's feet.

As she joined the game, Lily thought of her ma, long gone, and how nice it would be to have her around still. Not just to talk to her about her life and her work, which Lily now knew about thanks to the diary she had found last year, but also just to be with her. To have a mother in her life who understood who she was becoming. Like Robert and Caddy had with Selena.

And here they were, all together.

To anyone looking from the outside, they might've been a family. And perhaps, in that moment, they were.

The next day was spent recovering at the hotel, and the day after that seeing the sights of New York that they had missed when they were busy investigating things for Dane and spying on Miss Buckle and Matilda Milksop.

On their last night in the city, they did end up seeing the New York Metropolitan Opera, because when Miss Child understood they had recovered her diamond, she invited them all along as her special guests.

Miss Child was even more shocked when Lily told her she'd rescued the gem from the bottom of the ocean – they declined to explain the rest to her, for fear it might upset her delicate sensibilities. After she had regained her composure, Miss Child rang the opera house from the hotel lobby and made sure to stress that they should be given the best seats in the house – which turned out to be in the Grand Tier Box, right beside the stage.

Dane and his grandma came too and so did Kid Wink and the Cloudscrapers, who'd played such a large part in alerting the police to the location of Dane and the diamond in the first place.

The box was a bit snug with all of them in it, but the view was magnificent and there was plenty to admire in the splendid auditorium. Golden curtains that shimmered in the light and gilded boxes full of people that stretched all around Lily, making her feel like she was in one of those old-fashioned paintings of heaven. Only this heaven was stuffed with people rustling programmes and chatting to each other, rather than angels.

Behind Lily, everyone in the box was talking too. Papa was asking Kid Wink about her Wonderlite and promising to put her in touch with some New York professors who could help her develop it. Caddy had borrowed Robert's binoculars and was staring at the well-dressed crowd, *oohing* and *aahing* as if they were a bevy of brightly-coloured birds with exotic plumage that she was seeing for the first time.

Dane's grandmom was gossiping happily with Selena, and Dane was stroking Spook, who he had hidden in his pocket. Lily wondered if it was the first time a mouse had ever been brought to the opera. Come to that, she wondered if it was the first time there had ever been a fox at the opera, for they had snuck Malkin in too – hidden in her basket of course.

But soon Lily forgot all that, for the curtain rose and the performance started. It was an operatic version of *The Tempest*. Lily wasn't sure she could sit and watch a story with so much shipwreck in it after her time stuck under the sea, but luckily the magic distracted from the tragic parts – that and Miss Child's enthralling singing.

She played Miranda. She even wore the Ouroboros Diamond, now set in a much more low-key brooch and pinned to the lace collar of her dress. It glinted in the limelight, sending sparkling blue stars glittering over the gigantic room full of people, before they darted off and away like bold, luminous fish across the opera house's cavernous gold ceiling.

Lily could not take her eyes off Miss Child, nor the Ouroboros Diamond brooch. How lucky they were to escape from the Shadowsea alive, to rescue Dane and to be able to bring that magnificent rare diamond back to her.

Their final day in New York was a bright winter's day. Lily, Papa, Robert, Malkin, Selena and Caddy checked themselves out of the Murray Hill Hotel and took two electrical hansom cabs to Grand Central Depot, a block north.

The snow was melting and rivulets of water ran down the cobbled street and into the storm drains, which hissed with steam and moisture.

In the steam-wagon, Selena flicked through their copy of *Appleton's General Guide to the United States and Canada*, reading out various passages about Boston and Harvard and telling them all what they might see from the window of the train on the journey. She was dressed for travel in the outfit she had been wearing on the first day they arrived in New York. The glass beads of her long velvet coat twinkled in the morning sunlight beneath her black woollen winter cape, and her hair was pinned up beneath her large, felt, feather-trimmed hat.

Caddy wore her velvet jacket with the green glass buttons, and her matching green walking gloves and a scarf, plus a different bonnet, which was a little less Christmassy. Malkin had on his green woollen jacket and Lily her green blouson and tiger scarf. Papa wore a black bowler hat and a new black coat and gloves he had bought on a shopping spree on Fifth Avenue the previous day. Robert, of course, wore his da's coat and hat, as he always did.

Outside the entrance to the Grand Central Depot, newspaper boys stamped their feet and clapped their gloved hands together, huffing like horses. They shouted out today's headlines, vying to sell their papers as quickly as possible and come in from the cold.

"BIPLANE BUILT! NEW FIXED-WING AIRCRAFT TAKES FLIGHT!"

It sounded too intriguing a story to miss. Robert

bought a paper and stuffed it under his arm. He would read it later, on the journey.

They entered the station, crossed the concourse and climbed the few steps to platform nine, where their train was due to depart. Lily glimpsed their trunks, which had arrived before them, being stowed in the guard's compartment at the far end of the train. Then she saw something else.

Dane and his grandmom had come to the station. They were already on the platform, waiting to see them off. Dane waved cheerfully as soon as he caught sight of them, and his grandmom, beaming, held Spook up in a cupped palm so he might say goodbye too.

The engine of the train gave a deafening whistle and blew a long plume of grey steam from its smokestack, warning them that it was almost time to leave.

Lily was the last to step up into their carriage. She lingered for a moment in the doorway after Caddy, Robert, Malkin, Selena and Papa had already climbed aboard, and glanced back over her shoulder at Dane. He was holding his grandmom's free hand and he looked happy.

As all of them shuffled along the couchette car's corridor, searching for their cabin, Lily was reminded of the last carriage they'd been on – the Cloudscraper

Express, kitted out with inventions of Kid Wink and the home-made decorations of the rest of the Cloudscrapers.

When Lily found their compartment, Papa had already stowed their luggage in the overhead racks and Selena was busily stuffing her and Caddy's cases in beside those.

Robert was pleased his ma and sister were coming on with them. As things had turned out, he hadn't got to spend nearly as much time with his ma in New York as he would've liked, so it was good that they could be together for the next leg of the trip. Hopefully, there would be no more dangerous adventures on that part, but you never could tell…

Selena finished strapping her cases into the luggage rack and sat back down in her seat. Malkin lunged across her lap and pressed his snout to the window, staring out at the station platform. They had checked before they boarded and it seemed that mechanimals were allowed on this train, and so he was going to make the most of it this time.

Papa settled down opposite Selena in the middle of the cabin. He removed his black bowler hat and held it in his hands, seemingly unsure what to do with it, but that was all part of his awkward way. His hair was slicked back, but there was a tuft on top that would not be tamed and stuck up like couch grass, flecked with strands of grey. And that made Lily love him even more. She took the hat from him and hung it on a hook above his seat, before settling beside the window.

Robert nestled into the space opposite Lily, between Caddy and Malkin. He took his cap off and put it in his pocket. Now the train whistle was blowing and the guard was coming down the platform, closing all the doors. "ALL ABOARD!" he called. "THIS IS A NON-STOP TRAIN TO BOSTON! NEXT STOP SOUTH STATION, BOSTON!"

Selena grinned at all of them. "Well," she said, "I suppose that means we're on our way!"

"I suppose it does," Papa said, getting out his speech and correction pencil once more, which he'd tucked in his increasingly-tattered book of Shakespeare.

"Give me a moment." Lily stood and ran into the corridor, rushing to the far side of the train.

She pushed down the window and stuck her head out, searching for Dane on the platform. He was still stood there with his grandmom and Spook, only a few feet away.

"Good luck!" she called out to him, over the hiss of steam as the train started up.

"And to you," Dane shouted back.

"I hope to see you again soon," Lily called, but her words were drowned out by pistons pumping and wheels turning beneath her as the train began to move.

Soon the carriage was speeding away from platform nine.

Lily glimpsed Dane one last time. He was talking animatedly with his grandmom three-quarters of the way down the platform, grinning and waving wildly after the rapidly departing train.

And then he was a blur.

And then he was masked by a streaming line of buildings.

And then he was gone.

She stepped back to their cabin and stood for a moment in the open doorway, looking at her family and Robert's. Selena had the *Appleton's Guide* open and was flicking through more pages about Boston and Harvard. Caddy was reading the book they had given her: *The Secrets and Techniques of World-Class Spies*. Papa had his pencil out and was checking through the speech one last time, before he had to give it at the university in a couple of days.

"Shall I read you the new title?" he asked the rest of the cabin's occupants. "It's called: *Concerning the dangers of clockwork and electrical technology in the modern commercial world.*"

"It's not very catchy," Selena said, looking up from her book.

"My dear Mrs Townsend," Papa replied. "It's not meant to be. It's a scientific paper!"

As Lily returned to her window seat, she thought she could probably give Papa and the other professors at the conference a few warnings about the dangers of *both* electrical and clockwork technology, but she didn't say so, not just then.

She glanced at Robert, who was stroking Malkin's ears and looking through the glass with his binoculars. When he felt her eyes on him, Robert dropped the lenses and gave her one of his biggest, cheekiest grins.

They had come so far together, seen so many adventures, and now they would be travelling on to somewhere new. Lily was glad he was still with her. She hoped that Dane would be able to find a friend as loyal and true in his new life and she wished him the courage to begin to trust people again so that he might. But she knew such bravery took a long time – it had with her. Dane would never stop missing his lost parents, not really. All this time later, she still missed Mama more than she could say. Not a day went by when she didn't think of her in some small way. She knew that Robert felt the same about his da, for they had talked about it many times. But there were ways to remember and look back with love, while still moving on.

Papa had told her once that people didn't change, but that wasn't true. People changed too much. They woke up different every day. Learned new things, forgot others. You couldn't hold on, not really, not to the dead or memories, or the past, or even to your childhood, when you were growing up so fast. But wasn't that the joy of it? Not the stillness, but the growing. The changing adventure of each day...

To walk a little taller. To see from a higher angle. To grow and change and learn and experience new things – the endless good and bad that shaped your path. And, after all, wasn't that what being alive was all about? Brackenbridge may have been home, but home would always be there, waiting. It was just that sometimes you had to leave it to find out what you were missing.

She wiped a stinging feeling from the corner of her eye.

"Are you all right?" Robert asked her.

"I think so," she said. "I was wondering about Dane. I hope he can be happy now he and Spook are with his grandmom. But, just in case, I asked Kid Wink and the others to look in on him from time to time."

"Good idea," Robert said. "He'll need their help."

"And their friendship," Malkin added. "Like we three need each other."

"We four," Caddy added. She'd been listening from her seat across the carriage. "We six, in fact, because there's your papa and ma."

Lily laughed. "You're right. Friends and family together." She smiled around the carriage at all of them, but especially Robert. "Wherever in the world you are, that's my home. And wherever in the world I am, I hope you're with me. Because that's the best way to see the world, with the ones you love."

"There's so much world out there to see," Robert replied. "Big blue skies that stretch for miles and miles, and a million things to experience and do. And, along with Malkin and your pa and my sister and Ma, I can't think of anyone I'd rather see them with than you, Lily."

"Me neither," Lily said. "I wouldn't miss a moment of it. Wherever you go, I'll be there with you, along for the ride."

Lily gazed out the window, past Malkin, who was still pressing his forepaws against the glass. She stared at the strange new country as it unfurled before her: the gilded city, interspersed with blurring flashes of bright green leaves. Nature and the man-made.

Two different energies fused together, like they were

inside her. The regimented ticking rhythm of the Cogheart and her fizzing, bubbling mind, whose thoughts soared every day to new heights. The mixture had for so long seemed imperfect to Lily, a grating mismatch, but she knew now that was not the case. Its combination had helped her overcome so much adversity, made her who she was. Strong and unique. A beautiful blend of contradictions. Alive and, with those she loved, travelling on to see new sights.

The train clacked along it rails, its movement an incessant call to adventure, but a sudden and complete calm had descended on Lily. She felt whole and one at last and that feeling flooded everything around her, inside and out, until it became as deep and still and silent as a winter's day.

Lily pressed her freckled nose to the glass and watched the world glide by in all its gabbling, scrabbling, screaming, complicated glory, streaming towards her in one great river of life and light, and her heart went out to meet it.

A Thrilling and Treacherous

COGHEART ADVENTURES

Quiz...

1. What is the name of the Hartmans's (and Robert's) house?

2. Which lesson in Miss Octavia Scrimshaw's Finishing Academy for Young Ladies required Lily to carry books on her head to improve her posture, and what was the name of Lily's teacher for this subject?

3. Robert's da owned a shop in Brackenbridge; what did he do and what was the shop called?

4. What surname did Lily and her father first use in *Cogheart* to avoid being discovered by some nasty villains?

5. How many mechanicals live with Lily, Robert and Papa, and what are they all named?

6. In *Cogheart*, Robert and Lily make friends with a reporter from *The Daily Cog*, who also happens to live in a ramshackle zep. What is her full name?

7. Which notorious criminal broke out of Pentonville Prison in *Moonlocket* to come after Robert?

8. What organization is Papa, a mechanist, part of, what is their symbol, and in which *Cogheart Adventure* do Lily and Robert visit their headquarters in London?

9. In *Moonlocket*, Lily, Robert and Malkin escape from a moving zep...but what ingenious method do they use to get out safely? (Even if they do end up a little damp at the end!)

10. Which theatre were Selena and Caddy working in when Robert first met them in *Moonlocket*?

11. Which queen did Robert, Lily and Malkin meet at the end of *Moonlocket* – and on the back of which animal?

12. What is inside Robert's Moonlocket that he wears around his neck?

13. Where in the world did Lily and Robert find themselves after breaking out of the circus which had kidnapped them in *Skycircus*?

14. Who was Lily's governess in *Cogheart*, and what false name did she use in *Skycircus*?

15. Name the nasty mechanical from *Skycircus* who is described as having arms as "big as brick pillars"?

16. When is Lily's birthday? (Clue: she celebrates it at the beginning of *Skycircus*!)

17. What does Malkin avoid doing because he's worried it'll make his insides rusty?

18. Can you remember the names of all the police that the gang have encountered across the *Cogheart Adventures*? (Clue: they're all mentioned somewhere in *Shadowsea*…)

19. What magazines, full of daring adventures and terrifying tales, do both Lily and Caddy love to read?

20. What presents does Malkin receive for Christmas in *Shadowsea*?

21. Lily loves the scarf that Mrs Rust made for her; what colours did Rusty knit it in?

22. What is the name of the fancy hotel that the Townsends and Hartmans stay in in New York?

23. Kid Wink comes up with a brilliant invention that helps the gang see on the Shadowsea Submarine Base; what is it?

24. Which platform on which railway line does the ransom drop take place on in *Shadowsea*?

25. Lily's Papa loves reading Shakespeare, so he's delighted to find that Miss Aleilia Child has invited them to the opera in *Shadowsea*! But which Shakespearean play is the opera based on?

26. At the end of *Shadowsea*, Lily, Robert, Malkin, Papa, Selena and Caddy are all headed off to explore America... Where is their next stop?

ANSWERS: You can find the answers after the glossary and *Cogheart Adventures*...

A dictionary of curious words

A glossary of words which may be uncommon to the reader

Bioluminescence: when Lily encounters the school of fish glittering in the undersea dark, she's found what are called "bioluminescent fish" – fish that can produce their own light. Bioluminescence can either be due to chemical reactions inside the fish or bacteria in them which glow themselves.

Electricity: electricity is everywhere around us, from electric lights to telephones, trains to electrical cars... But what is it? Electricity is a form of energy, which can also be converted into other forms of energy, including heat and light. Scientists realized that electricity could be useful, and from the early 1800s, lots of scientists were researching what you could do with it. In 1809, an English scientist, Humphry Davy, invented the first electric light, and in 1879 Thomas Edison, an American inventor, made a long-lasting light bulb, while in 1876, Alexander Graham Bell patented the first telephone. For Robert and Lily, then, electricity was still a very new idea, very exciting and full of possibilities – particularly for Papa! (You might be there for hours if you ask him about it, though...)

Encyclopaedia: a large book or collection of books which covers everything one might need to know about, from aardvarks and angels to zeppelins and zoetropes! Mind you keep them out of the way of Malkin's snapping jaws...

Mechanimal: a mechanical animal, such as Malkin.

Minute steak and French fried potatoes: when Robert, Lily and Papa stop for a quick New York lunch, they eat minute steak and French fried potatoes. The steak is called a minute steak because it should only take a minute to cook! Confusingly, the "French fry" has a disputed origin, with some historians claiming it originally came from Belgium in the 17th century. French fries were, however, then taken up across Europe, North America and Canada. Indeed, President Thomas Jefferson is rumoured to have introduced them to America!

New York Elevated Railways: also called the "El" or "Els", were railway lines which ran across New York on metal rails elevated above the city below. First opened in 1878, it must have been quite a sight to behold as trains rushed by overhead. But as Lily and Robert discover when they first arrive, it was a little scary to stand underneath the rails, as ash and soot would fly off and coat anyone standing in the wrong place…not to mention making it very loud and very dark!

Ouroboros: a symbol of a snake eating its own tail. Originally used by the Ancient Egyptians, it has come to mean the eternal cycle of life and death. It's quite a difficult word to pronounce, so Robert suggests you might try it like this: "oor-oh-boh-rus".

Phonograph: a machine that could record and play music. The phonograph was invented by Thomas Edison (wasn't he a busy man!), and came in very useful on the Shadowsea Base to distract the zombies…

Submersible: a small vessel that can travel under the sea.

Zeppelin: a type of airship. It has an oval-shaped "balloon", beneath which is a rigid metal framework filled with bags of gas to keep the ship afloat. The passenger and crew area – or gondola – is usually situated under the main balloon, and can be quite roomy.

Find out where Lily and Robert's
thrilling adventures began in...

Lily's life is in mortal peril. Her father is missing and
now silver-eyed men stalk her through the shadows.
What could they want from her?

With her friends – Robert, the clockmaker's son,
and Malkin, her mechanical fox – Lily is plunged
into a murky and menacing world. Too soon Lily
realizes that those she holds dear may be the
very ones to break her heart…

"A steampunky tale of ambition, pursuit and revenge."
The Guardian

Follow their escapades
into the dark underworld of
thieves and trickery in...

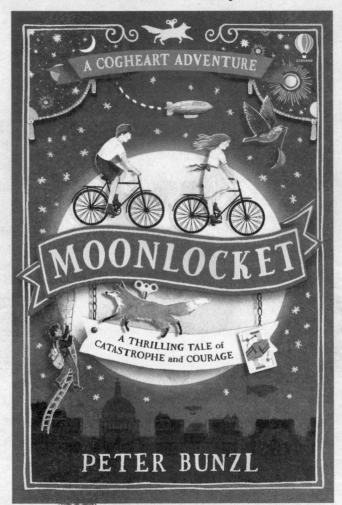

A COGHEART ADVENTURE

MOONLOCKET

A THRILLING TALE of
CATASTROPHE and COURAGE

PETER BUNZL

Storm clouds gather over Lily and Robert's summer when criminal mastermind the Jack of Diamonds appears. For Jack is searching for the mysterious Moonlocket – but that's not the only thing he wants.

Soon, dark secrets from Robert's past plunge him into danger, because Jack is playing a cruel game. Lily and Malkin, the mechanical fox, must stay one step ahead before Jack plays his final, deadly, card…

"A must-read for all fans of adventure –
children or not."
Kiran Millwood Hargrave

Step aboard the flying circus for
Lily and Robert's show-stopping
adventure of trickery and tight-ropes...

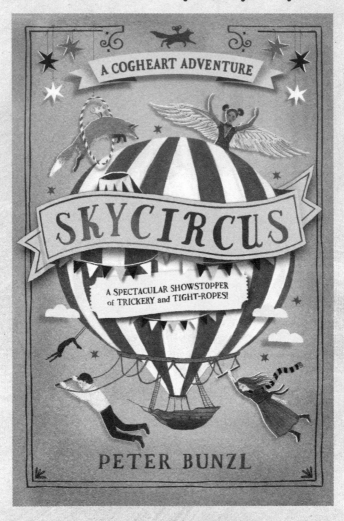

A COGHEART ADVENTURE

SKYCIRCUS

A SPECTACULAR SHOWSTOPPER
of TRICKERY and TIGHT-ROPES!

PETER BUNZL

Invited to a one-off spectacular show by Slimwood's
Stupendous Travelling Skycircus, Lily, Robert and
Malkin can't wait to jump onboard.

But behind the daredevil deeds of the bewitching
bird-girl and the lobster-handed boy, something sinister
lurks. And soon, the watchful ringmistress, Madame
Lyons-Mane, reveals a deadly plan for Lily. Could the
secrets of Lily's past hold their only chance of escape
from this terrible trap?

*"Dastardly villains, friendly mechanicals
and thrilling airship action."*
Kirkus

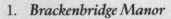

COGHEART ADVENTURES

Quiz Answers

1. *Brackenbridge Manor*
2. *Deportment with Mrs McKracken*
3. *He was a clockmaker at Townsend's Horologist's*
4. *Grantham*
5. *Four: Mrs Rust (Rusty), Captain Springer, Mr Wingnut and Miss Tock*
6. *Anna Quinn*
7. *Jack Door*
8. *The Mechanists' Guild. Their symbol is a golden cog, and they visit the headquarters in Moonlocket*
9. *They use the empty mail bags to sail down the mail line into the Hampstead Heath ponds!*
10. *The Magnificent Theatre of Curiosities*
11. *Queen Victoria, on the back of the mechanical elephant: the Elephanta*
12. *A painted miniature of Robert, his ma and his da, and a tiny photograph of Caddy and his ma*

ACKNOWLEDGEMENTS

An ocean of thanks to the following people... My excellent editors Rebecca Hill and Becky Walker, without whom I would still be drowning in streams of incomprehensible plot and words. My wonderful agent Jo Williamson for aiding me once again in navigating the stormy sea of publishing.

To everyone at Usborne who helped bring this book and the whole series to life. Most especially, Kath Millichope for her gorgeous design work and Becca Stadtlander for her stunning illustrations. Sarah Cronin for her beautiful type. Katarina Jovanovic for her publicity know-how. Stevie Hopwood for her marketing brilliance. Jacob Dow for his able assistance. Sarah Stewart, Anne Finnis and Gareth Collinson for copyedits and proofreading. Christian and Arfana for their sales prowess, and Lauren and the rights team for taking the *Cogheart Adventures* to so many far-flung places.

To Michael for being my co-pilot through the storms and squalls and becalmed seas that seem to come with writing.

And, last but not least, to you, dear reader, who've braved each fantastic voyage of danger and daring, catastrophe and courage, trickery and tightropes, terror and triumph!

I hope you've enjoyed reading the stories as much as I've enjoyed writing them. I shall miss Lily, Robert and Malkin terribly, but I can always relive their adventures by reopening one of their books, just as you can.

Right now they're headed off on a train to somewhere new, and this is where we must leave them. I have another place I'm excited to visit too. A world filled with pirates, princesses and wild boys, and I hope you'll be along for the ride as I embark on that new, as yet untold, adventure…